STRAIGHT
DOWN THE MIDDLE
— A NOVEL —

MARGARET DAVIS

Kelso Books

ISBN: 0-9825046-2-4 | ISBN-13: 9780982504628
Library of Congress Control No. 2009939208
Printed in the United States of America.

For Ray, with love

ACKNOWLEDGEMENTS

My heartfelt gratitude goes to the many people who have read and critiqued different versions of this book. They include Frank Baldwin, Teresa LeYung Ryan, Sara Marion, Ruth Paya, and Mil Pribble. Finally, a big thank you to Terez Rose who has advised and supported me throughout the writing process and to Judith Marshall for her invaluable help in getting this book published.

CHAPTER 1

My story begins on a gray February evening when the Neanderthal from across the street comes bounding up the steps to our porch and bellows at Cindy and me, "So which one of you wants to get pregnant?"

The setting is San Francisco. The year is 1984. We've only just arrived home from work; Cindy hasn't even unlocked the front door. The Neanderthal's name is Sam. He moved into the house across from ours a few months ago with his friend, Roland. Cindy and I have often talked to Roland but this is our first conversation with Sam. If you can call this a conversation!

I glare at him and snap, "Couldn't you say that a little louder?" He laughs and claps a hand to his mouth. Cindy snickers but I'm too annoyed to see any humor in this situation. Anyhow, Roland is the one I should be venting my wrath upon. Where *is* he?

Sam's bulky body is blocking my view so I push him aside to look down the steps. And there's Roland, clinging to the rail as if he hopes it will hide him. I shout, "Okay, Roland, what's going on?" Sheepishly, Roland disentangles himself from the rail and comes up the steps to stand beside Sam. You couldn't find two more dissimilar men. Roland is slight of build, blond, with fine pale features. Sam is dark, muscular, hairy, and everything on his face juts out—brow, cheekbones, jaw. Archetypal caveman.

Roland squeaks, "I'm sorry. I hope you don't mind but I showed your letter to Sam."

Cindy looks at me, her eyes wide. She murmurs, "It's kind of cold on the porch here, don't you think? Let's go inside." We all follow her into the house and she ushers our guests to chairs in the living room.

Cindy is my lover of five years. She's a beautiful woman. Honey-golden hair, porcelain-doll features, figure like a model. But this is no dumb blonde. In only five years with her company, she's risen from receptionist to assistant manager of the public relations department. And this is a Fortune 500 company we're talking about here. She can be other things too that sometimes catch a serious person like me off guard: playful, impulsive, a practical jokester.

The four of us sit around the coffee table. Sam looks at Cindy and me and says, "Hope I'm not speaking out of turn but Roland and I discussed your problem—about wanting to find someone to get you pregnant." I give Roland an icy look and he blushes. Sam continues, "Roland wasn't sure he was—er—quite up to it, so to speak." He grins again— he's always grinning—flashing a mouth full of big white teeth. Sort of like Burt Lancaster, but not that handsome. He says, "So we thought maybe I could stand in for him. I mean, are you particular?"

Are we particular? Out of the corner of my eye, I see Cindy swallowing a laugh. She's thinking, as I am, about the roller-coaster we've ridden over the past several months— hours of debate, last-minute doubts and mind-changing—to arrive at this very point.

I snap. "We are extremely particular."

But Sam isn't interested in me. He's looking at Cindy who's smiling at him in the vague, endearing way she has.

He's returning her smile with an eager expression that rather puzzles me. In this part of San Francisco when two people of the same sex live together, as Sam and Roland do, it's a fair bet they are a "couple."

"Sam, are *you* gay?" I ask.

His eyelids flicker and he shifts his glance for just a second toward me. "I guess you could call me bi," he says.

Cindy tells him, "It's very important to us to have someone who's willing to father the child and then just go away."

Sam says, "No problem. Babies leave me cold. Well... other than the conceiving of them." He laughs, a loud earthy laugh, those teeth flashing. He goes on, leaning back on one elbow and looking earnestly at Cindy, "I have good genes, if you're worried about that. I come from healthy stock. Now Roland here, everyone in his family died of some disease."

Roland looks startled.

Sam says, "Well, they died of something, didn't they? The ones who are dead?" He laughs again and Roland looks confused. I'm beginning to think Roland is a bit of a dope. I wonder, not for the first time, how on earth these two got paired up to begin with.

But now my stomach is rumbling. I stand up and say, "Sorry but we do need to get started on dinner now."

Sam asks, still looking at Cindy, "So what are the next steps? You'd like medical information, I guess?"

One thing Cindy is really good at is delivering an elegant coup de grâce. Now I watch her and wait for it.

But, instead, Cindy—still looking endearing—purrs, "Yes, of course, the medical stuff. But Sam, we don't know much about you, do we? So we'd also like you to write up a complete description of yourself. Sort of a résumé of your life:

family background, education, career, hobbies—that sort of thing."

"Résumé?" Sam sounds as astonished as I feel.

She purrs on, "Yes, like you're applying for a job. Which you are, of course." Then she too stands and walks toward the door.

I see Sam and Roland exchange glances. Sam asks, "When do you want this résumé?"

"A couple of days will be fine," Cindy assures him.

As soon as the two men leave, she swings around to face me and the laughter explodes out of her. "Diane—oh, baby—you should see your face!"

Her laughter is the final straw. Because, you see, our letter to Roland contained an unusually sensitive and personal request. Certainly not transferable to anyone else—and least of all to someone like Sam.

Huffily, I march toward the bedroom, shedding my coat and purse on the hall chair. "Okay, Cindy. I suppose this is one of your little jokes. Which will cause no end of confusion all round. And I can guess who'll have to clear up all that confusion."

Cindy follows me into the bedroom.

"Don't be mad, honey bunch. We can't let that arrogant jerk get away with that. *Are you particular?* As if we were picking out a garbage can. He deserves to pay for being so presumptuous."

As I change into my jeans and sweat shirt, I ask, "How is he going to pay exactly? And what do we do with the stupid résumé, if he produces it?"

Cindy appears to take the question seriously. She sits down on the bed to think, her brow furrowed. "'How about this?" she suggests. "After we get the résumé, we'll ask him to come in for an interview. Keep stringing him along to the last minute. Then we say, 'Sorry, we've changed our minds—you don't meet our standards.'"

"Cindy, that's so silly. In fact, it's really pretty mean."

She squeals with delight. "Oh, Di-dee, you're so upright and sensible. My Rock of Gibraltar. But even a rock needs to have a giggle now and then."

"If you say so. But you know something. That poor klutz doesn't realize that I have any part to play in all this. The way he was looking at you, he obviously thinks you're the one who requires his services. Couldn't you see it in his face, *Yummy, yummy, wait till I get my hands on this dishy blonde?*"

"Oh, barf." She gives another joyful squeal.

At the dresser, I comb my hair and study my reflection in the mirror. "Of course, when he reads that letter more carefully and finds out that *I'm* the one, he'll lose interest so fast...."

"Oh, stop it." Cindy, standing beside me, puts an arm around my shoulder. In spite of the reproach in her voice, she doesn't contradict me. Why would she? For a few moments, she too studies my reflection: the plain freckled face, receding chin, lanky brown hair.

She says, "As far as I'm concerned, sweetie-pie, you're the most beautiful person I know."

We both know she's speaking figuratively. But this is fine by me. Because I know my worth. Cindy would fall apart without me. Her income is higher than mine, it's true, but I keep our household running—managing everything from meals to money. And I keep her grounded. We go together. Her sparkle lightens my life. I bring sanity to hers.

We go to the kitchen, where I pull plastic bags of veggies out of the crisper and start to wash and chop. Stir fry tonight. Cindy sits on a barstool, swinging her legs, and talks about work. She updates me every night these days because there's some kind of battle brewing in her firm over who will succeed the manager of her department who is due to retire soon. I know Cindy hopes that person will be her but she has told me "the politics are ugly."

Tonight, I'm not listening too hard. There are things on my mind. When there's a lull in her monologue, I interject, "I guess it's back to the drawing board for us, huh? Pregnancy-wise."

"Finding a replacement for Roland, you mean? Yeah, what a bummer. Who'd have thought he'd be such a wimp!" She gets off the stool and comes to stand beside me, gazing down at the stove. "Honey-bun, this is all turning out to be so difficult, isn't it?"

"I never thought it would be easy."

As I get the onions started in the pan and turn to chopping up chicken pieces, I brood. Over the past year, Cindy and I have had endless talks about the best way to get a baby. When I asked at the local Catholic agency, they told me that getting babies for lesbian couples was a real iffy proposition as far as they were concerned. I don't take kindly to rejection so that kind of put me off. Anyway, I'm not really that enthusiastic about adoption. I'd much rather have my own.

So we assumed that artificial insemination would be the way to go. But then an acquaintance of ours had a horrible experience with this. She'd carefully checked out the donor ahead of time, but something went very wrong. The poor woman got some other guy's "donation" by mistake and she ended up with a baby *and* HIV. That really scared the pants off me even though people keep trying to tell me this was a fluke. It isn't much comfort if you're the fluke.

Then, recently, Cindy and I were at a party with a number of gay and lesbian friends and a woman there told us she had become pregnant by sleeping with a gay man the "natural way." She said if you could find the right man, it needn't be that bad an experience. Cindy and I immediately thought of our gay neighbor, Roland. Roland is a lot less revolting than most males. He's gentle, artistic, quiet, polite. And, over the past couple of months, we've become quite friendly with him. So, after considerable discussion and back-and-forthing, we composed a letter to him asking if he'd be interested.

We knew that Roland shared his house with a loud, primitive specimen of the male species. It didn't occur to either of us that he would share our letter too.

CHAPTER 2

A week goes by. Then two. And three. During this time, Cindy and I do absolutely nothing about finding a replacement for Roland. Sometimes I ask myself what on earth we're waiting for. Then I remember the answer: we have no idea what to do next.

On a Thursday night, almost four weeks after Sam and Roland visited us, Cindy and I arrive home to find a white envelope jutting out from under our doormat. Cindy picks it up. It's addressed to *The Ladies at 2013 Bayley.*

Cindy coos, "Oooh, what's this?" She rips open the envelope as she follows me into the house. "Whaddya know, it's your Neanderthal's application. I thought we'd heard the last from him."

"Obviously," I say, "he's reread our letter to Roland and realized that I, and not you, want to be the consumer of his services." I toss my coat and purse onto the chair in the hall.

"The thing is," Cindy says, "he's finally come through. Not that it matters a hoot given the plans we have for him."

There's dinner to get ready. We're in something of a rush tonight—or rather I am. They have a double header on TV tonight on the classical movie channel, starting at eight. Without bothering to change first, I hurry into the kitchen and put water on to boil for the pasta, pull out lettuce and assorted veggies from the fridge for salad, start warming pasta sauce.

Meantime, Cindy sits at the table, engrossed in Sam's résumé. She makes noises at intervals—"Oh?" "H-mm." "Ha." "Wow!" I take no notice. *Rebecca* starts in only an hour. After a time, she says, "Diane, this is pretty impressive stuff." Sensing my determined inattention, she gets up and follows me around—from fridge to sink to stove to table, quoting snippets from the pages in her hand.

"Just listen to this. Father is a bank president in Southern California. Mother is a federal appeals court judge. One grandfather is a former state senator. What else? Brother is a nuclear physicist—oh, wow! he was a runner-up for a *Nobel prize*." She waves the document at me and then flips the page. "His sister is a nationally known child psychologist; she's had four books published, one of them was awarded...."

"Not a bad pedigree for a bum, huh?"

Cindy protests, "According to this, Sam's hardly a bum. Let's see...." She buries her nose in the pages again. "He has a bachelor's degree from UCLA, where he graduated *magna cum laude and* Phi Beta Kappa—h-mm!" By now, she's practically drooling. "Also, a Master of Business Administration from Stanford where he was some kind of tennis champion. And now he's employed by Johnson, Harvey and blah-blah-blah, stockbrokers, in a—quote—senior position that puts him in line for a vice presidency—unquote."

I look up from the six different things I'm trying to do and comment, "Sounds to me he's in line for Bullshitter of the Year award. Anyhow, why do we care? Cindy, remember I'd like to be through by seven-thirty. Could you maybe wash the lettuce or something. Please."

With reluctance, she sets the résumé aside and puts on an apron.

We don't talk about the résumé any more that evening. But, at bedtime, when Cindy goes off to take a bath, I can't resist sneaking a peek at it. To be honest, it's more than a peek. I read it from cover to cover. Twice. It's fascinating to me how some people can be so inventive.

The next evening, Friday, we have a bit of excitement planned. Cindy's bringing two business colleagues home for dinner. I get off work early to prepare a bang-up dinner of roast beef and Yorkshire pudding. (My dear departed grandmother actually came from Yorkshire.)

As usual, early isn't early enough. Half an hour before Cindy is due to arrive with her guests, I am flying around in a state of dishevelment. The table is set, the dinner pretty well on track, but I still have to make the Yorkshire pudding, and I haven't even started to get dressed.

I get out the faded, food-spattered piece of paper that sets out the steps for making Yorkshire pudding. This is my grandmother's fail-proof recipe. First, heat up the oven to 475 degrees. Mix eggs, milk and flour into a batter. Put tablespoon of fat in baking pan and put pan in oven till fat sizzles. Only for a minute though—if it gets too hot, the fat will explode all over the oven. When fat sizzles, pour in the batter and bake.

Well, the fat is in the pan and the pan is in the oven and I'm half-crouched by the oven door waiting for the sizzle, when the doorbell rings. I hesitate. There's no way I should leave my post at this critical moment. But it might be Cindy arriving early; sometimes she forgets her key.

So I run to the front door, fling it open and gasp, "I'm in the middle of something," and turn to run back to the kitchen. It registers on my frazzled consciousness that it's not Cindy and her guests at the door.

It's Sam.

Pops and bangs are coming from the kitchen as I run to the rescue. In the nick of time I fling open the oven door and rescue the pan. Then I quickly give the batter a final stir, pour it into the hot pan, and slide the pan back into the oven.

As I relax, exhausted, from all this effort, I realize Sam has followed me to the kitchen and stands watching me, his big body lolling against the door-frame. I look at him and he looks at me. He says in a tone of mocking admiration, "Julia Child, I presume?" But there's no time now to be exchanging quips with him. So I go toward him with my hands in front of me like a bulldozer, not actually touching him but sort of shooing him backwards. "Sam, I can't chat right now. I have exactly fifteen minutes to take a shower, dry my hair, get dressed...."

I stop talking, because he's doubling up with mirth as he backs down the hall in front of me, bumping into one thing after another. He says, "Okay, okay. I get the hint." We reach the front door and he stands facing me, one hand behind him holding the doorknob. His eyes study my face, "You're Diane, right?"

"Right."

"And you're the one who wants the baby?"

The way he's ogling me raises my hackles. I ask, "And the reason for your visit?"

"I just came over to see if you got my résumé."

"Yes, we did."

He cocks an eyebrow at me and smirks. "And what did you think?"

The smirk does it. I can't wait to see this arrogant jerk brought down a peg or two. "We'd like you to come for an interview."

"An *interview?*" He cracks up again, leaning his face on the doorjamb, his big white teeth flashing as he rocks back and forth. I grit my teeth and wait for him to get his merriment under control. Just when I'm set to slam the door in his face, his guffawing becomes more restrained and he asks, "When? Only I'm leaving on Sunday for two weeks. On business."

"Oh, I don't care. When do you want to come?"

"Tomorrow? I'm busy in the afternoon so how about eleven o'clock?"

"See you then." I shut the door quickly before he thinks of something else to say.

The next morning, I sit at the dining table, pouring cereal and milk into a bowl, and reflecting with satisfaction on my culinary efforts the night before. The dinner was perfect. The guests raved about my cooking. Cindy raved about me. "I keep telling Diane," she told our guests, "she's such a fantastic cook she ought to make money at it. No, I'm not kidding. One day, when we have some money saved up, we're going to set her up in business. A little inn in the country."

Cindy has talked about this "inn in the country" before. In truth, being an inn keeper has never been a particular dream of mine but it probably beats being one-sixth of a six-person word processing pool—which is all I can currently aspire to with my lack of a college degree.

As I slice a banana into my cereal, a zombie-like Cindy sits across from me, sipping black coffee. My sweetie-pie drank a little too much wine last night. She says, "Oh, before I forget, would you help me put together a grocery list. I'm having a facial at eleven. I'll stop off at Safeway on my way back."

It takes a couple of seconds for this to sink in. Mouth full of cereal and banana, I mumble, "Eleven? No, that won't work. I forgot to tell you before but Sam came over yesterday. About his résumé. I told him to come back at eleven today for an interview."

Cindy, coffee cup wavering at half-mast, yawns. "Well, tell him to make it next weekend."

"No, that won't work. He'll be gone for the next two weeks."

"So what's the hurry? It took a whole month for him to get his résumé to us, didn't it?"

She has a point, but her attitude irritates me. She was the one who suggested the interview in the first place and now she's allowing things to drag on. All I want to do is put this stupid Sam business behind us. I finish eating in silence. A few minutes later, as we wash breakfast dishes at the sink, I say, "You don't have the facial appointment marked on the calendar."

"No, I just made it yesterday."

"Well, why don't you change it? Make it this afternoon instead."

"Diane. They did me a special favor by fitting me in today. They have nothing else until the end of the week."

"So?"

She clucks. "So I need to look my best for Monday. For my presentation at work. Remember, we were talking about it last night?"

I look at Cindy. Her skin is flawless. Anyone less in need of a facial I have never seen in my life. But it's no use arguing with her. She'll tell me I just don't understand the requisites of the high-powered executive circles she moves in. She knows that in my job I hardly ever get to see a customer. I could be covered with zits from brow to belly button and no one would care.

I turn away and keep washing dishes.

She says, "Oh, come on, you're not fretting about keeping him waiting, are you? What's the rush?"

"No," I retort. "I could care less about him. I just want this interview business over and done with. I can't stand these silly games."

There's a silence, then she says in a conciliatory tone, "I'm not sure why it so upsets you. But if you really want to get it done today, why don't you go ahead without me?" She adds, as if offering me a great bargain, "Tell you what. Why don't you do the interview and I'll write the rejection letter?"

There's one problem with this: I'm the one who can write letters and Cindy's the one who can bring people down pegs. But enough already.

I sigh. "Okay, let's do that."

Later that morning, I stand by the front window watching our testosterone-laden neighbor charge across the street to our house. He comes leaping up our steps with his usual cocksureness. When he rings the bell, I let him in and lead him into the living room. I sit on the couch by the coffee table where I have placed his résumé, a yellow lined pad, and a pen. He snickers at the sight of these items and throws himself down in an easy chair to my right, adopting that insolent macho sprawl—arms crossed behind his head, legs straight out and far apart.

Looking at him, lolling and grinning, I decide the first order of business is to get the smirk off his face.

"Sam," I say, in my most crisp and professional voice, picking up his résumé and waving it, "This is the most incredible résumé." The smirk grows broader. "Cindy and I split our sides when we read it."

The smirk vanishes. *Bingo!*

"Why?"

"Because we've never seen so much baloney in one document." I laugh—a hearty, albeit phony, laugh. Now he looks hurt as well as puzzled. But he straightens up and looks alert.

He says, "I don't understand what you're saying. What do you consider baloney?"

Quickly, I flick the pages of the résumé in front of me, looking for some obvious embellishment of the truth. I say, "For a start, you say you're some kind of vice president."

He reproaches me. "You obviously didn't read it carefully. I said I was in line for a vice presidency. My current job is one step down." Then he completely takes the wind out of my sails by pulling his wallet from an inner pocket and taking out a business card, which he hands to me.

The card looks very expensive; it's one of those that folds over so you can place it on the table like a tent. It reads: *Sam T. Bradshawe, Senior Account Executive, Johnson, Harvey, Burrows, Finch & Beckett.* This is followed by an address and telephone and fax numbers.

I study it for a moment. "How come this says 'Sam' rather than 'Samuel'?

Sam sighs as he puts away his wallet. "Because my name is Sam. Rather than Samuel." He puts his hands on his knees and leans forward. "So what other instances of alleged baloney did you come across?"

One item catches my eye as I flick through the pages. "Were you really a tennis champion?"

He says, "Yes, really."

"And you went to Stanford?"

"Yes, I did." Now he sounds testy.

"And, let's see, your mother's a judge?"

At this, Sam jumps to his feet. "Oh, for Christ's sake. Look, Diane, I'm sure we both have better ways to spend our time so I'll be running along."

"But I haven't finished yet."

"Well, I sure have." He turns his back on me and marches to the front door. I follow, aware that I have lost control of a situation I very much want to have control of.

"No, please wait a minute."

He stops and half turns toward me. He says, "This is all a set-up, isn't it? So that you and your half-baked friend can make fun of me. You're not seriously considering me to father a child for you."

"Of course, we are." But he ignores this and flings open the front door. As he starts to step outside, I call out, "Sam, do you really want this job?"

He pauses then and turns to look at me for a long moment. As I look back at him, I notice for the first time that he has very nice blue eyes. A pretty summer-sky blue. For a fleeting second, I forget how much I can't stand the rest of him.

Finally, he says, "Yes."

"Then you've got it."

By the time Cindy breezes in at one-thirty, I've worked myself into a real funk. She pushes her way through the front door, a grocery bag under each arm, face aglow. And I do mean aglow—a shiny, glycolic peel glow. She sings out, "Treats coming up! Hot barbecued drumsticks and French bread for lunch." My mouth waters—that barbecued chicken from the supermarket is my very most favorite snack. I help her put the groceries away while she chirps away happily about her morning with the esthetician whom Cindy seems to find a barrel of laughs.

When we're ready to eat, Cindy pulls the plastic wrap off the chicken and slices the bread. I make the tea. We take the food to the table and sit down. Cindy says, as though she's just thought of it, "Oh, did Sam come for the interview?"

Between bites, I relate the story. Cindy laughs as I tell her about getting rid of the smirk and the slouch. When I express surprise about the business card though, her face gets serious. "You were the one who was skeptical about his résumé, Diane—not me. I always say you can't judge a book by its cover."

"Whatever. But guess what? I ended up offering him the job."

She stops eating and gives me an *Are you serious?* look. "You told him you're going to sleep with him?" Then her face lights up. "Oh, I see. This is part of leading him on right to the very last minute. And then we can squash him."

I feel sick at her interpretation of my motives. "No, no. That's not what I had in mind at all. How can you think I could be that mean?"

Cindy's bubbliness fizzles. "I'm sorry, I don't follow. I thought you said you couldn't stand him. But now you want to go through with it?"

"No, of course, I don't. Not with him. It's just I couldn't stand the way he was stomping out of here with his nose in the air. He was actually yelling at me for questioning his stupid résumé. I wanted to pull the rug out from under him."

The tears well up and I wail, "Oh, what are we going to do?"

Cindy moves her chair next to mine and puts an arm around me, cradling my head against her shoulder. "There's nothing to worry about, babykins," she coos. "Just send him a letter saying you've changed your mind. And you don't even have to bother doing that for a couple of weeks, do you?"

She feeds me tissues as I snuffle into her shoulder. "Come on, sweetie. He's not worth crying over."

I sit up and blow my nose. "Oh Cindy, that's not why I'm crying. I'm crying because we're not making any progress here. When I withdraw my offer to him, Roland and every prospective father for miles around will get to hear the story. We're never, ever going to get this baby."

She kisses my wet face. "Of course, we will." She adds in her soothing voice, "And even if we don't, it's not the end of the world, is it?"

I consider this for a moment. And start crying again.

CHAPTER 3

On Saturday morning two weeks later, I'm in the bedroom getting laundry ready for Cindy to take to the Wash 'n Dry. I've stripped off the beds and stand in a sea of sheets, towels, and clothing that I'm about to sort into "warm" and "cold" piles.

Sam is due back this weekend. I had intended to write him by now to tell him I'm withdrawing the "job offer," but haven't got around to it. Frankly, it's the least of my concerns.

Over the past couple of weeks, I've agonized constantly over this pregnancy business. There simply isn't any ideal solution. There are times—usually when I'm in bed and can't sleep—when I feel I'd do anything to get pregnant. But in the cold light of day, I know that's just not true.

The phone in the kitchen rings. Cindy answers it and I catch the word "Sam." Quick as a flash, I drop the sheet I'm folding and run into the kitchen. Cindy's saying, "Diane? Sure." She holds the phone out to me but I shake my head. She says into the phone, "Just a minute," and mouths "*What?*" at me.

I mouth back, "You tell him." She nods as if she understands. But then she says, "Diane isn't available right now. I'll ask her to call you later." I wave and mouth again but Cindy turns her back and holds out an arm toward me, as though telling me to go away. She's still talking to Sam, seeming to repeat what he's saying. "You're going out in an hour, back by five? Right. I'll tell her. Goodbye." She hangs up.

"Cindy, didn't you understand me? I don't want to talk to him. Anytime. Ever. I was hoping you'd tell him I'd changed my mind."

Cindy looks patient in a strained sort of way. She says, "Diane, sit down. And simmer down." She takes my arm and pushes me to a chair to enforce her first command. Then, sitting down herself, she says slowly, "Point number one. *You* made the arrangement with Sam. He might not believe *me* if I tell him it's cancelled. Point number two. Don't you think it'd be a good idea to keep our options open?"

I gasp. "What are you talking about? You think he's an option?"

"Now, Diane, let's just think this through for a moment. I know we decided to try impregnation in the natural way." She draws a breath. "But you must admit our efforts to find a father are a flop so far. The man we're willing to consider isn't willing to consider us. And vice versa." She tilts her head to one side, earnestly looking into my face. "And really I don't think either one of us is eager to go running around the neighborhood looking for other candidates. Or am I wrong?"

"Of course not." I turn away from her.

"Diane, this baby isn't just going to drop out of a tree. So if we don't want to adopt, we'll have to rethink artificial insemination." Her voice quickens. "I know you have this hang-up about it but you know with that HIV case I don't think we heard the full story. I bet that woman's HIV had nothing to do with the baby. I bet she got it some other way and just blamed the sperm bank."

My jaw dropped. "How could anyone lie like that?"

Cindy says. "Much easier than admitting the truth."

"Well, I wouldn't find it easy."

"Easier, I said, not easy. Anyway, back to our situation. If we pick a donor we know with good health and good genes, there's no reason things wouldn't work out. We know Sam has good health and with his family background, he must have good genes. So don't deep-six him yet."

Solemnly, we look at each other. "I know," she says, "I can see you have so many objections you don't know where to start. Look, it's just something to think about. I'm going to fix us a cup of coffee before I set off on my errands."

She goes to the sink to put water on to boil and I return to the laundry in the bedroom. As I finish piling the last of the dirty clothes into the basket, I notice Cindy has come to the doorway and is watching me. She says gently, "This whole business is really stressing you out, isn't it, sweetheart? Maybe we should rethink the whole idea. Or at least postpone it for a year or two."

I shake my head and slump down onto the bed.

She says, "Diane, I've never seen you like this before. Nothing is worthwhile if it makes you this unhappy. Come on, the coffee's ready."

She leaves but I stay a few moments longer, too frozen with fear to move. Because at this very moment I'm convinced that I want this baby more than anything I've ever wanted in the world. My stomach hurts with longing every time I see an infant in its mother's arms. I can *feel* the new little being in my arms. I can hear myself boasting about her to friends, to people at work. At times during the day, I daydream about every step of her life unfolding: babyhood, childhood, teenage. I would be a good mother. I know all the things not to do to a tender young mind.

Now my baby's very existence is threatened. By me. By my fussiness and misgivings that are taking all the joy out of what should be such a joyous enterprise. I get up and hurry into the kitchen.

Cindy is already at the table sipping her coffee. She points silently to the cup awaiting me. I pick it up but don't drink. I say quickly. "You know, Cindy, I'm sure you're right. Going with a sperm donor is about the only option open to us. And we don't have to use Sam, do we? We could ask Roland...."

My voice trails off as I see her expression. "Forget Roland. Pathetic wimp! Do you have something against Sam?"

There is one huge thing I have against Sam but I hesitate to say it out loud. It sounds so...*superficial.*

"What?" she repeats.

I whisper as though he could hear us. "Oh, Cindy, do we really want a baby who *looks* like Sam?"

She peals with laughter. "Oh, Diane—you and all that Neanderthal stuff! He's not that bad looking. Somewhat *me-Tarzanish,* maybe, but well within the range of what's normal for males." Then she jumps up, carries her coffee cup to the sink, and heads to the bedroom to collect the laundry basket. "Okay, I'm off. I'll be back about noon."

After she leaves, I look at the clock. If Sam is leaving within an hour, I don't have much time. I find a pencil and a piece of paper and sit down to make some notes on what to say to him.

A few minutes later, I review what I've written. *Hello, Sam. This is Diane. There's been a change in plans. Cindy and I decided that we would like you to be a sperm donor. That way would be more satisfactory to us than the other alternative we discussed. I hope this is okay with you.*

Sounds good: polite but clear. Now to act quickly before I change my mind. I go to the phone.

Sam answers with an ebullient "Hullo."

"Hello, Sam. This is Diane. There's been a...."

"Diane. How are you?" Before I can respond, he asks, "Are you ready to go ahead?"

"Yes, I am. But there's been a change...."

"That's great. When would you like to get started? I'm free this weekend, tonight or tomorrow."

"No, Sam, wait. We've decided...that is, Cindy and I would like you to be a sperm donor."

A silence. Then Sam says in a silly voice, "I wasn't planning to donate anything else."

"No, what I mean is we want you to donate for that artificial..." Artificial *what*? My mind goes blank.

He says, "If you mean artificial insemination, the answer is absolutely not. That wasn't our agreement. I agreed to donate to a warm body, not a plastic cup."

Stunned, I bleat, "Are you sure?" It hadn't occurred to me for a second he'd refuse.

"Absolutely, totally, one hundred per cent sure."

A long silence follows. Finally, Sam says in a softer voice, "What's the matter? Did you lose your nerve?"

I sigh. "You could say that."

"Mm-m. I understand." He really does sound sympathetic. But then, after another pause, he says, "Let's see. Are you busy tonight?"

My mind is so befuddled at this point, I don't question his question. I say, "Tonight? Let's see, Cindy is going out to some awards banquet at her firm."

"And you?"

"No, I'm not going."

Sam says, "Fine. Why don't I come over about eight o'clock and we'll take it from there. Just see how it goes." After a moment, he adds, "Okay?"

It's cruel the way life sometimes puts you on the spot. What I say next will clearly have momentous consequences for all our lives. The obvious thing—the only sane thing— is for me to say *No*. But if I do—as the panicky thoughts jumbling around in my brain keep reminding me—think of what will happen next. *No baby* is what will happen next. Because I know exactly what Cindy will say when I tell her Sam's response. She'll say, "Fine. So let's just forget about it for a while." But I don't want to forget about it. Besides, I think, how awful could it be anyway?

So I say, "Okay."

CHAPTER 4

Just before eight o'clock that evening, I'm in the living room pacing up and down like a caged animal. Cindy's in the bedroom getting ready to leave for her awards banquet.

It's an understatement to say Cindy was surprised at what I'd agreed to in her absence this morning. But she respected my desire not to talk about it too much. She knows how easily I get doubts and reverse myself. And neither one of us wants to go back to square one.

Clip-clop, clip-clop, coming down the hall. Cindy has her heels on. She pops her head around the door. I look over at her. She says, "Oh, what a forlorn baby! Are you okay?"

"Sure," I say.

She takes my hand and leads me to the couch where she sits down beside me. "Are you sure you want to go through with this?"

"I've never been less sure of anything in my life." I give a grim laugh. "But now we've come this far, I sure don't intend to back down."

She looks at me anxiously. "I really wish I could skip this silly awards thing so I can be here with you. In fact, maybe I should call...."

"No, Cindy, please. It's going to be fine." I squeeze her hand. "Off you go. Stop worrying about me."

"Well, if you're sure."

A few minutes after she leaves, the doorbell rings and I let Sam in. For once, he isn't grinning. In fact, he looks a bit hesitant as though he thinks this may not be such a good idea after all. He's carrying some papers in his hand. I lead him into the hall and toward the bedroom. But he stops by the entrance to the living room and says, "Hey, where are you going?"

"You want to do it in the living room?"

"No, of course not." he says. "I want to show you the rest of my medical records."

"Oh, that's right."

He's already sent us results of various medical exams and blood tests and has promised even more evidence of his lack of disease. We sit down side by side on the couch and he shows me a chest X-ray, EKG, and heaven knows what else. I'm not sure how I'm supposed to evaluate this stuff but who cares? He'd hardly be showing it to me if there was anything bad here.

When he gets through, I say, "Okay, everything seems fine. But there is one other thing we haven't discussed." I hesitate. "How much do you want us to pay you?"

He smiles but looks embarrassed. He says, "How much did you offer to pay Roland?"

"We never discussed a dollar figure with Roland."

"So how much do you think I'm worth?"

He gives me a challenging look, his customary smirk playing at the corners of his mouth. I suggest, "Two hundred dollars?"

"Two hundred dollars!" There's the ear-to-ear grin again.

I say, "Well, you're not really doing this for the money, are you?"

At this, he roars with laughter, rocking back and forth in that way he has, and slapping his thighs with his hands. "Believe me, at those rates, I won't be giving up my day job." He finds it so funny he's almost in tears. I can feel my face getting warm. He catches my eye and stops throwing himself around. He says, "No, I'm not doing this for the money. I'm just glad to be able to help you out." I guess I look skeptical because he adds, "Also, it's neat to get new experiences. You know!" He watches me, the grin lurking.

For several hours, the tension has been building inside me. It feels like a steel cable connecting my head to my extremities with someone keeping it taut. People on the rack must have felt like this. As Sam smirks about "new experiences," the cable tightens. I can just picture him with those *Johnson, Harvey* people at work, swaggering around and guffawing about what he did on Saturday night.

Suddenly, he stretches back on the couch, yawns, and says, "You got anything to drink?"

"I don't know. I wasn't figuring on you coming over to drink."

As he turns to face me, his knee brushes against mine. I jerk my leg away. Sam gives me a thoughtful look. "Look, I'm not a machine, okay? I have to get myself into the mood for this sort of thing. So a drink would be nice." It dawns on me that Sam may be feeling as nervous as I am, but this doesn't make me feel any better. I get him a glass of red wine, and leave him with it while I go to the bedroom to prepare.

After switching on the lamp on my bedside table and turning down the covers, I pace around the room a few times. A couple of minutes later, I go back to Sam in the living room and say, "I want the light out."

He looks at me and says, "Okay."

"So I'll get undressed first and turn the light off and call you. But will you be able to find your way across the room in the dark?"

He snorts like a silly adolescent. But then he says, "Look. Why don't we both go into the bedroom at the same time. You stand one side of the bed, me the other. We'll turn the light off and both get undressed at the same time." This sounds surprisingly sensible. He finishes off his wine and follows me into the bedroom, over to what Cindy calls "our big brass bed."

We face each other across the bed like a couple of wrestlers in the ring. I say, "Okay?"

"Okay." His mouth twitches. Quickly, I turn off the light.

I undress—to the extent necessary, anyway—put my clothes on a chair behind me, and climb under the covers. In the darkness, I can just make out Sam as he struggles with pulling things up over his head and down over his hips. As he goes along, he tosses his discarded clothes onto the floor behind him.

Finally, he climbs in beside me.

Being an old bed, it has squeaky springs. "Part of its charm," Cindy always says. But there is nothing charming about the tortured shrieks that fill the room as Sam settles in.

He mutters and shifts around until his upper body is crammed up against me. There's a moment of silence. Then he says, "Diane, why the hell are you wearing a sweater?" I jump as he puts his hand on my midriff and slides it upward. I put my hand on his to push it away, but in a flash, he curls his fingers around to envelop my hand in his, holding it down on my chest.

I protest, "You have no right to be messing around up here. This has nothing to do with making babies."

Sam gives an exaggerated sigh and flings himself away from me onto his back, almost onto the floor. He rights himself by letting go my hand and reaching out to grab the night table. He says, "I keep trying to tell you I can't turn on and off like a tap." Now he turns toward me again, pushing up on one elbow and looking down at me in the dark. He says sternly, "Diane, I have a job to do and you have a job to do too. Your job is to help me in any way you can to do my job. And that means, for a start, getting rid of all this."

With that, he grabs my sweater and wrenches it upward.

A while later, I sit in the kitchen sipping the hot cocoa I have just fixed for myself. I feel the way you do when you've managed to survive some dreaded event like a performance review. A sort of relieved stupor.

Sam is in the bathroom. God knows what he's doing. I can hear the faucet being turned on and off. Presently, he appears, muttering something about forgetting his comb. I look at him and snicker. He's wet his hair in an attempt to smooth it down but there's an unruly black tuft sticking up at the crown. It reminds me....

He says, "Diane, what's that look on your face? It couldn't be—it's surely not a *smile?*"

"Smart aleck!" I retort. He grins and I tell him, "I was remembering a shaggy mutt we had when I was a kid. Long, black hair. He loved to go swimming." I run my eyes over Sam's head.

Unperturbed, Sam says, "And all I lack is a ball in my mouth. Arf, arf!" He sits down and eyes my cup. "What're you drinking? Whatever it is, I'll take it."

I get up to heat more milk.

Sam asks, "So what did you think of sex with a man?"

"Not much." It just pops out.

There's a split second of silence before the "ha, ha, ha" starts. In that split second, our eyes meet and I see an unmistakable glimmer of hurt.

31

As I walk over to the fridge, I find myself saying, "Shall I fix you something to eat? Scrambled eggs and toast?"

If he guesses this is a not too subtle attempt to compensate for my nasty response, he doesn't comment. "Great," he says.

Watching Sam wolf down the food—and wolf is truly the right word—I reflect there is some deep primordial satisfaction that comes of seeing someone so enthusiastically eat food you've prepared. Mere words can't possibly express such a high degree of appreciation.

When he isn't wolfing, he chatters away in his usual demonstrative fashion, with much waving of arms and flashing of teeth.

"Bedtime snacks like this always remind me of when I was growing up."

"You grew up in Southern California?"

"Yeah. Vista del Mar. My parents were kind of stunned when I moved to San Fran. Especially when they found out about the Castro District." He chuckles. "They're what you might call conservative. Especially my mother."

"That's right. I seem to recall you said she was a judge of some kind…"

"I'm not saying she was overly strict or anything. Far from it. If anything, my brother and I were kinda spoiled." He takes a mouthful of cocoa. A wave of sleepiness hits me and I struggle to stay awake.

"You have a sister too, don't you? A child psychologist?"

"M-mm. I was closest to my brother. We were just one year apart. We were always organizing things: camping trips, secret societies." Sam's expression is one of happy reminiscence. I feel a stab of envy. He asks, "How about you? Any brothers or sisters?"

"One sister, two years younger. Why did you move away from L.A.?"

"For a complete change of scene. I enjoy new experiences, experimenting with alternative lifestyles. I was fascinated by what I'd heard about the Castro. My home life was a bit too perfect. Oh, except it was pretty urban. That's one thing I'd really like to do some day. Live in the country. I have this dream of a big old house with a few acres. Dogs and chickens—that kind of thing."

I note, "We kept chickens once when I was growing up."

"Oh, yeah? You grew up on a farm?"

"Not exactly. My grandmother owned a few acres in the country in Northern California. She had an apple orchard. Also a couple of pigs and a goat. We lived with her for a couple of years."

"Man! That must have been a great experience."

"Actually—well, I enjoyed the country living but it was a sad time for all of us. My parents had just gotten divorced and we went to live with Grandma because we had no money and nowhere else to live. It took my mother a long time to pull herself together and find a job and everything."

I rub both hands around my warm cup.

Sam asks, "How old were you then?"

"I was thirteen and my sister Hazel eleven. For a while, my mother tried to find comfort in the bottle—following in Dad's footsteps." I glance up at Sam. His blue eyes are fixed on my face. "My grandmother was one of these no-nonsense people who couldn't stand people feeling sorry for themselves. At the time, she sometimes seemed a bit heartless. In retrospect, I realize that we all probably owe our survival to her refusal to let us wallow in self-pity."

There's a silence. Then Sam says, "Divorce sure is tough on kids."

I don't often talk about those times but I find myself saying, "When they were together, they fought like cat and dog. It was a horrible home life for us. But when my father finally left, my sister and I were devastated. We cried ourselves to sleep every night for the longest time."

A pause. Sam asks, "Do you see much of him?"

"We never saw him again. I'm not even sure he's still alive."

Sam shakes his head. There's a split second when his sympathy feels like a palpable thing and I half expect him to reach out and touch me. But he doesn't.

Suddenly, I see it's eleven o'clock. Cindy is due home any minute. I stretch and yawn and lead the way to the front door. Sam follows. As we near the door, he says, "So when do you think we should do this again?"

"Do what again?" Visions of scrambled egg suppers flash through my mind.

"Well, we'll need to do this a few more times, won't we? Unless we strike it lucky the first time, which seems kind of unlikely."

It's a good thing I'm in front of him and he can't see my expression. What a dolt I am! Of course, people don't always strike it lucky the first time. And here I am basking in the idiotic illusion that all I have to do now is wait nine months. By the time I reach the door and turn to him, I have my face under control. "Let's just wait and see. I'll let you know."

"Okay." He reaches into his pocket for a pen and another of those business cards and scribbles something. "I'm writing down the days I'll be away in the next couple of weeks. Otherwise, I'm usually home by six. Of course, you can also call me at work if you like."

He looks and sounds so earnest, I have a mischievous urge to make a silly crack about how I'd rather kill myself than go through this again. But I remember that hurt look in his eyes and resist the urge.

At the door, we say goodnight and smile at each other in an almost formal way.

Cindy gets home some fifteen minutes later. She comes into the kitchen where I'm cleaning the scrambled egg pan. "Don't tell me you fed the beast!" She puts her arms around my waist and I turn my face to be kissed. "You don't look *that* devastated. How was it? Or shouldn't I ask?"

"Well, it sure wasn't fun. Painful and uncomfortable. Just as I'd expected." I put the cleaned pan on the draining board. Cindy gets a dish towel to dry it.

She says, "Poor baby. It must have been hideously embarrassing for you." I think about this as I rinse out the sink.

"I suppose it was, especially at the beginning. But, you know, Cindy, in retrospect, the whole thing seems more funny than anything else. Like one of those old Abbott and Costello routines. We both kept getting entangled in ridiculous positions and we never stopped grumbling. Sam grumbled about the bed—he said it was noisy and too short. I grumbled about everything he was doing, and then he grumbled about my grumbling."

Cindy laughs. She says, and now there's a sly edge to her voice, "Well, at least you got your curiosity satisfied."

"What on earth do you mean?" I try to look indignant but it's no use—I can't stop the corners of my mouth turning up. "Oh, okay, I suppose I was curious. A bit. After all, you've had sex with a man. I never have. So now we're even."

"And now you know what you've been missing," she teases.

"Cindy, that reminds me. The poor sap actually asked me what I thought of sex with a man." I flash her a big grin. "And I told him."

"O-oo, Diane." We both giggle. Unexpectedly, the memory of his hurt expression flashes into my mind. Cindy seems to sense it. She says, "Never mind, it's all over now. Although—well, let's hope this one takes."

A little later, we go to bed and I cuddle up to her. As our two bodies lie curled, spoon-fashion, into each other, I slide my hands up her front to cup her small, firm breasts and think of Sam's effrontery in trying to do the same to me.

"How deliciously *smooth,*" I purr, "How deliciously— how shall I put it?—*hairless!*"

She chuckles and strokes my arm. I nestle my face into her neck. Sleep is a long time coming tonight. I think about sex with Sam. It was predictable—"having sex," not "making love." Yet I don't feel like the sacrificial lamb Cindy is imagining. Partly because he was so patient and persistent, in spite of the noisy bed and my ranting. If I'd been in his place, I'd have given up within the first ten minutes. Also, our little sojourn in the kitchen afterwards was kind of pleasant.

But I still don't want a baby who looks like Sam!

CHAPTER 5

Two months pass by. It is now late May. And I am still not pregnant. Sam and I have had several follow-up sessions. We approach these quite scientifically these days, unlike our first hit-or-miss attempt, with me carefully charting my daily temperatures to identify the fertile periods. We also throw in some extra sessions for luck.

Starting with our second "date," we moved our base of operations to Sam's house. Sam suggested this because, to quote, "I have a decent bed, not like that old wreck of yours." My indignant response that the so-called "wreck" was, in fact, a true antique brought a cheerful, "You can say that again," from him.

Roland, tactful soul that he is, always manages to be out when I go to their house. He doesn't seem to be in the least bit jealous of my association with Sam. Sad to say, the same cannot be said of Cindy. This is in spite of the fact that I am careful not to schedule time with Sam unless she has some social event of her own scheduled that evening.

But then there was one occasion when her plans fell through. "It's okay," she said, a martyred tone belying her indifferent shrug. "Go ahead. I've plenty to do." I got home that night to find her glaring at the T.V. and refusing to meet my eye. It took me back to the times when my mother used to sit up waiting for my father to get back from a binge.

And these days if I so much as whisper Sam's name she comes down on me with some snide comment.

One Monday morning in late May, Cindy and I are having our usual rushed cereal-and-coffee breakfast before leaving for work. It's especially rushed today because Cindy is leaving straight from work to fly to Albuquerque on a two-day business trip. She says, "I'll call you this evening. Although..." She grimaces. "Didn't you say you were going to Sam's tonight?" I nod and brace myself. "So you can take your time," she meows. "Not have to hurry back to me."

I put my cup down. "Cindy, please don't talk like that. You don't think I enjoy these sessions with Sam, do you? For heaven's sake, *you* were the one who insisted he isn't that bad and has such good genes and all."

I'm tempted to add that I'll call the whole thing off if it so upsets her. But I learned long ago not to make threats unless I'm willing to carry them out.

She pushes aside her cereal bowl and leans forward, looking earnestly into my face. "Diane, has it occurred to you he may be infertile? Or maybe the chemistry is wrong between the two of you and you could never produce a baby. You've been doing this for months now. How long are you going to keep trying?"

"It's not months, only a few weeks. I did ask the doctor though. About how long we should keep trying."

"And?"

"She said we should try for at least a year before giving up."

The other night when I told Sam this, he chuckled and said, "Oh, good."

Cindy doesn't share this sentiment. Her mouth set in a hard line, she pushes back her chair, stamps to her feet and carries her dishes to the sink. "Diane, can you imagine what it's like having someone you love being so intimate with another person?" She glares at me over her shoulder. "Have you even thought about that? About what I go through every time you go over there?"

"Cindy, darling, you shouldn't let it bother you so much. You couldn't possibly be jealous of *Sam*. That goofus caveman!"

"Somehow you seem to be getting very comfortable indeed with that goofus caveman. Well, I have news for you. I've had enough. It's time we tell Sam to take a hike."

My mouth is dry as I watch her turn the water on in the sink and rinse her dishes. "Cindy, you don't know what you're talking about. For heavens sakes, I feel sick every time he comes near me. I can't wait to have all this over and done with. But it seems silly to give up now we've come this far. How about just another month?"

She thumps her rinsed plate down on the counter. "Come what far? You haven't left the starting gate. No, Diane, I've come to the conclusion this is the worst way possible way for you to get pregnant. We both must have been mad to even consider it."

Briskly, she dries her hands on the dish towel. "From now on, it's artificial insemination or nothing. You tell Sam there's to be no more rolling around in the sack. If he doesn't want to be a regular sperm donor, we have no more use for him. You tell him that. Tell him tonight."

She marches out of the room.

There's a tiny seed of guilt inside me that her words are feeding. I know at some level I'm being deceitful. I wasn't lying when I said I don't *enjoy* my sessions with Sam. But, in truth, I don't hate them as much as I feel I *ought* to. Selfishly, I've tried to ignore Cindy's growing unhappiness in spite of the heavy toll it's taking on our relationship.

I go in search of her. She's packing the last of her toiletries into her carry-on bag. "Cindy, I'll talk to him tonight. I promise." The look she gives me is skeptical rather than pleased. But I forgive her. She's been through a lot lately. As I help her finish packing, I think that Cindy hasn't specifically forbidden tonight's assignation, has she? So I *will* see Sam tonight but will have to tell him it's our last date.

That should be interesting.

That evening, after Sam and I dispense with the business portion of our rendezvous, we drift into the kitchen for our customary après-sex snack. As he starts the coffee, Sam asks, "How long can you stay, Cinderella?" Then, remembering, he says, "Oh, that's right. Dragon Lady's away for a couple of days, isn't she? Hey, hey! The possibilities are endless."

Now is the time to tell him. I take a deep breath. And chicken out. "Know what, Sam. I didn't have much dinner tonight. Shall I fix us some scrambled eggs? Do you have enough eggs?"

"Sure do. Bacon too. And how about waffles? Roland has a waffle iron around here somewhere."

Sam finds the waffle iron in a cupboard, along with waffle mix, and we prepare a little feast. I've never made waffles and watch with interest as he mixes up the batter and pours it into the waffle iron. When everything's ready, we take the food into the dining alcove. Then Sam turns on the radio and finds some dreamy, old-time music for our dining pleasure!

The food tastes great. As we eat, we make appreciative mumbles—Sam about my bacon and eggs, me about his waffles and coffee. A haunting tune wafts from the radio, and I stop eating to listen. "Sam," I say, "I love this song. Do you know what it's called?"

He listens a moment. "Something about, *Love Walks In*. Gershwin." He half-hums, half-sings along, "Great dance music. Do you dance, Diane?'"

"No, I don't. The only dancing I've done was in high school. Our P.E. teacher gave us lessons in ballroom dancing to prepare us for the prom." I giggle. "The poor woman didn't realize that our proms didn't exactly feature waltzes and foxtrots."

Sam picks up a piece of bacon in his fingers and chews it. "H-mm," he says. "So how does that work? Did you go to the prom with a girl?"

"Are you kidding? I didn't go to the prom, period. I didn't have many friends in those days of either sex. You see, through my teens, we never stopped moving so I was always changing schools...and it was hard to make friends." Sam, his elbows on the table and still eating the bacon, fixes his eyes on me and I find myself blushing. "To make things worse, I was the most unappealing adolescent you could ever hope to meet—skinny, spotty, tongue-tied, hopelessly uncool."

"Sounds like the ugly duckling that grew into a beautiful swan."

I look at him sharply. "Yeah, right. Some beautiful swan!"

Sam says, "Don't be so down on yourself. You look good to me."

It's hardly an effusive compliment. But nice.

Sam finishes the bacon and slurps some coffee. He says, "So are you saying that back in your teens you weren't a lesbian? Or didn't know you were?"

I'm surprised he's this interested in my history. I'm surprised I'm this willing to talk about it. Cindy is the only other person I've confided in to this extent. I say, "I don't think I was anything. Frankly, I couldn't stand boys. They always seemed noisy and rough. And they sure didn't think much of me. I was never asked for a single date. My mother was always lecturing me to smarten up lest I become a—horror of horrors!—old maid."

I laugh as I say this but still feel a stab of pain, remembering those self-esteem shattering squabbles with my mother. Sam goes on eating and watching me, saying nothing. "At the same time," I say, "I didn't like girls either, not in any sexual way."

Sam says, "And then one day love walked in. With Cindy!"

"Well, yes, it did."

Sam pours a second cup of coffee for each of us. We sit and sip, the radio keeps playing sentimental songs, and I tell Sam about Cindy.

"When I was nineteen, I left home and went to live in the city in a boarding house. There were several lesbian women living there. They were kind to me. For the first time I didn't feel like a total outcast because of my lack of popularity with the opposite sex."

"Ah, so they corrupted you?"

"No, they really didn't. As I said, I didn't have any kind of love life in those days. When I lived at home, my mother was always on my case about boys. She left my self-confidence so shattered, it was a real joy to be with people who didn't keep bugging me about it."

Sam, his hands wrapped around his coffee cup, smiles at me. Looking at him across the table, I think how nice he is when he's quiet like this. So different from the guffawing braggadocio who emerges when other people are around!

I continue. "Then, a couple of years later—I was twenty-two by then—Cindy moved into our boarding house. She'd just moved to San Francisco from Chicago and was staying at our place until she found an apartment of her own."

My voice gets dreamy, thinking about it. I tell Sam, "I'd never met anyone so full of life as Cindy. She had a sparkle to her; people turned to look at her in the street. Just about everyone in our boarding house fell in love with her. As did I, although I didn't realize it right away." I chuckle. "I guess I'm not a love-at-first-sight kind of woman."

Sam smiles back and I go on. "From the start, Cindy was extra nice to me. Even so, I could hardly believe it when she asked if I'd like to share an apartment with her. I mean, here was the most attractive, charismatic woman I'd ever met choosing *me*. I was so excited and flattered."

Sam nods. But I'm starting to feel uncomfortable under his steady gaze. His expression is kind but I think I see a trace of amusement there. I say, "Enough about me. Has love ever walked in for you?"

He laughs. "Scores of times. It keeps walking right in and then walking right out again!"

"Tell me about Roland."

Cindy and I still haven't figured out what's going on with Sam and Roland. The two of them are so dissimilar. Of course, they say opposites attract, and heaven knows Cindy and I are hardly carbon copies of each other. But we do enjoy being together and doing things together, whereas the two men appear to live quite separate lives, coming and going at different times with different friends. At least, from what we can observe.

Sam says, "Oh, Roland..." But then there's the sound of a key in the lock and the front door opens. "Here's Roland now."

Roland closes the door and slinks into the living room, peering to see if anyone's in there. He jumps when he sees us in the dining alcove, and says, "Hi. I don't want to interrupt anything."

Sam says with a smutty laugh, "We don't do anything interesting in here. Only eat. In fact, why don't you join us?"

Roland seems mildly horrified at the idea, but Sam persists, "Come on, there's plenty of coffee in the pot. Decaf. Help us drink it up."

Roland relents and the three of us sit around the table drinking coffee. As the men chat about some night club Roland's just visited, I tell myself I mustn't forget to tell Sam what Cindy said.

Finally, there's a break in their conversation. I look at my watch. "You know, it's almost midnight. I'd better be getting home."

Sam gets up too; he always walks me across the street after our dates. As we step out into the misty night air, he says, "How about coming again tomorrow night? Might as well go at it all we can while Dragon Lady's out of the lair."

"Now, Sam. Quit calling her that."

Now I *must* tell him. But he launches into a story about a woman in his office whom they call the Dragon Lady—all the while laughing and gesticulating in his usual demonstrative fashion.

At the bottom of our steps, he stops to say goodnight. I take a breath. "You know, Sam, there's something I need to tell you."

"Yeah?" As he looks down at me, the light from the street lamp is behind him, casting his face in shadow. All I can see is the white flash of his teeth—but I can picture the whole face: eyes crinkling up at the corners, lips twitching in their cheerful, mischievous way. Something thumps in my chest.

"It's late. I'll tell you tomorrow." I turn around, climb the steps, and give my customary wave before opening the front door.

It takes a long time to go to sleep. That song keeps running through my mind, stirring up all kinds of thoughts. About me and boys and my teenage years.

And Cindy.

At the time Cindy and I first moved in together, we were not yet lovers. In fact, from her occasional comments to me about the "dikey" nature of some of the other women in our boarding house, I'd assumed she was unsympathetic to non-heterosexuals.

Our first apartment was a two-bedroom sublet—a lovely place overlooking the park. It was available for one year and too expensive for Cindy to rent by herself. Lucky for me, I thought, that she considered me non-dikey enough to invite to live with her.

Things changed about a month after we moved in. One evening, we were looking through a photo album of mine. Cindy paused at a picture of me with a male cousin. "Your boyfriend?" she asked.

Immediately, I felt defensive. I was sure that Cindy—with her glamorous looks and bubbly charm—had spent a lifetime fighting off admiring males. "No," I responded. "There's no one special in my life."

"Oh?" This was said with a challenging look that made me feel sure she could guess what a dismal failure I was in the boyfriend department.

"Cindy, you have to remember that most of the time I was growing up, we did nothing but move. We never lived anywhere long enough for me to put down roots and make friends."

"Well, I moved a lot too."

"And that didn't stop you from having a slew of males chasing you. Is that what you're saying?"

I laughed to make this a joke but inside I was squirming. Maybe, I thought, moving in with Cindy wasn't such a good idea after all. At least, at the boarding house, no one ever browbeat me about my lack of a sex life.

"Yes, they did." She sighed—adding, "Unfortunately, I can't stand men."

There was something tentative in her voice, in the way she looked at me through her lashes. Then I said, "Oh, I get it. The 'money means nothing to me' syndrome."

"What?"

"You know, when you read interviews with the filthy rich, they so often say something like, 'The money means absolutely nothing to me.' Like fun, it doesn't. Or maybe it doesn't, when you're swamped with it."

She looked hard at me and said slowly, "Do I take it you'd like to be swamped with men?"

By now, I could feel my face burning. "Maybe this is hard for you to imagine, Cindy, but, yes, it would be nice to have a lot of friends. To be popular."

"Well, sure. But *men*? I rather thought you liked women."

"Sure I do, but…" I looked at her a long moment, feeling confused and a bit alarmed. Then her face relaxed and she reached out a hand to take mine.

"Diane, I firmly believe that people always get what they really want. Any woman who really wants a man can get one, no matter how often she moves house. Now how many boyfriends have you had in your life?"

I hesitated.

"Any at all?"

I shook my head.

"Now *that* tells me something."

I told her, "Men have always been a giant turnoff for me. I don't know—bullying and intimidating."

Cindy tossed her head. In those days, she wore her hair in a pageboy bob which she brushed until it literally dazzled the eyes. "Believe me, you haven't missed much. I've known lots of men—dated 'em, slept with 'em. One even tried to get me to marry him. But, Diane, in my heart I know that I could happily live my whole life without any of them."

I stared at her. "But, Cindy, surely...won't you want to get married some day?"

She laughed. "You're swallowing your mother's propaganda, girl! How about this? I've been looking all my life for someone just like you to come along. Someone..."

The phone rang at this point. She hesitated a moment—then blew me a flirtatious kiss before going to answer it. I remained on the couch, my eyes following her—stunned and intrigued by what she'd been saying. What *had* she been saying? Slowly, it sank in that perhaps—maybe—she wanted me to be her "partner." This was a term whose special meaning I had learned for the first time during my stay at the boarding house.

She talked on the phone for quite a while, her back to me, the golden hair sparkling as she moved her head. And, as she talked, a torrent of emotions flooded over me. Uncertainty, fear, excitement. And joy. Because at that moment it suddenly seemed that everything in my unsettled life was finally falling into place.

And now, on this Monday night five years later, the joy is with me still. As for Sam, I'll worry later about how to tell him. I fall asleep cuddling Cindy's pillow.

CHAPTER 6

That conversation with Sam never did take place. The very day after Cindy so unequivocally put her foot down, Sam's father suffered a major heart attack. Sam took off right away to be with his family in Los Angeles and I've hardly seen or heard from him the past couple of weeks.

On a Thursday night in mid-June, we arrive home to find a message from him on our answering machine. "Diane, I'm flying back to San Fran tonight. I'll give you a call this evening."

His timing is perfect. Because I have a different—and considerably easier—message to deliver now.

He calls shortly after dinner.

"Sam, welcome back. How's your father?"

"He's doing great, out of the hospital and well on the road to recovery. About time too. I've used up all my vacation time."

"Roland told us it was a triple bypass?"

"Yeah, but he's passed the worst of it. And I sure have had enough of family for a while. I mean, they're all great but I can only take so much of being clung to. Know what I mean? My mother's a real clinger and she makes me feel edgy. I just don't have a bottomless reserve of sympathy to draw on."

"Now you sound like my late grandmother. Everyone put their stiff upper lip forward. And all that."

"We-e-ell, what's the point? You have to get on with things, don't you? Life goes on. And that's why I'm calling. So we can get back to unfinished business. Up for a date tomorrow night?"

Speaking slowly, savoring the moment, I say, "Guess what? Our dating days may be over. For it is just possible that I, Diane Dawson, may be pregnant."

He whoops. "No kidding!"

"I'm trying not to get too excited. I went to the doctor today and she's having some tests done. She'll call me tomorrow."

"Hallelujah!" He lowers his voice to a dramatic growl. "How come all this happened while I was away? Huh? Are you *sure* this baby is mine?"

"Oh, you funny man, you! Anyway, I'll let you know tomorrow."

"Sure." He pauses. "Maybe we should have just one more go at it. To cement the deal, as it were."

"No, Sam." My voice is firm but I can't help smiling thinking how Cindy would flip if she could hear him. "The doctor said nothing about cementing."

He gives a ho-hum sigh. "Just testing."

The next morning, at breakfast, I fidget and pick at my food. Cindy is floating on air. She chirps, "It will be so good to know for sure about the baby. Also, it will be *wonderful* to see the back of Sam."

"M-mm." What will be even more wonderful, I think, is to have a sunny-tempered Cindy back in my life. I say, "If all goes well, we can go look at some baby furniture this weekend."

"Oh, yes." Cindy's eyes shine. We both love buying stuff.

• • •

Around ten o'clock, I'm at my post in the law office of Lawrence Jackman & Sons, my employer. As I tap away at my word processor, I see Miss Byrd mincing her way over to me. Miss Byrd is the supervisor of our word processing pool. She likes us to call her by her first name, Alice. So we do, to her face. But, behind her back, she's always Miss Byrd. This is because it's such a good name for her. She's tall and thin and a bit stooped, sort of like a crane, and has a long hooked nose.

We all love Miss Byrd. In spite of her frail physique, she defends us staunchly from the puffed-up-with-their-own-self-importance Mr. Jackman and his progeny who pile on the work, set ludicrous deadlines, provide confusing and contradictory instructions. And then blame us when things go wrong. But Miss Byrd always takes our side.

Also, she never fails to observe if one of her *girls*, as she calls us, is sick or down in the dumps. We snicker about it sometimes, but actually it is quite comforting when you're in a melancholy mood to have the old dear take you aside to comfort you and offer some homespun advice. Advice that's out of date maybe, but always well-intentioned.

Miss Byrd reaches my side and leans down to whisper, "Phone call." We're strictly forbidden to accept or make phone calls in the office, but I've told Miss Byrd I'm expecting an important call from *the doctor*. Her eyes widened in excitement when I told her. I didn't explain why the doctor would be calling. I get up and follow her into the glassed-in cubicle that is her office. She hovers by an open file drawer in the corner, pretending not to listen.

"Hullo," I say into the phone.

"Mrs. Dawson?" That's the doctor's nurse on the other end. I mutter "*Ms.*" but she doesn't hear me. She says, "Congratulations are in order. The tests came back positive."

Even though I've been expecting this news, and would have been crushed not to have received it, I still feel like a rocket just exploded inside me. Spontaneously and quite literally, I leap into the air and squeal, "That's wonderful! That's wonderful!"

Miss Byrd, I note out of the corner of my eye, flinches at my leap and then stands stock still. I can almost hear her muscles quivering in concentration. I don't care. At this moment, I love the whole world. Dear Cindy for putting up with all the Sam shenanigans. Dear Sam for his persistence. Dear Miss Byrd. Talk about ears pricking up! I swear hers have grown an inch in the past sixty seconds.

The nurse tells me about a program they have for ex-pectant mothers and that I'll need to call back next month to schedule an appointment. I agree and hang up. Miss Byrd lowers her head and peers at me over her eyeglasses. Deliberately, I pause—partly to tease her but also I'm not sure how this sweet spinster lady is going to take my news.

Finally, I say, "Alice, I'm going to have a baby."

A strange mix of expressions crosses her face—astonishment, dismay, and, after a few long moments, a sort of determined delight. "That's wonderful, dear. I didn't know you were...." Now, she blushes.

I help her out. "No, I'm not. Married, that is. But my partner and I have been trying to have a baby for some time."

"Your partner?" I nod. The poor woman looks bewil-dered. She says, "Well, congratulations." We talk a little about things like when the baby is due, maternity leave, and so on. Then, as I'm about to leave her office, she asks, "Will you and your partner be getting married? Now that you're having a baby?"

I ponder my response. She obviously doesn't suspect that my partner is female. In fact, the whole gay revolution has no doubt completely passed her by. Well, there is such a thing as same-sex marriage, so I don't have to lie totally. I reply, "We haven't really discussed it, but who knows."

Miss Byrd nods her head in vigorous approval. "I do think it's a good idea for the baby's sake."

Comes lunchtime, and I am itching to share the news with my significant other. We have to use the pay phone in the basement to make personal calls, so after munching my peanut butter sandwich, I grab some change and make my way downstairs.

When I step out of the elevator, I see a small man—one of the janitors, I think—talking on the only phone. At the sight of me, he hangs up and retreats to a spot a few feet away. I call Cindy's office but she's out power-lunching somewhere so I leave a message. "Cindy, I have *great* news."

Aching to get someone's real-time reaction, I think about Sam. There's a directory by the phone and I look up his firm: Johnson, Harvey and something. I find it and call the number. The switchboard directs my call to his phone. A female voice answers, "Mr. Bradshawe's office." When I ask to speak with him, she says, "He's in a lunch meeting but I may be able to interrupt him if it's urgent. May I ask who's calling?"

"Diane Dawson."

"And your company?"

"Er, Lawrence Jackman."

Now why did I say that? It won't mean a thing to Sam and he'll probably refuse to take the call. But after a couple of minutes, he comes on the phone. "Bradshawe speaking."

I'm taken aback for a second. It's hard to reconcile the somber cadence of this businesslike voice with my exuberant bed-bouncing companion.

"Sam, it's Diane. I have good news."

There's a pause. Then, "Oh, *Diane!*"

"Yes, the results were...." I notice to my annoyance that the little man still hasn't left and has the nerve to be eavesdropping. I mutter, "Positive."

Sam says, "What? I can't hear you."

I raise my voice. "Positive—the results."

Sam says, "So we have a baby? That's terrific."

I make a face at the wretched little man and he turns his back. Sam's voice drifts through, "Diane, are you there? This is pretty exciting."

"Yes, it is." This pushy little man is ruining my concentration. Sam's voice has a tense feel to it, and I remember he had to leave a meeting to take my call. I say, "Well, I just thought I'd let you know."

"Yes, I appreciate it. Look, Diane, I have to go now but I'll call you tonight."

I hang up, feeling a bit flat. As I turn away, the little man advances. He waits until I board the elevator before picking up the phone. Spitefully, I consider leaping out to stand beside him and see how he likes being eavesdropped on. For some illogical reason, I find myself blaming him because Sam hung up so quickly.

By the time I get on the trolley to go home, I'm back on my wave of elation. Happily, I dream away the dreary journey, oblivious to the weary-faced commuters jostling around me. I think about shopping for baby furniture, about transforming our tiny spare room into a nursery. I've seen just the right wallpaper: two shades of pink with a sconce of silvery lambs and puffy white clouds.

When I get home, Cindy is there ahead of me. She greets me with her arms outstretched and we hug. "Sweetie, what wonderful news. I was longing to call you back this afternoon, but you know your company and its stupid rules!" I am so happy to see Cindy so happy. For a moment, I slide my face along the side of her head and breathe in the lemony smell of her hair. How I have missed my cheerful Cindy these past Sam-filled weeks. She burbles on, "I had to celebrate somehow so I treated some of my colleagues to coffee. They were thrilled for me. For us."

Surprised, I react, "You told people at work?" For all the lip service paid these days to gay rights, I still harbor dark fears that one day Cindy's nonconformist personal life will topple her off that corporate ladder she's climbing so speedily.

She says, "Of course. Didn't you?" I tell her about my awkward exchange with Miss Byrd, and she laughs. "Don't be surprised if that old goat is a lesbian herself!" I decide not to tell Cindy about my call to Sam. It would probably upset her to think he got the news before she did.

Cindy says, "Now you take it easy tonight. I'll get the dinner." This announcement doesn't exactly thrill me because Cindy's cooking is of the slapdash variety. However, she means well so I make murmurs of appreciation.

We both get changed; then I sit at the kitchen table while Cindy prepares the food. She pan-fries chicken breasts and fixes flavored rice from a packet. Soon, the smell from the frying chicken becomes overpowering. Oh dear, could this be the start of morning sickness? And it isn't even morning. While Cindy has her back to me, I hold a napkin over my nose and try not to breathe in too much.

The phone rings. Cindy bounces over to answer it after pulling the pan off the heat. "Hello." Right away, her voice cools. "Oh, hi. No, she's not available right now."

She glances at me. I know it's Sam, and now Cindy's going to know I've already told him. She listens, her brow furrowing. Then, she says, "Well, thank you. I guess you'd like us to send you your two hundred dollars now. Or do you want more? Seeing it took so long."

I tense. Cindy's being nasty. While Sam talks, she tries to interrupt him. "Okay...okay... Look, Sam, a deal is a deal. So we'll mail it to you tomorrow. And remember the other part of our agreement—no more contact." She listens some more. "Thank you, but we have other plans." More listening. "Yes, I'll tell her. Goodbye."

She hangs up and raises her eyebrows at me with a half-smile. "Can you imagine, he wanted to see you. Pushy, isn't he?" She mimics in a gravelly baritone, "*How about I take you both out to dinner to celebrate?*" She gets two plates from the cupboard, puts a chicken breast on each and adds a scoop of the rice mixture. Then she pours each of us a glass of milk and carries the food over to the table. "There you are. *Bon appetit.*"

But the chicken has become over-greasy after sitting in the pan while she was on the phone. The very sight of it turns my stomach. I take a forkful of rice and a sip of milk. Cindy looks at me and says, "Not hungry? I'm not surprised. The thought of that oaf is enough to make anyone lose their appetite."

"What was it he wanted you to tell me?"

Cindy mumbles through a mouthful of food, "Oh, something about how he didn't have time to talk when you called him today, and he's afraid he may have sounded abrupt. And some nonsense about how you sounded distracted." She glances at me. "Obviously just trying to prod me into calling you to the phone."

"No, he's right. I was distracted. There was this annoying little man by the phone. He wouldn't go away."

Cindy gives me a puzzled look and I realize that *distracted* is what I must sound right now. After a long moment, she says gently, "Look, Diane, Sam has done what we are paying him to do. You do still agree that we must make a complete break with him now? I mean, we *all* understand that, right?"

"Yes, of course."

Suddenly, the smell of the food is making me feel really ill. I cover my face with my napkin again and say, my voice thick, "But you might have been nicer to him."

"No, Diane. We have to make a clean break, otherwise he'll keep hanging around and we'll have to be increasingly rude. Sometimes, you have to be cruel to be kind."

There she goes with her corny clichés. But I know she's absolutely right. This baby is ours—Cindy's and mine. Sam was the means to an end. From now on, there's no place for him in our lives.

CHAPTER 7

After that conversation with Cindy, Sam doesn't call at 2013 any more. We still see him occasionally when he goes out to his car and often hear his booming voice when he's talking to a neighbor.

One day, insistent honking from a car horn lures me to the front window. There's Sam in a new green Porsche parked by the curb outside his house. It seems Roland is in the house and Sam is trying to attract his attention with the honking. What attracts *my* attention is the tall blonde with long bedraggled hair who is sitting beside him in the car. Where did *she* come from? When Roland emerges from their house, I move away from the window so he won't see me peering. It's none of my business anyway.

A Saturday night. Cindy and I are getting dressed to go to a party. The past few weeks, I've been plagued by morning sickness—or, more accurately, morning-noon-and-night sickness. But now it's definitely on the wane and it feels wonderful to be socializing again. Humming to myself, I select one of my favorite dresses. It's a dress that just makes you *feel* pretty. A soft silky cotton in a sort of Indian print of gold and brown.

When I go to zip it up, the zipper stops part way. For a moment, I can't figure out what's wrong and then I realize.

Cindy comes out of the bathroom at this moment, toweling her damp hair. She giggles at my cursing. "Now, Diane, not in front of the baby." She looks at the halfway zippered zip and adds, "We'll have to get you outfitted at the *Ladies in Waiting* store, won't we?"

As I search through my wardrobe for something less formfitting to wear, I go through the motions of grumbling at the inconvenience. But it's all a sham. Bubbles of joy are percolating inside me at this fresh evidence of my budding motherhood. Cindy, sitting on the bed behind me, says, "Oh, Di-dee, how I envy you!"

"My fat waist?"

"No, silly. Your *glow*. Pregnant women always seem to have this incredible glow."

"H-mm." I look into the mirror, holding up against me a cream two-piece I have selected. "I don' see no glow, honey-chile. All I see is the same ole' me. Now with expanded mid-section."

Cindy laughs. "You don't fool me. You're loving every minute of this motherhood stuff, aren't you?"

There's no way I can deny that. At this moment, I feel like the luckiest woman in the world.

Cindy comes to my aid as I struggle to pull the cream top over my head. "It helps to unbutton *all* the buttons, honey-bunny," she says. When my head finally pops through the opening, we smile at each other, eye to eye.

She says, "Have I ever told you how wonderful it is to have you back?"

"Have me back? Where did I go?"

She frowns a little. "I'm not sure. But you definitely left me for a time."

We gaze solemnly at each other in silence. Finally, I say, "You're talking about Sam?"

She nods. "For a while, I thought I was going to lose you."

Her eyes fill with tears. Mine do too. "Cindy, we must clear something up." As I speak, I put my arms around her and pull us both down into a sitting position on the bed. "About Sam. Sure he can be polite and sweet when he wants to be, *but...*" Here I look hard into her eyes with the most earnest expression I can muster. "The man is loud, he's coarse, he's crude, he's...."

"A Neanderthal?" She smiles through her tears.

"Exactly. I mean okay to have sex with but..."

At this, we both shout with mirth. I continue, "But, seriously, as someone to spend time with on a *voluntary* basis—I don't think so."

Cindy kisses my cheek. "I'm sorry," she gasps, "It was stupid of me to react like that. I promise I'll never be that neurotic again."

"I hope you'll never have any call to be." I stand up. "This cream outfit should do, don't you think? The top sort of disguises the waist."

"It looks great." She goes off to the bathroom to blow-dry her hair. After she leaves, I take a few deep breaths and remain sitting on the bed a while longer. An unspecified dread has gripped me while we were talking and I have just realized what it is. Since we've been lovers, I have never for a moment envisioned a life without Cindy. The prospect is inconceivable to me. But her words seemed to imply such a prospect is not inconceivable to *her.*

For a moment, I remain sitting on the bed, rubbing my stomach as though that could smooth away the panicky feeling inside.

Our friend Phyllis is giving the party. It takes ten minutes to drive to her house, and another ten to find a parking space. Phyllis greets us at the door. She's about sixty, with iron-gray hair down to her waist, ruddy complexion unadorned by makeup, and a faint Scottish burr to her speech. Tonight she's wearing what can only be described as a multi-layered tent that accentuates rather than hides her bulk.

This goodhearted, bag-lady-look-alike is an activist. Her causes cover a broad spectrum from gay rights to the saving of whales. She's someone you just have to respect for her sheer energy and passion—although Cindy and I sometimes pretend not to be in when we see Phyllis marching up the walk with yet another bunch of petitions under her arm.

Phyllis' living-cum-dining room is crammed with noisy people, drinking and laughing. But immediately, above the din, I recognize a distinctive *ha-ha-ha*. Sure enough, there's Sam off in one corner in the midst of a group of equally rowdy party-goers, including—well, whaddya know!—the Bedraggled Blonde.

Cindy says to Phyllis. "I see Sam's here."

"Yes," says Phyllis, "and just check out that gorgeous woman he has with him." *Gorgeous?* I look again. Blondie is a healthy-looking Germanic type. I bet she hikes mountains in the rain. She's probably called Brunhilda.

I find a chair in the farthest corner of the room from Sam. Cindy gets me a can of ginger ale. "I'll round up some munchies for you. What would you like? Veggies and dip?"

"It's okay; I'll help myself in a while. You go off and mingle."

"If you're sure." I nod, and she floats off to check out the crowd. I watch her as she greets and hugs and kisses cheeks. Everyone knows Cindy and she knows everyone. She has a vivacity that draws people like a magnet. Males and females alike. And she knows it and loves it! I watch her with pride and think, not for the first time, how much I would love our baby to look just like her. Unfortunately, fat chance!

As I sip my ginger ale, I look thoughtfully down at my belly. It doesn't really look fatter but it must be. Zippers don't lie. A shadow dims the light from the room. I look up and somehow am not surprised to see Sam standing there. He says, "Hi, Diane." There's no spare chair so he crouches on the floor beside me. Thank goodness he didn't bring Blondie over with him. "How've you been?"

His solicitous tone annoys me. It seems downright hypocritical considering he hasn't attempted to make contact even once since he found out I was pregnant.

"Well," I say, "I'm okay now, but I sure was sick there for a while."

Now he looks anxious. "But the baby was never at risk, was he?"

"Well, no," I admit. His eyes travel toward my belly and rest there a moment. Then he looks up, meets my eye, and smiles a little self-consciously. He says, "When is he due?"

"February 15. And what makes you think it's a *he*?"

His smile grows cocky and he tips his head to one side. "Do you have evidence to the contrary?"

"I just know it's a girl."

"And I just know it's a boy." But his eyes are twinkling, and I giggle.

Then his face gets serious and he glances around before speaking. "Diane, I know Cindy is determined to keep me away from you, but please let me know when the baby is born. Won't you?"

"Sure."

He nods and stands up. Then he leans toward me and speaks softly. Come to think of it, he's been speaking softly the whole time, no doubt to avoid attracting Cindy's attention. He says, "If there's ever any way I can help you or the baby, just let me know. Anything at all."

"Pots of money would be good."

"Money's no problem. I'd be glad to help out."

"Oh, no, Sam. I'm only kidding."

"I'm not."

He flicks a hand in farewell before walking off. A few minutes later, I hear raucous shouts and laughs from across the room and look over. There's Sam, appearing to wrestle with Blondie. She's writhing around on his lap, undoing his shirt buttons and pulling his chest hair. All this is accompanied by knee-slapping hilarity from onlookers. I look away.

Driving home later in the evening, a tipsy Cindy inquires, "So what the hell did Sam want?"

"He was just asking about my health. Oh, and he'd like to know when the baby is born."

"He would, would he!"

I glance at her. I'm glad we don't have far to go. At times like this, I could kick myself for not learning to drive Cindy's stick shift. Not that I'd be much use tonight even if I had. Suddenly, I'm so sleepy I can barely keep my eyes open. As she drives, Cindy is getting herself whipped into a small frenzy. I hear snatches of what she's saying in between spells of nodding off.

"As long as we live close to him, we're never going to be free of him, especially...." Here, she stops to poke my arm. "Diane, are you listening to me? Especially if the baby is a boy."

Half-asleep, I protest, "No, not a boy."

Her voice continues to come and go in waves as I struggle to stay awake. "He'll drag the kid off...teach it football...turn it into a macho ape like him." In my slumberous state, I picture Sam and Brunhilda driving up in the Porsche, their arms outstretched. *Give us the baby, Diane. We're going to Little League.*

We pull up at the curb in the front of our house. The garage we rent for Cindy's car is a couple of blocks away, but tonight she'll leave it parked in the street. It embarrasses me to have it parked outside our house because Cindy got this dumb personalized plate for it. It says *Hot2Trot*. She thinks it's cute; I think it's downright unprofessional.

Now, she gets out of the car and glares over at Sam's place. "There's only one solution. We have to move."

Stumbling behind her up the path to the house, I plead, "No, Cindy, surely that won't be necessary."

"Yes, it will. Otherwise, he'll be in our hair forever."

Inside the house, she closes the front door and puts on the safety catch. She keeps talking as we go into the bedroom and get undressed. "You see, Diane, I'm not as naïve as you when it comes to men. I battle with them every day in the office. Sam doesn't care about babies, *per se*. For him, as with so many men, it's all a matter of power and dominance. He'll try to take control of the baby just to prove he can."

Climbing into bed, I recall the way the springs screamed like live creatures when first Sam came aboard. I put my face into the pillow so Cindy won't see me smile.

She keeps talking even after putting out the light. All about the corporate world and men and power plays and ways to thwart them. About how Sam has another think coming if he imagines us little girls will sit by helplessly while he moves in on our baby. "One day, he'll wake to find us gone. No forwarding address. That'll fix him." I know it's the wine talking. Tomorrow, she'll have calmed down. Heck, tomorrow, she'll be too busy nursing her hangover to be bothered about Sam.

Thoughts blur into fantasy, sharpen, and blur again as waves of sleepiness come and go. I relive the evening. Sam's offer to help us was kind of nice. But that's probably just another ploy in the power game Cindy was talking about. As the saying goes, there's no free lunch. And how about that blowsy blonde and the scandalous way she was carrying on, taking his shirt off? Well, why should I care? We're finished with him anyway.

But as I give in and let sleep overcome me, it occurs to me that even if we are finished with him, Sam still complicates things for me in ways I don't completely understand. Cindy's right. If we stay here, he'll be in our hair forever. Moving is the smart thing to do.

CHAPTER 8

It's a Friday in the last week of January. I've been home on maternity leave for a week now, seven wonderful days of rest and self-indulgence. And there are still two whole weeks to go before the Big Day.

Cindy comes home at six o'clock. She walks into the house, calling out, "Oooh, what a lovely smell! What's for dinner?"

"Roast pork tenderloin," I call back, "prebraised in garlic, mashed potatoes, applesauce and sprouts."

Cindy hangs her coat up in the hall and comes into the kitchen to hug me. "I'm *drooling* in anticipation."

She's not the only one. The past few months, I've recovered both the joy of cooking and the joy of eating. As I putter about in the kitchen—mashing potatoes, slicing the meat—Cindy pops into the bathroom, then to the bedroom to change, then back to the kitchen. She chats as she glances through the mail, entertaining me with tidbits from her day on the fast track.

As I put the food on the plates, something in my midsection stirs ominously. I've had a backache much of the day so maybe I'm overdoing things. Well, after dinner, Cindy will do the dishes, as she does every day now, and I can zonk with my feet up in front of the TV.

Suddenly, what feels like a giant vise grabs me around the middle. The pain is excruciating. I drop my knife and fork and clutch the edge of the table. Cindy is mid-anecdote. "So I said to him, if you feel like that, perhaps we should both go talk to Mr. Fillmore...." She stops abruptly. "Diane, what's wrong?"

"Nothing." The pain recedes as quickly as it came, but I'm still gasping from the shock. "I had a pain but I'm okay now." I pick up my knife and fork. This is too delicious a meal to even think of wasting.

Cindy goes on staring at me, her mouth hanging open. Then she says, "Do you think you're getting labor pains?"

"No, of course not. I'm not due for two whole weeks. And first babies tend to be late, not early." She shrugs, and we both continue eating. Cindy gets back to her anecdote, but pauses now and then to give me a concerned look. I'm determined to think positive. I have fourteen days of freedom left and intend to enjoy every one of them.

We both fairly polish our plates. Cindy says, "Diane, that was a superb meal. As usual."

"Thank you. I do think this meat was especially tender. And now...." I push back my chair and rise, gathering up the dirty plates, "Just wait till you see what's...*for dessert.*" My voice rises in a shriek on the last two words as another of those damned pains knocks the stuffing out of me. I slam the plates back down on the table and clutch my stomach. "Ohmygod, this is awful."

Cindy stands up and comes over to ease me back into my chair. She says, "I don't care how many weeks are left. I'm calling the doctor right now."

Twenty-four hours later, I'm in the maternity ward of St. John's. Cindy drove me to the hospital just after midnight. The baby came about nine o'clock this morning.

Thinking back, it's all a blur: excitement, rush, noise, bright lights, grinding pain. And a voice saying, "It's a boy. A beautiful baby boy."

Cindy hung around at the hospital until late afternoon when she finally went home to get some sleep. She won't be coming again till tomorrow.

From my propped-up position in bed, I look around the bland room. Oodles of cream and gray-blue. It's a semi-private room but I'm the only occupant this evening. My bed is near the window—a sheet of black reflective glass at this time of night. Between me and the window, there's a little bassinet for the baby. He's not in it at the moment; the nurse has taken him somewhere for weighing or something.

A candy-striper comes to the door. "Juice? Snacks?" Dinner wasn't that long ago, but I take an orange juice and a couple of cookies. I should be reveling in this pampering but I'm not. It's hard to revel when you feel so darn sore. Also, I feel kind of down.

It's a good thing we did the baby's room in yellow, as Cindy urged, rather than go with my choice of pink. But that isn't much comfort to me at this moment. It's my fault, I suppose, that I was so taken aback at having a boy. I could have found out the sex of the baby before birth, but I just didn't want to. I really was sure it would be a girl. And, frankly, if it wasn't going to be a girl, I didn't want that unsettling news to overshadow my pregnancy.

The news doesn't seem to bother Cindy one bit. In fact, she is positively running over with enthusiasm for our baby. As I lay blubbering on the delivery bed, she was cooing things like, "Just look at that dear little face. What a doll!" On and on. And, finally, "Oh, come on, Diane. Little boys can be adorable too."

I don't know about that. Besides, it really doesn't seem fair to the poor kid being raised by two women.

I mean, neither of us is the slightest bit interested in sports or whatever it is little boys like.

As I sip my juice, I fret over something else. There's something I've been putting off that I can put off no longer. Telling my mother.

My grandmother died after I'd been living with Cindy only a few months. Cindy didn't attend the funeral with me. This was mainly because I had not yet found the courage to "come out" to my family. They knew only that I was living with a female friend.

On the evening following the burial, the three of us— my mother, sister, and I—were sitting around the kitchen table in my mother's apartment. My sister lived, and still does, only a few miles from Mom in the Northern California town of Redding. At that time, Hazel was engaged to be married to a pasty-faced and—in my opinion—rather boring young man; he had found himself something else to do on this evening of mourning.

The three of us sipped tea and looked gloomy. Conversation lagged. Then my mother—nose hovering just inches above her cup, her voice thick—proclaimed, "There's not much point in living any more, is there?"

Hazel and I raised our eyebrows at each other. We'd heard similar outbursts before. After my father left us, my mother passed through one emotional phase after another— from deep depression to obnoxious acting out to a sort of embittered complacency. Her moods saddened and frightened me as a young girl. But, as I grew older, I lost patience as I saw them more as a bid for attention rather than a genuine expression of a soul in torment.

Hazel said, "Because Grandma's gone? But, Mom, you never got along with her. You hardly ever went to see her in the nursing home."

My mother cast her eyes around the room in a desperate, caged-animal, fashion. "No, but at least she was someone not to get along with. You girls..." She waved a hand at the two of us. "You don't give a fig about me. How often do you ever come to visit? Even you, Hazel. And you live right around the corner."

Hazel sighed, opened her mouth and closed it. She looked at me again. My mother continued, "All I can hope is one day there'll be grandchildren I can enjoy. At least from you..." to Hazel again. "If you and that good-for-nothin' ever get married."

A snort of laughter escaped me. I said, "Mom, you're too much."

Immediately, her pale gray eyes turned in my direction. Her mouth tightened in thin-lipped venom. "At least," she snipped, "Hazel has found a man. More'n you've done."

My heart thudded as I recognized this as the perfect moment to tell her about Cindy. Not meeting her eye, I said, "Nor do I plan to, Mama. I've already found the person I'll be loving for the rest of my life."

The two of them gawped at me, wide-eyed. My mother asked, "What are you talking about?"

"My Cindy."

In the ensuing silence, I watched a trickle of tea dribble out of my sister's mouth. Then my mother stammered, "*Cindy*? But that's a...that's not a...."

I nodded and tensed for the outburst to follow.

"What are you talking about? You're not trying to say you're one of *those* women. No, I won't have it. I won't have it." She glared at me—hoping, I suspect, for a denial from me. An acknowledgment that this was a silly joke. When it didn't come, she threw her head upward and rolled her eyes around. "Thank the Lord your grandmother isn't able to hear this. Dear God in Heaven, what have I done to deserve a daughter like you? Have I been such a bad mother?"

Hazel dragged her startled eyes away from me and reached for my mother's hand. "Mama, don't take it so hard. These days, lots of people…"

"I know about those people. That still doesn't make it right. It's…it's *disgusting*." She shuddered as if the very thought of my iniquity was too sickening to bear. "What do you mean by it? Huh? What do you have to say for yourself?"

As chirpily as my trembling voice would allow, I said, "Well, I have heard tell that the parents of gay people sometimes take the news hard. I guess those weren't just rumors."

This appeared to infuriate her further. Eyeballs veritably popping out from her head, she snapped, "It's nothing to snicker about, Missy." Whereupon, she rose to her feet and stomped from the room. Hazel and I heard her climbing the stairs and shutting her bedroom door behind her. And there she stayed for the rest of the evening, refusing even to come down for the casserole my sister had prepared and brought over specially for the occasion.

As I packed that evening, I had just two thoughts in my mind. To get out of my mother's house as early in the morning as I could. And never to return.

Which I did. And haven't.

Amazingly enough, she wrote to me very soon after I returned home from that visit. It was a chatty letter full of sentimental reminiscences about Grandma. She asked if I'd like to have something of the old lady's: her pearls, silver teapot, oak dresser. At the time, I skipped through these niceties in search of some mention of Cindy. There was not a word. Since then, we've exchanged birthday and

Christmas cards. She never mentions my partner or my life style, nor do I.

Hazel, my sister, got married three years ago but has not yet produced a child. My mother's Christmas note last year complained about this. She wrote, "I can see I'm going to die without ever becoming a grandmother."

"Hypocritical old cow," I commented to Cindy after relaying this prophecy to her. "She made sure there was precious little joy in the lives of her two daughters. Now she wants a chance to screw up some grandkids."

My mother knows nothing of my pregnancy, mainly because I haven't known what or if to tell her about Sam. Now, I suppose she has to be told. But what would be the consequences of that telling? Under no circumstances, do I want her playing the grandmother and interfering in our lives. On the other hand, if she acts as she did with Cindy and just refuses to acknowledge my baby's existence....

The hurt would be more than I could bear.

My gloomy reverie is interrupted by the sound of laughter and scuffling in the hall—male voices counting off room numbers. Then, "Here she is!" Sam and Roland fill the doorway. Sam's holding a huge basket of flowers. Spectacular, garish flowers—a profusion of scarlet, gold, purple, and white.

He charges into the room, a barrel of noisy energy. A more subdued Roland follows. I'm surprised to see them. I haven't talked to either of them since that party at Phyllis' house last fall. Cindy must have phoned to tell them the news. Sam puts the flowers on the window ledge. He says, "How're you feeling?"

"Horrible."

My reply is drowned out by Roland who peers into the empty bassinet. "Oh, no, someone stole the baby!" He and

Sam snort and slap each other's shoulders and Sam makes silly remarks about the invisible baby and how you have to add water to make it reappear. They're like a couple of ten-year-olds.

"Oh, you have visitors." The nurse has reappeared with the baby. She looks from Sam to Roland and back again. She says to Sam, "You're the father, right?" Sam nods in a proud, self-conscious way. "I knew it," she says, "The baby looks just like you." Sam beams. Roland snickers and retreats to a corner by the curtain. My brain is too fuzzy to react.

"Here, would you like to hold him?" While Roland snickers ever louder, Nursie presses the little guy into Sam's muscular arms. She shows him how to support the head and all that. He looks down at the baby as though viewing some rare specimen someone's dug up in a cave.

Nursie looks at me. She says, "I'm glad I've caught the two of you together. I'll be right back." She leaves.

Sam sits down at the bottom of my bed still holding the baby. He says, "He's incredibly tiny."

Roland pipes up, "Well, he's premature, isn't he?"

"He is *not*." I'm full of indignation. "He's full term."

Roland looks at Sam and says, "We thought he was early. Sam had the date marked on the calendar." Awkwardly, Sam hands the bundle over to me and I look down at the little face. What makes that woman think he looks like Sam, for heaven's sake? He looks like a baby; they all look pretty well alike at this stage.

I say, "So I guess Cindy called you about the news?"

Sam and Roland exchange glances. Sam says, "Actually, I called her. I got back from a party around midnight and saw Cindy loading you into her car."

Roland chuckles, "We guessed something was up. So, today, Sam called Cindy. Many times."

"Yeah," Sam said, "No one answered. So I kept leaving messages."

"Cindy's been here with me most of the day. But she did eventually get back to you, I guess?"

Neither of them comments. At this moment, the nurse comes back carrying a clipboard. She says briskly, "Now I need some information for the birth certificate." She goes through the form, asking questions and jotting down the answers: mother's name, address, date of birth, father's name and date of birth—but not address, I note.

"Now, the baby's name?"

That's a good question. Cindy and I already have a name for a girl, Charlene Elizabeth. Well, I know Cindy will be happy with Charles. I don't know about a second name though.

Sam says, "How about Robert Alexander?"

I look at him in amazement. Nursie flaps her eyelashes at him and says, "That's a nice name."

She's actually about to write the name on the form when I find my voice. "No way! His name will be Charles... something."

Sam has the gall to argue. He says, "Alexander was my late grandfather's name. Just before he died, I promised him I'd name my first son after him. Robert...well, I just like the name Robert."

Indignation is making me sputter. The baby rolls into my lap as I sit upright and shout at Sam. "What the hell does it have to do with you? Butt out."

Nursie hastens forward to rescue the baby. She takes him from me and lays him in the bassinet. "There, there. Don't get so upset." And to Sam, "Maybe you could compromise." The poor woman obviously thinks this is a marital spat.

Sam looks at me. He has a calculated glint in his eye. Darn him, he knows exactly what he's doing. Cindy was quite right about the power trip. I'm about to start yelling obscenities again when he says quickly, "How about Charles Alexander?"

I stop mid-yell. *Charles Alexander.* It has a nice ring to it, a rhythm. Shades of kings and emperors. Nursie looks at me anxiously. "How about that, dear?" Well, there's no point in saying "No" just to be spiteful, so I nod and she writes it on the form. She puts the clipboard on my bedside table. "I'll leave this with you to review and sign."

She bustles off, and Roland emerges from behind the curtain. I pick up the juice glass to take another sip. My hand is trembling so much, I almost spill it. Sam is still sitting on the bed, watching me. His face is softer now. He picks up my free hand and half-whispers, "I didn't realize it would upset you so much. Of course, it's up to you to name the baby." Stroking my hand, he turns to look down at the sleeping baby, and adds, "But I'm really glad he has my grandfather's name." I'm too weary to say any more.

Sam stands and says to Roland, "I guess we've caused enough ruckus for one day. Maybe we should leave." Roland is already half-way to the door. Sam says, "He's beautiful, Diane." He looks down again at the little squashed face. "Well, for a baby, that is." The two men *heh, heh* in their silly way. I know they're just joking around, but even so the tears well up at the implied insult to my infant. Sam squeezes my hand before letting go. He says, "Remember, call if you ever need me."

After he leaves, I read over the form the nurse filled out and see that she's shown Sam's address as the same as mine. And, to my fury, she's listed the baby's name as Charles Alexander Bradshawe. I take the pen she's left, slash out the *Bradshawe* and substitute my own last name, *Dawson.*

. . .

Cindy phones about nine-thirty that evening. "I'm about to go to bed but thought I'd check on our new Mommy. How's everything going?"

"I feel sore. And kind of depressed."

"Oh, poor love. Would you like me to pop over to see you. I can be there in a half-hour."

"No, no, Cindy, I think visiting hours are about over. Besides, I really would like to get some sleep."

Cindy clucks, "Don't tell me Phyllis came to see you and left you worn out. She called this evening and I told her where you were. But I did try to persuade her not to visit tonight."

"No, she didn't, but Sam and Roland did."

"*What!*" Cindy sounds furious. "I just don't believe this."

"Sam said he called you."

"Yes, he left innumerable messages. He finally caught up with me after I got home. But I refused to tell him where you were. I said you were not to be disturbed."

"That's strange. I wonder how he...?"

"I bet Phyllis told him. I'll have to tell her how much we don't appreciate that. I'm so sorry, honey-bunch. I hope those morons didn't upset you too much."

She doesn't know the half of it! Wait till I tell her about the baby-naming business. Come to think of it, perhaps I won't tell her about that. Otherwise, she'll want us to come up with a different second name. And I've become rather attached to *Alexander*.

After I hang up, the night nurse comes in to get the baby and me settled for bed. You no sooner get used to one nurse than they change shifts. This one stops partway across the room, seemingly transfixed by the flowers on the windowsill. With the lights turned down, they look more dazzling than ever, their splashy colors reflected against the backdrop of the black glass. She says, "Wow, something completely different! We usually get subdued pink carnations on this floor!"

"Yes," I agree. "You could hardly call them subdued."

She grins at me. "Positively in your face, I would say. But they sure make you feel alive—light-hearted, cheerful—like a summer day."

I murmur, "Sort of like the guy who brought them."

She goes over to the flowers and pulls out a card, which she hands to me. It's a standard florist's card, with little flowers around the edge and a big printed *Congratulations* on it. Below this, in a bold spiky hand that must be Sam's is written, *"Love, Sam,"* followed by a single big X for a kiss.

Suddenly, I think of his sheer gall in disobeying Cindy, his bold-as-brass arguing with me over what to name the baby. I just can't help it—I smile. And I start to laugh. And then I find myself howling with stomach-wrenching gasps, tears coursing down my cheeks.

The nurse looks puzzled at my hilarity but smiles sympathetically. "Men!" she says. "Sam is the father, I assume?"

"Oh, yes," I gasp, " He sure is."

CHAPTER 9

My six-week maternity leave goes by so fast, I can't believe it. I keep feeling I've only just come home from the hospital. Next Monday, only three days from now, I'm to start work again. It was a struggle but we finally found a sitter for Charlie. She's Mrs. Ziebowski, a middle-aged Polish woman who lives a couple of miles away. Cindy will drop Charlie off and pick him up in her car on her way to and from work.

Everything in my life these days is baby, baby, and yet more baby. In between bouts of feeding and changing and laundry, I try desperately to catch some sleep. As for sleeping at night, I can forget it. This kid cries all night. He'd better mend his ways by next week.

About five, I put Charlie down for a nap and lie down myself for a ten-minute rest. Before I know it, I hear Cindy's key in the door. It's past six already. Quickly, I tumble out of bed and hurry to the kitchen, apologizing for not being ready. "I'm afraid it's going to be frozen dinners again tonight. Let's see...." I drag two boxes out of the freezer. "Roast turkey and dressing sounds tasty. Good, they can be microwaved. Only ten minutes, Cindy."

Cindy is in a super-good mood tonight. She murmurs, "Fine, fine," to my description of dinner plans, and then floats around the kitchen, humming to herself, as she helps me clear up the clutter. Breakfast dishes still in the sink, countertops and table covered with bottles, formula, bibs and wash-cloths. I can't believe what a slob I've become. How on earth will I cope when I go back to work?

When the food is bubbling, I remove it from the microwave—which, I note, also needs cleaning. We sit down with our plastic trays before us and tear off the film covers to reveal...well, a pretty revolting-looking set of contents, to tell the truth. Maybe I overdid the microwaving.

But Cindy doesn't complain. She lifts her fork, looks down a moment, and says, "Diane, our lives are about to change."

Sometimes, Cindy makes dramatic pronouncements like this but it turns out to be nothing much. For instance, she said something like that the day she ordered a garbage disposal. So I keep pushing my way through the soggy mess in front of me. "What on earth is this wet cardboard-like stuff?" I exclaim. "Oh, I suppose it's the dressing."

Cindy puts her elbows on the table and flicks her fingers at me. "Diane, you remember I told you those Peterson people have been trying to recruit me for a company in the East Bay?"

"Are those the headhunters?" Cindy is regularly "hunted," if that's the word.

"Yes. Anyway, today they said the client wants me to go for a full day of interviews next week." Her voice is a little shaky. "They say their client is tremendously impressed with my credentials. They think I'm almost certain to get an offer."

I frown. "But, Cindy, you told me before that the job they have available is Manager of Public Relations. You're expecting to get that job in your present company. Is it really worthwhile moving?"

Cindy plants her elbows on the table and looks at me earnestly. Slowly, she says, "This job would be the opportunity of a lifetime. The company is a leader in communications technology. They're headquartered in New York and are just starting up a Northern California office."

I say nothing. With a sigh, she tackles her food again. After a couple of mouthfuls, she tries again. "Don't you see, I'd be in on the ground floor. Not only would I be creating the PR department from scratch but I'd be a member of the top management team. I'd be helping to shape the whole branch operation."

To be honest, I don't know what to say. I'm a bit afraid of anything that might rock the boat at this stage of our lives. After a while, I ask, "And it's a lot more money?"

"Not much more than my current salary to start but if I do okay there'll be a *big* raise in six months. Also, there'd be fantastic stock options and those alone would make the move worthwhile. This company is really taking off."

Now, stock options and companies taking off are things I don't know much about. Some things I do know though. "Cindy, this company is in the East Bay. Didn't you say in San Ramon? That's *miles* away. What time would you have to leave in the morning? How will you get Charlie to the sitter and pick him up? There's no way *I* can do it—that's much too far for me to walk with the baby."

"Of course, you can't do that. For that matter, I wouldn't dream of commuting all that way—not for long anyhow." She straightens up and a little smile appears on her face. "Here is the most wonderful thing about this whole business. If I get this job, we won't need to renew our lease here. House prices across the Bay are way cheaper than in the city." She leans toward me, her eyes shining. "We could buy our own home. Wouldn't that be fantastic?"

The lease on this house is coming due for renewal the end of May. I'd quite forgotten about it; we generally renew it without any discussion. I look around the kitchen. It took us a while to fix up this place to our liking but now it's a perfect little home. Compact, comfortable, close to stores and transportation. And we've just done up the baby's room. Owning our own home has been a goal of ours ever since we started living together. But I hadn't anticipated it happening for a while yet.

"Cindy, you do realize we only have about $30,000 in our house fund? We'll need way more than that. There's the downpayment, closing costs, house insurance."

Impatiently, Cindy pushes aside her plate and reaches across the table to grasp my forearms. "Di-*ann*, these places I'm talking about are available with next to nothing down. We could get a brand-new condo with two bathrooms and a double garage—and, yes, we *will* be able to afford it. The Peterson man hinted that by the end of the year I'll be getting double my current salary."

"Double? Good Heavens."

But it takes only seconds for me to find something wrong with this rosy scenario. "Cindy, hold on. What about me? If we move, then *I'll* have to do the commuting. I can't do that with Charlie."

As if on cue, Charlie starts to wail. I jump up and head toward the bedroom. Cindy calls after me, "Don't be silly. Of course, I wouldn't expect you to commute. You'd have to quit your job. Which you've been longing to do, right? Since the old goat retired. I'll find a job for you in my new company. How about that?"

It's true about dear Miss Byrd. She's retired and my friend Kitty from work phoned recently to report that our new supervisor, Miz Lucinda Morales, is Queen of Slimeballs. It seems the girls had fun with her to start by calling her Luce.

It took her about a week to figure out what they were sniggering at; from then on she insisted on the full Lucinda.

I take Charlie out of his crib and into the kitchen, handing him to Cindy. She holds him in her lap and coos at him while I fix coffee and heat up his bottle. "Just think," Cindy says, "Once we're all settled in over there, we'll only have a tiny commute—maybe ten minutes. All the more time to spend with *this* little doll." With her finger, she strokes his forehead.

"About this job," I say. "would I be in a pool or someone's personal typist?"

"Oh, come on, sweetie. Forget the typing. What I had in mind was having you be my administrative assistant."

"Really? Wouldn't I need a college degree for that?"

"Don't worry about the degree. I'll have the authority to create any kind of job I want. To start with, I'll tailor it to fit your current qualifications. If we decide later to expand your duties, we'll arrange whatever extra training you need."

Charlie's bottle and the coffee are ready. I take him and my coffee into the living room and settle in my rocking chair to feed him. Cindy follows. "Oh, let me feed him. *Please*, Di-dee. Wasn't that the whole point of switching to the bottle?"

She's right. I'm in the process of weaning Charlie off the breast and onto the bottle. I decided to do this partly because it makes things easier with me going back to work. But also because it enables Cindy to share in the feeding. Reluctantly, I let her take my place in the chair and hand Charlie over. She settles him in the crook of her arm with her face so full of love, I feel ashamed of my possessiveness.

As she feeds him, I sit on the couch with my coffee and mull over the administrative assistant business. The idea is growing on me. My lack of a degree has always been the bane of my work life. I know I have the smarts of any college graduate; I just need some employer to let me prove myself. The position Cindy is describing sounds ideal. We can help each other succeed. My heart leaps thinking of it. We'd have it all. Two upwardly-mobile young business-women, with an elegant new home and a beautiful baby.

Suddenly, Charlie makes a choking sound. "Uh-oh, what's wrong with him?" Cindy pushes the bottle and Charlie toward me. I'm aware of reaching out eagerly. She comments as I pat his back and settle him back into her arms. "You really are much better at this mothering stuff than I am."

"No, of course I'm not." But I feel an inward glow at her words. "It's just that I've been looking after him more. You'll catch up as soon as I go back to work." I add, "Sob, sob!"

Cindy laughs. "Never mind, my love. In fact, something wonderful occurred to me today. Once I get my big raise, you'll be able to stay home for a few months with Charlie. Wouldn't that be great?"

Looking at her shining eyes, I can't be a wet blanket. "It's a heavenly thought!" I say. "But I'd have to work out our budget very carefully."

She talks over me. "Here's another heavenly thought. We'll have room for a washer and dryer too." There's a mischievous tilt to her mouth as she nods toward my make-shift washing line across the corner of the kitchen. She knows how much I hate hanging out at the Laundromat.

"Cin-dee, just how much of a raise are you expecting?"

She giggles and nods at her empty coffee cup. "More coffee, please, madam administrative assistant?" As I take our empty cups to the kitchen, she calls out, "It will have to be enough of a raise for a washing machine. You don't find Laundromats in San Ramon on every corner as you do in the city."

Cindy doesn't have the temperament to worry about how to pay for anything. So I do the worrying. But, right now, even as I feel the familiar urge to tut-tut at her lack of frugality it's hard to contain my excitement. New job, new home, a washing machine. When I return to the living room with our refilled cups, I glance out the window at overcast skies. New weather, even.

Cindy follows my gaze. She says, "And another wonderful thing is it will get us away from here. From certain of our neighbors, if you follow me."

It takes a second for this to sink in. "If you're talking about Sam, I haven't seen or heard a word from him since he visited me in the hospital that day."

Cindy looks smug. She says, "I know, and I know why. After you told me he'd been to see you in the hospital, I realized drastic action was called for. Remember, I'd specifically told him he wasn't to bother you? But he just ignored me. So I called and told him in no uncertain terms that if he valued his life he was not ever to come near you or Charlie again."

The image of dainty little Cindy threatening the life of muscleman Sam is mind-boggling. I say, "And was he scared?"

Then I burst out laughing and Cindy joins in. She says, "It seems he got the message." It seems he did, although I can't imagine how she pulled it off.

Charlie finishes the bottle. I take him from Cindy and put him against my shoulder, patting him on the back to burp him. As I pace around the room with him, my eye falls on the bureau and the letter I wrote this afternoon. "Cindy, I wrote that letter to my mother today. See what you think."

She picks up the single sheet of paper and reads aloud.

"Like many same-sex couples, Cindy and I wanted to have a baby. And now we have one. His name is Charles Alexander..." She continues scanning the page in silence. "You don't say you actually gave birth to Charlie. From this, she might think we've *adopted* him. Or found him on the doorstep."

"So? If she wants details, she'll be forced to ask me."

Cindy shrugs and goes over to the TV. "Now for my nightly wrestle with this damned thing. We're down to only two stations and they're fuzzy. That's another thing we need, Diane—a new TV."

This comes out sounding like a happy observation rather than a grumble. My girl is riding high tonight. As she continues to fiddle with the controls, I think how devastated she will be if this job doesn't come through.

So what if it doesn't?

I sit down on the couch and lay Charlie on his back on my lap. We'd renew our lease on this house. Life would continue as usual. I look down at my little son. His eyes are closed, dark eyelashes resting on his cheeks, unruly tufts of black hair sticking up from his head. That nurse was right. He does look like his father.

Again, I look up and out through the window toward the house across the street. All along, I've been sure that one day Sam would come charging over here to visit his baby boy—and me, for that matter. It's hard to believe he'd let a phone call from Cindy stop him from doing something he wanted to do. But if we move...

"I give up." Cindy turns the TV off and comes to sit beside me on the couch. "Oh, the littlest angel is falling asleep. I wanted to play with him."

"There'll be plenty of time for that," I say. "Years and years."

She cuddles up to me, tucking her head under my chin and sliding her arms around Charlie and me. With my free arm, I encircle her shoulders, pulling the three of us close. My little family, I think, linked together with bonds of love and trust. It would be good to think those bonds could never be broken. But I know better. Bonds like these are fragile. They need to be protected. From people like me, no less. It dawns on me that this is what Cindy's been trying to tell me all along.

Suddenly, the last vestige of my ambivalence about Cindy's news flies away. She *must* get this job. We *must* move. Far from here. Leaving no forwarding address.

CHAPTER 10

Two months later, nothing is turning out the way I'd like. Cindy was offered the job in San Ramon and accepted it. We're not renewing our lease; the new tenants are to move into our dear little home in less than three weeks. I hate my new supervisor at work. Lucinda Morales is a petty tyrant who throws a fit if you're two seconds late and always takes the client's side against you—even when you're obviously not to blame for whatever the screw-up is. All in all, life these days is the pits.

It's nine o'clock on a Monday night, and I'm putting Charlie to bed. Charlie is the one thing in our lives that couldn't be better. He's fourteen weeks old now—cute, cuddly, with a happy disposition that makes me ashamed of my constant bellyaching. And he's finally figured out that civilized people sleep at night. At least some of the time.

Cindy isn't home yet. Her commute these days is well over an hour in each direction in heavy traffic. Also, her new boss—a harridan called Marigold—seems to think twelve-hour days are mandatory for someone in Cindy's position. This makes life impossible for all of us. Cindy leaves for work at the ungodly hour of six a.m., dropping Charlie and me off at the sitter's en route. The Ziebowskis are barely awake at that time, so I wait with the baby in their living room for over an hour. Then Mrs. Z. takes over and I leave for work myself.

It's even worse in the evening. I get to Mrs. Z.'s before six but Cindy can't get there for another hour, or two, or more. After a couple of days of this nonsense, Mrs. Z. talked her husband into driving us home on the days Cindy is running late—which has turned out to be just about every day. Mr. Z. is not happy about the situation. Neither am I.

One major problem we hadn't anticipated has been the chronic shortage of suitable places for us to rent in the San Ramon area. All the decent apartments require long leases—no good for us, of course, since we plan to buy a house within a couple of months.

Now, as I tuck the quilt around Charlie, he snuggles into his pillow and I sing to him. "*Sing a Song of Sixpence, A Pocket Full of Rye.*" He makes contented baby grunts. What an angel.

Half an hour later, I hear Cindy's key in the lock. I call out, "Hey, Cindy, welcome home," and hurry off to heat up some stew and get the coffee going. When she comes into the kitchen, I give her a kiss. I can hardly bear to look at her these days. Her usually perky face is lined with weariness and she's acquired dark circles under her eyes.

After she finishes eating, we relax in the living room with our decaf. I say, "Cindy, you'll just have to tell that miserable Marigold woman you can't keep up these crazy hours." Incidentally, Marigold is the big cheese, director of Northern California operations for J&B Systems.

Cindy says, "It really isn't Marigold's fault. She's working as frantically as I am to get things up and running. If we don't make this branch a going concern by the end of the year, the people at head office may close us down."

"H-mm." I've never met Marigold but as soon as Cindy first mentioned her, I envisioned one of those illustrations in

Alice in Wonderland of flowers with grotesque human faces. I see Marigold as a round pudding face on top of a long stick of a body, with carrot-colored hair sticking out all round her head like a punk rocker's. "Didn't you say Marigold was going to give you some ideas about solving the housing problem?"

Cindy nods, "Yes, we had a talk about that today. Unfortunately, she doesn't know of any places we could rent. She thinks we can probably find a place to buy quicker than we could find a rental."

"Not much help, is she?"

"Oh, really, she is. At heart, she's a most generous person. She's very concerned about my long commute and seems to be willing to bend over backwards to make life easier for me."

Cindy stares at her coffee cup, cradling it as if to warm her hands. "Marigold rents an apartment close by work. She says she has an extra room and would be happy to have me stay with her till I get something lined up. She wouldn't even charge me my share of the rent; I'd just have to share in expenses like utilities and food."

"Cindy, that's marvelous! How very kind of her." I'm wiggling with excitement. "You know, if she'll let you, why don't you move right away. Before this damned commute kills you. Charlie and I can join you at the end of the month when the lease is up."

And next week, I think, I can hand in my notice.

Cindy won't look me in the eye. "Diane, I'm not sure how to tell you this but it isn't that easy. You see...." She drains her cup and finally looks up at me, smiling. "This coffee's wonderful. Any chance of another cup?"

"It's only instant." I pick up the cups and go to the kitchen, feeling cross. I hate being kept on tenterhooks. She calls after me, "Everything you fix tastes wonderful.

You must have the equivalent of a green thumb in the kitchen. What would that be—a greasy thumb?" She laughs heartily but I don't respond. For no particular reason, I feel uneasy.

When I return with the coffee, Cindy takes a deep breath and swivels around on the couch to face me. She speaks in a quick, determined way. "Diane, the fact is that Marigold didn't specifically include you and Charlie in her invitation. She was mainly concerned about my long hours. Also, she doesn't have that big a place. It might be pushing her generosity a bit too far to have all three of us move into her spare room. Don't you think?"

"Oh." I will myself to be calm. "So what's supposed to happen to us?"

She starts off, "Well, maybe in three weeks when we have to move out of here, I'll have found a place for us in San Ramon. If not..."

"If not, Charlie and I can make ourselves comfortable in a little cardboard box under the freeway."

Cindy says, "Oh, come on. Listen, Marigold suggested we try to find someone in the city for you and Charlie to stay with. Just till things are settled. Di-dee, please don't look like that. How about Phyllis? You know how much she loves Charlie. And then there's that friend of yours at work. Kitty, is it? Maybe she has a spare room."

"I doubt it."

My eyes well up. I am deeply hurt that Cindy would even contemplate having the two of us live apart for any length of time. My sorrow is compounded by the realization that I will not after all be marching into Morales' office on Monday with resignation in hand. I take out a tissue and dab my eyes.

Cindy puts down her cup and strokes my thigh. "Honeybun, believe me, it's going to kill me to be away from you and Charlie all week, but we'll be together every weekend."

I snuffle, "I was so looking forward to starting my new job."

Cindy sips at her coffee. "Well, that's another thing I was going to tell you. We'll have to put the administrative assistant position on hold for a while." She adds hastily, "Marigold is heartily in favor of my creating this job for you. But she says we can't do anything about it until next year's budget gets approved. Probably in October."

It's now the middle of May. Mentally, I count off the months. "Cindy, you're saying we'll have to live apart for another *five* months."

"No, no. I'd quit if that were the case. I'll find somewhere for us to live if it kills me. Even if it has to be a motel."

"But what's the point of my moving if I don't have a job to go to?"

"You can be a stay-at-home Mom for a while." Cindy's face brightens. "Remember we discussed that? That would be perfect, wouldn't it?"

"But we can't..." I sag back into the couch without finishing the thought. I was going to remind her that her "big raise"—which may not be as big as she expects—won't be coming for many months. Motels cost lots of money. So I'll have to keep earning money too for now. But I don't have the heart for this discussion right now.

Cindy says, "Meantime, it really does make sense to line up a temporary home for you in the city, doesn't it? In case we need it."

Later, getting ready for bed, I think I really shouldn't be so selfish. Cindy's health is suffering with all this commuting. But the idea of crashing with Phyllis or some other friend really bothers me. I hate feeling obligated. And with

Phyllis, I know she'll constantly be dragooning me into collecting money or signatures or something for one of her many causes.

Then the ultimate objection occurs to me.

"The baby-sitter! Cindy, I couldn't stay with Phyllis; she lives even farther away from Mrs. Z. than we do here. And Kitty lives light-years away." Cindy and I had such a hard time finding a good sitter, I know she'll agree replacing Mrs. Z. is not an option.

Wearily, Cindy says, "Maybe Mrs. Z. has a spare room." I shudder at the thought. Mrs. Z. is a motherly soul who dearly loves babies and I am delighted with her as a sitter. Mr. Z., however, is another matter. Definitely not a baby person. "Or maybe..." Cindy says as she climbs into bed and punches her pillow, "Mr. Z. could rent you an apartment."

Mr. Z. is some sort of slumlord. He owns some decrepit apartment houses in their neighborhood on which he spends many hours each day. Probably spying on the tenants or something because he certainly doesn't appear to be fixing up the buildings.

I mutter, "Thanks a lot." Even though I know she's not serious.

At seven o'clock the next morning, after a pretty well sleepless night fretting about everything, I'm sitting in front of the Ziebowskis' TV with Charlie, waiting for Mrs. Z. to be ready. She and her husband are in their kitchen and I can hear their voices rumbling. It sounds to me as if they're arguing and keeping their voices down for my benefit. After a while, Mrs. Z. comes to the living room door. I stand up to get my coat, but she waves me to sit down again. "Please, Diane, I need to talk to you before you leave."

Uh, oh! She looks distressed. She sits awkwardly on the arm of the couch and says, "Unfortunately, Mr. Ziebowski say he can't give you ride home tonight. So you call Cindy, tell her to pick you up early. Okay?" She cocks her head on one side and looks appealingly at me.

"Oh."

I resist adding an expletive. She knows full well I can't control Cindy's hours. And, of course, I don't have a baby carriage with me and I can't possibly carry Charlie and all his things the two miles or so to Bayley Street. Finally, I say, "Well, okay, I'll take a cab home." I stand up again but she hasn't finished.

She squirms. "You see, Diane, Stan—Mr. Ziebowski—his plans change. Now he don't know if he can drive you no more after work. You tell Cindy she *must* come home early. *Every* day." Poor lady, she doesn't know how funny she sounds.

I sigh. "Mrs. Ziebowski, it breaks my heart to say this but I may have to find a new sitter. Cindy's going to be living in San Ramon during the week and just coming home at weekends. And I don't know where Charlie and I will live but it may not be close enough to bring him here."

For a moment, she looks really upset. Then her face lights up. She says, "We have good luck. Stan has nice apartment vacant just two blocks away. Very cheap." I almost laugh out loud, remembering Cindy's sardonic suggestion last night. From the look of his apartment buildings, Stan has a nerve to charge for them at all. But now I wonder if I'm being too hasty in my judgment. After all, it would be close to the sitter. I could even take the same bus to work.

"Well, Mrs. Ziebowski, I'm not sure but I guess I could take a look. Maybe you could mention it to Stan sometime."

"Yes, today. Maybe tonight when you get back from work, he show you the place." She looks a bit sheepish as she says this, no doubt remembering Stan was supposed to be busy tonight.

At least, I think, I'll probably get a ride home after all.

CHAPTER 11

Lucinda Morales' plump body bobs across the room to my work station. She waves a document at me. "Mr. Baldwin in Accounting wants you to make some changes in this report. I told him you'd have it by five."

With an irritated sigh, I say, "Lucinda, you know I'm working on this batch of letters for that class action suit. They're needed by tonight too. Also, remember I'm leaving work early today."

Of course, that's the crux of the matter. It never fails. Ask to leave early for some very good reason and Lucinda will bend over backwards to find some way to keep you late. I'm leaving early today because Charlie is sick and I have an appointment with the doctor at five.

Lucinda glares at me. "I said you could leave early as long as you got your work finished."

"And I will get these letters finished. But don't keep piling on more stuff." I'm feeling braver than usual today because last night Cindy called with the news that she's found a house to buy in San Ramon, which means I won't have to put up with Misery Morales for much longer.

Morales, who seems breathless at my insubordination, says, "Diane, I expect you to get all your work done before you leave. You can't expect special privileges if you can't keep up." And with that she stomps off. What especially angers me is she knows I'll make up the time by staying late another night. She just plain enjoys harassing us.

It's past four by the time the last of the letters rolls out of the printer. I check them over and place them in a folder in my out-basket. Then I cast a surreptitious eye around the office. As luck would have it, Morales has stepped out. I log off my computer, grab a sheet of paper and scribble: *"Lucinda—I'll finish up the Accounting report first thing in a.m. Diane."*

Leaving the note in plain view on my desk, I get my purse and slink to the door. Kitty, who sits next to me, flashes me a conspiratorial grin as I pass her. The only consolation in having such a martinet reign over us is that it really bonds us serfs together. Believe me, we've had some fun at her expense. But I'm not looking for any confrontations right now. I get my coat from the rack, keeping a nervous eye on the ladies' room door nearby. It stays closed. Then off I hurry, across the lobby and down the stairs to the street.

What a ridiculous way for a grown woman to carry on just to take a sick child to the doctor. By rights, I should have left even earlier; now, I'll have to take a cab to Mrs. Z.'s and then to the doctor's office.

The doctor says Charlie has an ear infection and pre-scribes antibiotics and plenty of warmth and rest. I carry him across the street to the pharmacy and pace up and down, shushing my fretful baby while they get the medicine ready. Then I get another cab to take us home and dole out the remainder of my cash to pay the fare.

"Home" is the small apartment I'm renting from Mr. Z. A palace it is not, but also it's not as bad as some of the truly crummy places he landlords over. The building is two stories high, with a flat on each floor, plus a basement. We have the ground floor flat with steps leading up to a small porch and our own private entrance. No one lives in the basement, which was flooded some time ago and is still uninhabitable. There is a tenant in the apartment above us—a shady figure whom I have never seen but often hear moving around.

Inside, the accommodation is adequate but gloomy. There's a large living room, part of which is curtained off to form the bedroom. The plumbing and appliances work, more or less. The outside, like all Mr. Z.'s properties, sports peeling paint and sagging masonry. And the neighborhood is scary with furtive figures lurking in doorways. I never, but *never*, go out alone after dark.

After giving Charlie his medicine, I change him and put him to bed. He isn't hungry but the doctor said this is to be expected. "He'll probably be ravenous in the morning," she said. "Just let him sleep it off." The poor little guy moves around restlessly and cries while I croon softly to him. After a while, he drops off into a snuffly sleep. I go into the kitchen to find some food for myself, smiling dreamily—as I've been doing on and off all day—about Cindy's phone call last night.

On Saturday, Cindy will take me to see the townhouse she's found. I can hardly wait. Charlie and I have been in this dreary apartment for over three weeks now and I feel lonesome. Cindy comes for the weekends, but, as I complained to her, they're only short weekends; she arrives late Saturday morning and returns Sunday afternoon. She says Marigold likes everyone in the office to get together on Friday nights. And it would be churlish to deny Marigold some well-deserved TGIF-ing after all her generosity to Cindy.

The moment I open the fridge door, I remember that I was supposed to buy groceries on the way home tonight. We're almost out of milk and, much worse, don't have a single drop of infant formula. This is a major nuisance. I don't want to wake Charlie and drag him out into the damp evening air. But if I don't buy the formula tonight, I won't have any for the morning when the doctor predicted Charlie would be ravenous. And the stores won't be open in the morning before I leave for work. And I'm supposed to be there extra early to do that darned Accounting report.

There's a little corner store that's open late every night and it's only a block away. I know I shouldn't leave Charlie alone but I'm sure he'll be okay for the five minutes or so it will take me to run down there. I get my coat and put my keys and checkbook in the pocket. No point in taking my purse; I barely have enough change for the bus tomorrow after paying all those cab fares. But Mr. and Mrs. Liu at the store have always accepted my checks, so that's no problem. I tiptoe into the bedroom to take a final peek at Charlie—sleeping heavily now—and quietly leave the house.

It isn't yet dark but there's a low cloud ceiling that makes it seem later than it is. It feels like it's going to rain any minute. As I approach the corner store, something looks wrong. There are lights on but, as I realize when I come up to it, these are just a couple of lights they leave on in the middle of the store when it's closed. I check my watch. It's not even nine o'clock yet. They're *always* open at this hour. I rattle the door handle and bang on the glass. No one comes. Oh, heck, what do I do now?

Turning to retrace my steps, I suddenly remember the all-night convenience store that Cindy and I used to go to sometimes when we lived in our last house. I think it was on Johnson Street, only two blocks to the east of where I'm standing. I hesitate. I should get back to Charlie. But I must get that formula. I swing around again and jog two blocks east to Johnson, and looking to the right, I can indeed see store-type lights a few blocks away. A bit farther away than I'd like, but I'll walk fast.

As I walk, I try not to look around. In this part of the city, the houses are old and tall with no lights on outside. There aren't many people about.

Two blocks, three, four...the wretched lights keep receding like a mirage in the desert. At last, after five blocks, the lights I've been aiming for loom up in the next block. But these lights don't represent food for sale; they come from a Christian Science bookshop. And as far as I can see looking south there are no other remotely hopeful illuminations.

Now what? I try to quell my rising panic and think logically. Maybe the convenience store is on Harley, another block eastward. This is like a bad dream. I'm already much farther from home than I'd ever intended to be. But the thought of returning empty-handed after coming this far is too much to bear. I'll try just one more block before giving up.

The block between Johnson and Harley is the darkest yet. I recall what my mother once said, "People can smell your fear, just like dogs can." And I'm getting increasingly fearful as this ceaseless quest for infant formula proceeds. I can't really see or hear sinister beings in the doorways but I can *feel* them. I move off the sidewalk and walk down the middle of the street.

At the corner of Harley, I glance to the right. And there's the convenience store, less than two blocks away. It's not a mirage; I can read the sign from here. Hallelujah! I run the rest of the way.

Inside, I make my way over to the baby products shelf in the far corner. Now, please God, let them have Similac! They do. I pick up two cans and carry them to the counter. While waiting for the teenage clerk to finish with the customer ahead of me, my eye falls on a counter display of candy bars. Fudge with almonds. I think I deserve a treat after all my travails tonight. I set a bar on the counter alongside the cans of formula and pull out my checkbook.

The clerk has pimples, I note, and a wary look on his face as he observes my checkbook. He rings up my purchases. "Seven-oh-seven." I write out the check and hand it to him. He looks at it and demands, "Driver's license." I tell him I don't have one. He sighs. "I need picture ID." Damn! My ID is back home in my purse, but I didn't think to bring it. Mr. and Mrs. Liu never ask to see it.

I say, "Okay, I'll just take one can of Similac instead of two. And forget the candy bar."

He looks suspicious. "And you'll be paying in cash, right?"

But of course I have no cash. I argue, "But one can is only, what, three something? Can't you trust me for that?" I explain about my sick baby, how I must have the formula, how the store I usually go to never asks for ID but for some reason they were closed tonight. He's immovable. Pointing to a placard behind him, he drones, "Store policy. No checks without picture ID." I ask to speak to the manager but apparently this insipid youth *is* the manager tonight.

The clerk looks past me at someone standing in line behind me. "I'll be with you in a moment, sir." His raised brow conveys his apology for neglecting a respectable customer for a deadbeat like me. I feel sick. I can't believe this is happening to me.

Suddenly, the man behind me reaches his arm around me and plunks a six-pack of beer on the counter beside my things. There's a twenty-dollar bill in his fingers. The man says, "This is to cover the beer *and* this other stuff." The voice is familiar. I look down at the hand. It's a big, hairy hand. Unmistakably Neanderthal!

Overjoyed and almost in tears with relief, I cry, "Sam," and swing around. He glances down in acknowledgment of my presence, but then the pimply one engages him in about as irritating an interchange as I've ever heard. The clerk wants to know does Sam want to buy the items for himself or for me, does he want just one can of Similac or both cans and the chocolate bar, should the two purchases be rung up separately or as one? I barely hear all this. In my happiness, I babble my gratitude over and over, through the clerk's questions and Sam's increasingly testy replies.

Finally, it's all resolved. Sam puts away his change, picks up his six-pack in one hand and the plastic bag with my things in the other, and makes his way to the door. I scurry along behind him. He pushes the door open with his shoulder and waits for me to walk through. There's a steady drizzle coming down now. We stand under the partial shelter of the narrow awning and look at each other.

He says, "So how're you?"—adding, without waiting for my reply, "I thought you'd moved over to the East Bay somewhere."

"Yes, Cindy has a new job in San Ramon. We'll be moving in a couple of weeks."

He grunts and holds up my grocery bag. "Where's your car?"

"Oh...I walked." Sam looks around at the night and back at me. He must think I'm some kind of lunatic to be walking in this weather. I say hastily, "I'm living close by— over there," and wave a hand.

"Oh. Goodnight then." He hands me my groceries but as he turns away, I hear him mumble something that sounds like "...if you're sure you don't need a ride." My ears perk up. A ride is the one thing I need most of all in the world right now. But Sam isn't exactly twisting my arm here; he's already hightailing it down the walkway toward his car.

It would be impolite to accept an offer tendered with so little enthusiasm.

The plastic bag is weighing down my arm. I look at the rain and the dark and think of having to walk back through those mean streets. What would become of Charlie if I were murdered by a crazed drug addict? Charlie! I've been gone for so long. He's sick and alone and may be crying his heart out at this very moment. I feel a sudden surge of panic.

"Sam, I would love a ride. If it isn't too much trouble."

He stops in his tracks. Then, not even turning around, he says in a flat voice, "Sure, no problem." He waves an arm toward his car and walks on.

When we reach the car, Sam puts our purchases in the back seat and we climb in. I glance at him curiously. Sam has many faults but lack of friendliness has never been one of them. It dawns on me that he may be impatient to get home because someone is waiting for him there. I somehow can't imagine he's that desperate to get back to Roland, so it's probably someone else. Blondie! That's who it must be. I picture the leggy creature, frizzy hair flowing, stretched out on the couch. Draped in a negligee. No, scratch that—she's not the negligee type. Draped in nothing and wondering why Sam's taking so long to get the beer.

In the car, I give directions. "Turn left at the street, left again, and I'll tell you where to turn next." We set out.

There's silence for a minute. Then Sam asks, "So where are you staying these days? With friends or something?"

"We've rented a small apartment. Just for a couple of weeks until we move to our house in San Ramon." I can't help boasting, "We're buying the house. It's brand new."

"So meantime you commute across the Bay every day?"

"Not me. I haven't left my job in the city yet. Cindy's staying with a friend near her job. She comes back to the city every weekend."

"Sounds complicated," he says. Then, "I've just bought a house myself. In Mill Valley. I'll be moving as soon as I find someone to sublet my place here."

"Oh, that's nice. And Roland will be moving with you?"

"No, Roland moved out a while ago. He's living over by Ocean Beach with a friend."

Interesting! I wonder if anyone else will be moving to Mill Valley with him. "When you move to Mill Valley, will...?"

He interrupts. "This is a hell of a long way. Did you really walk all this way?" I reprise the saga about Charlie's being sick, having to get his food for the morning, the corner store being only a block away and how they're always open, but.... He finishes the story for me. "Yeah, they were closed tonight you said." We fall silent.

Finally, we arrive. Sam pulls up in front of the house and peers through the car window. "You live *here*?" It's a good thing he can't see it in daylight; the streetlight is quite a way off and the house is in darkness. Of course, that in itself makes it look pretty spooky.

With a little laugh, I say, "I try not to go out after dark."

Sam says, "I bet."

I'm bursting to get into the house to check on Charlie. Quickly, I open the car door and say, "Sam, there's no way I can ever thank you enough for this. You have no idea how helpless I felt in that store. And this ride home is wonderful."

He looks at me. There's just enough light from the overhead dome lamp to make out the serious set of his face. He says, "May I come in and see the baby?" I hesitate, but for only an instant. For a start, I don't want to spend time arguing about it but also how could I deny him such a request after all his kindness tonight?

We get out of the car. Sam gets the grocery bag from the back seat and follows me up the steps. As we walk into the house, I feel very conscious of how this funereal place must look to him. We go into the living room, through the curtain into the bedroom section, and I hurry to the crib. Thank goodness, Charlie's still sleeping peacefully. Sam makes his way over to stand beside me, peering in the dim light coming from the living room lamp. He whispers, "I can't really see him. Can I pick him up?"

"Oh, no, please. We mustn't wake him. He's sick."

Sam stands beside the crib, one hand resting on the rails, and looks intensely down at the little body. At one point, he leans down to put his face close to Charlie's as though he wants to make sure he's breathing. After a couple of minutes, we walk back out through the curtain, and then into the kitchen where I relieve Sam of the groceries. Sam stands for a moment, looking thoughtfully up at the ceiling. There are some horrible exposed pipes up there—heating or water or something. Mr. Z had the misguided notion to paint them dark brown to disguise them.

Sam says, "This place could sure use some higher wattage lights."

"M-mm." I don't tell him that when I first moved in I replaced all the 40-watt bulbs with 100 and 200 watts. The fuses blew. Mr. Z. blew a fuse too; he railed at me for jeopardizing the safety of the building. "Don't ever do that again," he warned. "The whole place might go up in flames." I was quite ready to believe him.

I say to Sam, "How about a cup of tea?"

"Oh, no, thanks. I have company. They're probably wondering what on earth's happened to me." So I was right! We make our way back to the front door. Sam complains, "I really couldn't see the baby at all what with the poor light, and also he had his arm sort of across his face." He illustrates with his own arm.

Without really thinking, I say, "Yes, I'm sorry. Maybe you could visit in the daytime one day." I then start gushing all over again about how grateful I am to him for paying for the baby food and driving me home.

He says, "When?"

"When what?"

We're at the front door, and he turns to face me. "When can I come and see him in the daytime?"

"Well...er... not at the weekend."

"How about one night right after work? Thursday?"

Thursday is the day after tomorrow. Charlie will probably be feeling better by then, so I agree. We settle on six-thirty.

After Sam leaves, I call Cindy. I want to tell her about Charlie's illness. Also about Sam.

Cindy is sympathetic about Charlie and my run-in with Lucinda. "Don't let her intimidate you," she says. "In just a few weeks, you'll be able to tell her what to do with her stupid job."

"Believe me, I'm savoring that thought. But then, Cindy, you wouldn't believe my adventures this evening. The doctor said Charlie will be ravenous in the morning but after I put him to bed, I found I had no Similac in the house. None at all."

She laughs, "Oh, what a pain! The same thing happened to me last night. Only it wasn't Similac, of course.

It was coffee. And here Marigold had borrowed my car because hers is in the shop and I was dying for a cup of coffee. And, you know, I don't have a little corner store as you do. Our nearest stores are miles away."

"Well, as it happens…."

But she keeps talking—about how she was envisioning no coffee for breakfast, but then Marigold got back early and they got the coffee after all, blah, blah, blah. Then she starts talking about the weekend. By this time, I've sort of lost steam in terms of what I'd been planning to tell her about Sam.

Well, there's no hurry really. I'll tell her all about it the next time we talk.

CHAPTER 12

Sam rings the doorbell at six-thirty on Thursday evening. Charlie—fed, washed, and changed—is in his infant seat on the living room floor, playing with a plastic teething ring. He looks up at the sound of the bell. When I open the front door, Sam, looking a bit uncomfortable, says, "Hi." I lead him in and point him toward Charlie.

The two of them look at each other solemnly for a moment. Then Sam smiles and, to my surprise, so does Charlie. One of those captivating toothless grins that send mothers into orbit. Sam says, "O-o-o-h," in the sort of sappy tone I might use. "Hi, little guy." He gets down on the floor beside Charlie. Charlie waves the teething ring at Sam as though inviting him to play. Sam says, "I guess he's recovered from his illness."

"Yes," I say, "Babies are remarkable. You think they're at death's door one minute and then...." I watch nervously as Sam picks Charlie up and hoists him into the air. "Be careful, he's just eaten." Charlie, arms and legs dangling, gurgles happily down at Sam. Then Sam lowers him till his little feet are touching the floor and dances him up and down. The two of them look ridiculously happy.

I say, "How about a cup of tea?"

Sam looks at me over the top of Charlie's head and gently rubs his face against the silky-soft tufts of dark hair.

He says, "Thank you but I need to go get a quick dinner somewhere. I have to eat and be home by eight. Some folks are coming to look at my house tonight; they may be subletting it." He adds, "I thought maybe you and Charlie would like to come with me. Have you eaten?"

"No, I haven't."

Sam says, "There's a coffee shop at the corner of Market, just a couple of blocks away. They have great hamburgers."

My mouth waters at the thought of a hamburger. It's ages since I've eaten out. At the weekends, I cook for Cindy but the rest of the time I fix myself whatever's easiest, usually canned soup or an egg dish. I say, "Sounds good," and go to get sweaters for Charlie and me. On our way out, I reach for the stroller in the hall but Sam says, "We don't need that. I'll carry him."

Sam's "couple of blocks" turns out to be a fast-paced fifteen-minute hike. As we walk, Sam chats away to Charlie. He points out things. "Look, Charlie, doggie!" Charlie glances at the passing dog and then turns his adoring gaze back at Sam. Talk about a mutual admiration society!

At the coffee shop, we sit in a booth. The waitress— thin, middle-aged, with unbelievable red hair—brings a baby chair which Sam places on the seat beside him. The waitress makes cooing sounds at Charlie. "How old is he?" she asks.

I tell her, "Almost five months now."

To Sam, she says, "He sure takes after his dad."

Here we go again, I think. But Sam draws himself upright and says with mock sternness, "Madam, that's my son you're insulting."

She looks surprised, and then bursts into great cackles of laughter. Indicating Sam, she says to me, "Quite a guy, isn't he?" I smile. Sam meets my eye but doesn't smile back.

He has an odd expression, as though he's challenging me in some way.

The hamburger is delicious—and the peach pie and ice cream too. Sam and I eat heartily. Sam offers Charlie bits of everything on his plate—bun, meat, tomato. Charlie's not impressed until Sam gets to the ice cream. Then he sucks in and almost simultaneously spits out the strange cold stuff. Sam says, "I guess I'm not that good at this feeding business." But he beams proudly at Charlie as he speaks.

When the check comes, I say, "Sam, let me pay my share at least. You know, I still owe you that seven dollars."

Sam declines. "I invited you. I'll get it." He glances at his watch. "Sorry to rush but we'd better head back. I really want to be home when these people come tonight."

"Yes, of course." I lean across the table and wipe the ice cream off Charlie's face with a napkin. A mother and her young son walk past our booth on their way out. The boy is carrying a large toy dinosaur which he waves in Charlie's face. We all laugh as Charlie eagerly grabs for it and the boy quickly moves it out of reach. I say to Sam, "It's funny how the kids these days all seem to love dinosaurs. I'm not sure what the attraction is."

He says, "A hankering for prehistoric times, I guess. You know, when dinosaurs and Neanderthals roamed the land."

I jump. It's a long time since Cindy and I used to joke about "my Neanderthal"—but then it's a long time since Cindy and I have discussed Sam at all. It seems odd he should bring up that word. His head is down as he gets money from his wallet to pay the bill, so I can't gauge his expression. I say, "I didn't realize they roamed the land at the same time?"

Sam gives a little cluck—disgust at my ignorance, I suppose. "They didn't. The Neanderthals were much later."

He raises his eyes to mine. Again, that odd challenging look. I note he doesn't pronounce the "h"—he says Neander*tols*.

"I thought it was '*thols*,' not '*tols*.'"

"That's how it's spelled. Most scientists don't pronounce the 'h'."

"Really? I didn't know that." Sam unstraps Charlie from the baby seat and picks him up, preparing to leave. I have a hunch I should simply drop this subject. Against my better judgment, I ask, "How come you know so much about Neander*tols* anyway?"

Sam gets to his feet, draping Charlie across one shoulder. He says, "I don't. Just that you think I look like one."

"What! What are you talking about?" But I'm sputtering to myself because he's already halfway to the cash register.

After Sam pays the bill, we set off for home. As I struggle to keep up with his giant steps, my little gray cells work overtime. As far as I know, Cindy's the only person who's heard me liken Sam to a Neanderthal. I pant, "Was it Cindy who said...?"

"Uh-huh." Thank goodness, we've come to a red light and have to pause before crossing the street. Catching my breath, I prattle, "It was all a silly joke, you know. Cindy and I were watching you from our window when you and Roland moved in across the street from us. When was it, a couple of years ago now?"

He ignores my question. The light changes and we continue walking. I press on. "We saw Roland first. As you know, he's kind of slight of build. Then *you* appeared carrying an armchair on your shoulders and I said, 'Oh, here's one who looks like a Neanderthal.'" I'm panting again. "Sam, please slow down." He slows down. I look at his face, appealing for understanding. "Cindy and I are always joking around like that, making silly remarks about the neighbors and people we meet at parties. You know."

"I see."

Right now, it doesn't sound particularly funny to me either. But then...this is all such a tempest in a teapot. As we speed along, I start to feel indignant at the way he's making me feel guilty about this. To tell the truth, I really don't know what Neanderthals are supposed to look like but surely it's not *that* much of an insult, is it? Where's his sense of humor?

By the time we get back into the house, my little one is fast asleep on Sam's shoulder. Sam goes to the crib and carefully places Charlie in it. I take off Charlie's sweater and booties, and cover him with a quilt. Then Sam makes his way to the front door while I close the curtain that partitions the bedroom. I say, "Sam, before I forget, let me write you that check."

He says over his shoulder, "Sorry, no checks without picture ID."

My spirits lift at his playful imitation of the pimply clerk. Maybe he's just pretending to be piqued at me. I summon up the courage to ask something that's been puzzling me. "Sam, *when* did Cindy tell you about the Neanderthal thing?"

We're at the front door. He opens it and turns around to face me. "She called me the day after I visited you in the hospital. When Charlie was born."

I give a disbelieving laugh. "She called you specially to say, 'Diane thinks you look like a Neanderthal'?"

Sam looks at me. I remember he looked at me in this thoughtful way on that long-ago day when I asked him if he really wanted the job of fathering my child. The day I noticed his blue eyes. He says, "Cindy gave me a real earful on the subject of what *you* think of *me*." He turns, walks across the porch and starts down the steps.

"Why, what did she say?" I follow him outside.

He glances back as he skips down the steps. "Look, Diane, I'm sorry I brought this up. I really don't have time to talk right now."

"*Sam, what did she say?*" I'm on the top step now, and lean forward, sliding my hands down the railing toward him. I don't care that I'm shouting or that there might be all kinds of undesirables lurking about who will hear me. Suddenly, it's become very cold. As often happens in San Francisco on summer evenings, a blanket of fog has rolled in, obscuring the evening sun. My teeth start to chatter.

At the bottom of the steps, Sam stops and looks down at his feet for a moment, as though wondering whether or not to respond. Then he looks up at me and says, "Cindy said you told her I was the most obnoxious, unattractive person you'd ever met. A goofus caveman. Loud, vulgar, arrogant. She said I literally made you feel sick." He pauses. "And other stuff along those lines."

He turns and steps off the curb to walk around the front of his car. I climb down a few more steps and wail, "But, Sam, you surely don't believe all that. You couldn't." In the midst of my angst, it strikes me this is rather like the balcony scene in reverse: a frantic Juliet grimly climbing down in pursuit of a hastily retreating Romeo.

Sam shuffles with his car keys. Then he walks a little way back toward me and says in a low voice that I have to strain to hear, "Well, as it happens, I said something like that to her. I said it certainly didn't seem to me that you found me *that* offensive. And she said...." He gives a humorless laugh. "Cindy said you're always too timid to tell people what you really think of them. Apparently my visit to you in the hospital was the last straw. So Cindy thought she'd better tell me what you couldn't bring yourself to say."

And now Sam quickly goes around to his car door and unlocks it. He calls out to me as he climbs in, "It's cold out here. You'd better get back inside."

I'm freezing. The damp air is seeping into me. And inside my stomach there's what feels like a puddle of ice water that's chilling me from the inside out. I hurry back into the house and slam the door.

Indoors, I fix a cup of hot tea; then sit on the rock-hard futon in the living room, wrapped in a comforter, trying to get warm. I sit there a long time. But there are things to do for tomorrow and eventually I get up and do them: collect Charlie's stuff to take to Mrs. Z.'s, make my sandwich for lunch, find clothes to wear to work.

At ten o'clock, I go to bed, still feeling cold. I keep telling myself how stupid I'm being. I'm completely overreacting. Why should I care what Sam thinks of me? In only a few weeks, Charlie and I will be in the East Bay with Cindy; Sam will be moving north to Mill Valley. We'll probably never see him again.

Every time I toss and turn over, my eye lights on the luminous alarm clock on my bedside table. Ten-thirty, ten forty-five, eleven o'clock. There's no way I'll get any sleep tonight. Finally, I sit up, pull on my robe and slippers and grope my way across the room, past the curtain into the living room, and then down the hall to the kitchen where I turn on the light. Even though it's been a while, I still remember Sam's number. I sit at the table by the phone and dial. As I listen to the phone ring at the other end, I realize the time. Almost eleven-thirty.

"Hullo." His voice is sleepy.

"Sam, I've only just noticed the time. I hope I didn't wake you." I add, "This is Diane."

He says, "Yes, I know. No, you didn't wake me."

Now, I've always believed that at moments like these it sounds phony if you rehearse ahead of time. Better to be spontaneous—let the words flow from the heart. So I open my mouth but, to my surprise, what comes out is...small talk. I thank Sam again for the hamburger. "You're very welcome," he says. I ask if he got home in time for his visitors and did they like the house.

If he's surprised at my chosen topics for this late-night call, he doesn't show it. He sounds excited as he tells me about his visitors. "They loved the house. They're going to sublet it. That means I'll be able to move out in a couple of weeks."

"Oh, that's great." There's a silence. I take a deep breath. "Sam, I don't know how to begin to apologize for all the hurt we've caused you." He says nothing. I say, "I most certainly don't find you obnoxious and all that other stuff. I think you're kind and patient and gentle and humorous. I really like you. In fact, each time we got together I liked you more and more." This is the truth.

He says, "So Cindy just made it all up?"

Whoa! Now what? It would be easy to blame Cindy and leave myself in the clear. But that would be really dishonest. Cindy exaggerated and threw in some strange little inventions—like saying I was too timid to speak my mind. But she certainly didn't "make it all up." As I think back, I believe I really did say or imply most of those things in one way or another. But Cindy, of course, took everything out of context. The context was that of an insecure Cindy feeling increasingly threatened because Sam was playing such a big role in my life.

"Sam, you must understand that Cindy came to feel very jealous of you. She got more and more upset each time we got together. I had to be really careful not to let her think I liked you too much."

Silence. I say, "Obviously, I'd no idea she'd ever talk to you the way she did but she was afraid you weren't going to leave us alone after Charlie came. Remember, you were supposed to cease all contact with us once I became pregnant? I think Cindy got desperate trying to find some way to discourage you from coming around."

"She found a way all right."

"I'm so sorry. I would never ever want to hurt you like that."

After a few seconds, Sam says, "Don't worry about it. I'm a big boy now. I guess I can take it." Not as forgiving a response as I would have liked, but it's the best he's offering. We say goodnight and I go back to bed. I fall asleep almost as soon as my head hits the pillow.

The next day, I work late to make up for taking time off on Tuesday, and it's past six-thirty by the time I pick up Charlie and head for home. Deep in thought, head down, I swing around the corner into our street and am almost at our house when I notice the car parked at the curb. Sam's green Porsche. And Sam standing there, leaning against it. He says, "I hope you don't mind. I was on my way home and just wanted to talk for a minute."

"Sure." I unstrap Charlie and Sam lifts him out of the stroller with the *whee*-up-in-the-air gesture that men seem to love. He then tucks the baby against his shoulder with one hand, grabs the diaper bag with the same hand, lifts the stroller with the other, and proceeds up the steps and onto the porch. And to think of the performance I go through

117

every day to get Charlie and his associated paraphernalia up and down those steps by myself. It takes me at least two trips.

Indoors, I relieve Sam of the bag, then the stroller, and then the baby. Sam follows as I carry Charlie into the kitchen and place him in his infant seat on the dinette table. Then Sam and I face each other across the small kitchen. He smiles at me in a way that at one time I might have described as cocky. In my eyes now, he just looks awkward and unsure. He says, "I came by to apologize for being in such a rush to leave after our dinner last night. My behavior must have seemed really shitty to you, given we were in the middle of such a...er...sensitive dialog."

"No, I understand. You were in a hurry to get home."

"And then when you phoned later, I must have seemed..." He struggles to find the words. "Well, not as gracious as I should have been." He grins. "Of course, I was half asleep."

"It was a pretty pathetic apology," I say. "I'm really not that good at apologies."

"No, on the contrary. Your call really helped. In fact, the more I thought about it, the better I felt. Just the fact you bothered to call at all...."

All at once, listening to his earnest voice, I'm overwhelmed with emotion. I say, "Oh, Sam," and walk over to him at the same moment he reaches out to pull me up against him. I slide my hands under his jacket, and snuggle my face into the soft cotton fabric of his shirt. His body is warm and smells pleasantly talcumy. With his arms holding me like this, I feel...well, I feel a lot of things. Forgiven, of course, but also somehow *safe*.

Crash! Wail! Sam and I jump apart as Charlie shatters this tender tableau. Charlie has rocked his infant seat, sideways and then back again, and is slowly sliding out of it.

I forgot to strap him in. Sam laughs as he rescues the lit-tle tyke—*whee*! up-in-the-air—and Charlie responds with a gummy grin. Sam says, "He's reminding you he hasn't had his dinner yet." To Charlie, he says, "Okay, okay, I'm leaving."

"Can I fix you something? I was about to have a cup of tea." But Sam glances at his watch and shakes his head. "Sorry, no. I have to get home and change. I have a date tonight."

A date! I guess something shows on my face because Sam touches me gently under the chin and says, "I know. You're thinking this is the third time in a row I've turned down your offer of tea. Really, I love your tea, Diane—and your scrambled eggs. And anything else you have to offer." This with a slightly smutty grin. He says, "I promise I will one-hundred-percent-for-sure partake of your tea before I move out of the city."

"Oh? You're sure you can fit me in between all your dates?"

He laughs. "Now, now. Let's see...." He furrows his brow. "I'm going to be really busy in the next week or two. I need to get contractors in to do some things at the new house, and then I have to get packed and clean up the old house. How about I give you a call next week and let you know how things look?"

"Okay." I put Charlie back in his seat, making sure he's locked down this time. As I turn around, I bump into Sam who's still standing close to me. He puts up a hand and lightly pats my hair. He says, "Incidentally, when I said 'date,' I didn't mean a woman-and-sex date. I'm go-ing to a bachelor party for some poor slob who's getting married."

I tease, "But I thought bachelor parties *were* all women and sex."

"Really? Hey, I hope you're right." I laugh at his air of mock excitement and think how glad I am that things are okay between us again. Looking into his face, I know he's glad too. He says, "You tend to Charlie. I'll see myself out." And off he goes.

Later that evening, after much thought, I decide I'm not going to tell Cindy any of this stuff about Sam. At least, not yet. If I tell her about meeting him that night in the convenience store, then the issue of her hostile call to him will undoubtedly come up. And if that happens, she'll get all defensive, we'll probably argue—and our eagerly-awaited visit to the new townhouse this weekend will be spoiled. There's no sense in stirring up a hornets' nest. At some time in the very near future, Sam really will be out of our lives for good.

Some time, that is, after we have that cup of tea.

CHAPTER 13

Today, Saturday, we have a three o'clock appointment with the realtor. We'll tour the house and then we plan to submit a formal offer. All day, it's been hard to contain my excitement about my first visit to our new home. On the drive over to the East Bay, I pump Cindy for information. She says, "There are two large bedrooms plus a small den, two bathrooms, a living room with a vaulted ceiling. Diane, I'm sure I've already told you all this."

"I don't mind how many times you tell me. I love hearing about it."

We cross the Bay Bridge and head inland. East, through the long Caldecott Tunnel that always gives me the creeps. Then south toward San Ramon. In dreamy ecstasy, I gaze out the car window at the sun-baked hills of the Diablo Range. It will be lovely to move to a place with so much sun; we see far too much fog in the city in the summertime.

Shortly before three, Cindy pulls up at the curb outside the townhouse complex, and eagerly I drink in the prospect before us. The townhouses are Spanish Mission style: cream stucco, red-tiled roofs, with plantings of spiky yuccas and aloes in beds of crushed red rock.

"Oh, Cindy, it looks really pretty."

"I'm sure you'll love the inside too. As Marigold says, it's quite compact but the space is extremely well utilized.

Also, it has big windows and pale walls that make it look spacious and bright."

One discordant word catches my attention. "What does Marigold know about it? Has she seen the house?"

"Oh, yes. Marigold comes with me on most of my house-hunting expeditions." She adds casually, "In fact, Marigold will be meeting us here today."

"Why?" I scowl. "If she's seen the house already, why does she want to horn in on us today?"

"Diane, she's not horning in. I invited her. For one thing, I'd like you to meet her, and vice versa. Also, she's a pretty sharp businesswoman. Neither of us has any experience in house-buying so it will be good to have her there when we make the offer."

I calm down. Although I still feel Marigold has no business intruding on our special day, I am curious to meet her.

Two cars drive up—the realtor and Marigold. We get out of our car and Cindy helps me lift Charlie out of his car seat and into the baby carrier which I strap around my shoulders. Marigold walks over and Cindy introduces us.

Marigold is a complete surprise to me. Of course, I didn't really think she'd look like one of those *Alice in Wonderland* stick flowers. But I'm not prepared for this big-boned, mannish woman with close-cropped graying hair and a drill sergeant voice. She directs a brusque, "Good to meet you," to me, ignores Charlie, and then turns her back on us to talk to Cindy.

The realtor walks over with key in hand. He's a deferential little man who smiles a lot and finishes every sentence with a nervous titter. As we proceed on the house tour, Marigold takes charge. She grills the realtor: Is there hardwood under the carpeting? Will the builder redo the shoddy paintwork on the banisters? How about the land-scaping in the back yard? The little man practically curtsies as he answers each question.

It rather bothers me that he seems to have lost sight of the fact that Cindy and I, not Marigold, are the potential purchasers. But Cindy cheerfully ignores the two of them while she shows me around. She points out the sparkling kitchen with its black glass and stainless steel appliances. I gape at the impressive "cathedral ceiling" in the living room, and we giggle as we speculate on ways to dust cobwebs off the rafters—swinging on the chandelier, standing on each other's shoulders, and other nonsense.

Then Cindy takes me upstairs and we survey the bed-rooms, which, unfortunately, have a rather sterile view of the treeless street and more houses.

"Not much of a view, I'm afraid," she says.

"Look on the bright side, hon. At least we can see open hills and fields on the horizon."

"Not for long, I'm afraid. They're planning to build all over those hills too."

We can hear Marigold downstairs harassing the poor real estate man. Cindy turns to wink at me. I hiss, "Marigold seems to think *she's* buying the bloody house. Why is she getting so involved?"

Cindy shrugs. "Marigold likes to take charge. I'll talk to you later about her. Here, why don't you let me carry Charlie for a while; he must be getting heavy." She takes the carrier and Charlie off me. We go downstairs and out into the back yard. There's a small cement patio outside the sliding doors of the living room. The rest of the prop-erty consists of a narrow strip of bare earth sloping sharply upward to a fence. Both sides of the yard are hemmed in by the fences of the adjoining townhouses.

Cindy says, "It's what you call a low maintenance yard." She laughs at her own joke. "Seriously, we can terrace it to make it more usable, and put in shrubs and things."

"And some grass." Marigold's voice suddenly booms behind us. "I've been telling him we expect to see some grass." Why would anyone want grass, I wonder? You couldn't possibly mow a lawn on that slope. Marigold barks at Cindy, "Now you have some questions for the man, don't you? Don't forget to get it straight about the homeowner thing."

Cindy says, "Right. Time to get down to business." She hands Charlie back to me and goes inside to talk to the realtor, leaving Charlie and me alone with Marigold. It seems to me all three of us feel uncomfortable.

Marigold snaps, "How old is he? It is a *he*, isn't it?"

"Yes. Almost five months."

She looks at Charlie with disapproval. Charlie turns his face away. She says, "They're not too interesting at this age, are they? Not walking or talking or anything." I turn and walk back into the house. I'm darned if I'm going to keep up any kind of conversation with this fool. Walking and talking indeed!

Inside, Cindy and the realtor stand at the kitchen counter poring over papers. I feel a surge of pride watching and listening to Cindy. She looks so calm and capable and pleasant in manner. It's crazy to think that old battle-ax is her boss. How on earth does Cindy stand her? The battle-ax has followed me into the house and now barges her way into the negotiations with the realtor. The poor man flutters while Cindy continues to act serene. But I've had enough. "Cindy, I'll go wait in the car. Charlie needs a drink."

It's over half an hour before they all emerge. The realtor calls out to Cindy that he'll have the papers ready in a couple of days. He goes to his car, and the two women walk over to me. Cindy bends down to the open car window. "Diane, Marigold has very kindly invited us to have dinner with her."

My reaction is swift. I purr, "Oh, that's awfully kind of you, Marigold. Unfortunately, Charlie will need to be fed soon so we'd better be on our way."

Cindy gives me a look. She knows I packed enough food to enable Charlie to survive in the desert for a month. I give Cindy a look right back. There's no way I'm giving in on this one. Cindy turns to Marigold, "I'm sorry, Marigold. We'll have to take a rain check."

Marigold looks so disappointed, I almost feel sorry for her. But then she harrumphs, "Maybe next time you could leave the child with a sitter." Cindy hastily changes the subject before I can react to this impertinence.

"Marigold, I can't thank you enough for your advice. I don't know what we'd have done without you."

I tune out Marigold's response—a whole bunch of what sound like commands. More "advice," no doubt. She finishes with, "Now don't forget to let me know about the other thing as soon as possible." Cindy says she will.

Marigold leaves, Cindy gets into the car, and we're on our way. As we go, I direct a hostile stare toward Marigold's back. "What a very unpleasant woman!"

"Oh, Diane! True, diplomacy is not her strong suit. But she's absolutely brilliant when it comes to technical and marketing issues. She pretty much single-handedly opened up the California market for J&B's products. We still have a long way to go, of course, but we'd be nowhere without Marigold."

"Huh! I'm surprised she doesn't scare all the customers away."

"The customers put up with her because she really knows our products and is so good at tailoring them to our customers' needs. It's another matter when it comes to employees though. In fact, I recently learned something rather interesting." She pauses a moment to peer at the freeway signs looming up. "It seems someone else—some man—was hired for my position back in January. He quit after a month because he just couldn't stand working for Marigold—or so rumor has it."

I smirk. Cindy continues. "That apparently caused quite a ruckus at head office. Since I've been sharing her home, Marigold's started to confide in me. It seems her boss in New York is always lecturing her on how important it is to develop and retain good people. She keeps asking for my advice on how to be a better people person."

"Well, my love, either it's been lousy advice or she hasn't been taking it." I smile at Cindy as I speak, but now she's muttering crossly as she comes up behind a very slow-moving vehicle and looks for a chance to overtake.

She says, "I'll be so happy not to have to take this trip into the city every weekend. I hate this drive." I can empathize. Also, I think she'd probably like to talk about something else.

For the next half hour, we talk about the house, how we will furnish it, even who we'll invite to the housewarming. "I suppose," I say, "We'll have to invite Marigold. Ugh! Gag!" I glance at her and laugh but Cindy seems to be far away. Then I remember something. "Cindy, what did Marigold mean when she said to let her know about 'the other thing'?"

Cindy says, "Oh, that. Well, when we worked out the amount of money we'll need up front, it seems we may be a few thousand dollars short. I'd underestimated the closing costs and there are things like the homeowners' association dues that we need to prepay. Marigold is willing to lend me the money at a minuscule interest rate. That'd save the bother and expense of having to get a second mortgage."

Alarm bells ring for me. "Surely we don't want to get mixed up with Marigold any more than we have to. She seems to be overly-possessive about the house as it is. Look at the way she was carrying on today. In fact, Cindy, I'm just starting to realize how difficult things must have been for you recently. I've been moaning and whining about *my* boss, but compared to Marigold, Lucinda is a positive... well, Fairy Godmother."

Cindy laughs. "I know the woman must seem like a real pain-in-the-butt to you but there are some pluses in this situation. For some reason, Marigold really likes me and she's a wonderful mentor. I've learned more about company operations from her in a couple of months than I could in a couple of years without her. Also no one else in the office can stand her so they tend to use me as a go-between." She glances at me. "Do you understand what I'm saying?"

I'm not sure I do, but now my mind is on other things. We're plunging down into the darkness of that damned tunnel again, and I grip the comforting armrest. I hate this tunnel. There was a horrible fire in it some years ago when a tanker truck exploded and many people died. As we travel cheek by jowl with the cars in adjoining lanes at what seems to me an alarming rate of speed, Cindy continues to chat. I pick up the word *Marigold* now and then, but I'm really not paying much attention. At last, daylight emerges ahead of us. Cindy's saying, "...and she's going to arrange that meeting in the next month or so."

"What meeting?"

"I just told you. With the company founders. Mr. J. and Mr. B."

We're in the sunlight now. I'm still holding tight because the lanes have multiplied in number, and the highway swings switchback-fashion, down and up and curving around, as we get closer to the Bay. But the worst is behind us. It occurs to me I'll have to get used to that tunnel when we move; there are bound to be many times we'll take the trip to the city to visit friends.

Cindy says, "It would be fantastic to get to meet the top people in the company. It's worth putting up with Marigold's quirks just for that." She throws me a sidelong glance. I wish she would stop looking at me and keep her eyes on the road. She says in a disappointed tone, "Don't you agree? You don't sound very impressed."

"No, really I am. I can see why Marigold is so important to you." To prove I've been paying attention, I ask, "Are they really called Mr. J. and Mr. B?"

"Jack Jackson and Bert Bronson."

"Sounds like a circus act," I hoot. The Bay Bridge is in sight and I loosen my grip on the armrest. Soon we'll be home.

The next day, Sunday, Cindy drives us to Ocean Beach. We have a cup of coffee in the Beach House, sitting by big windows overlooking the sands and sea. Later, we call on friends in the old neighborhood. Thankfully, we don't bump into Sam. I tell myself next weekend for sure Cindy and I *must* have a talk about Sam.

We get home shortly after four, and I fix our evening meal of lasagna and salad. I always fix dinner early on Sundays so Cindy can get back to San Ramon at a reasonable hour. "Diane, you make a mean lasagna." Cindy dabs her mouth. "I really miss your cooking." She stands. "Now let me do the dishes."

"No," I say. "Why don't you take Charlie into the living room and play with him for a few minutes. You two don't get nearly enough time together."

"All that's going to change very, very soon." She sings to him as she lifts him out of his seat. "Cindy's little baby-love, Char-lee, Char-lee." Unfortunately, she loses her grip for an instant and he slips. He lets out a high-pitched protest and looks appealingly at me.

Cindy says, "Okay, kid. Keep your shirt on." I laugh. It strikes me that maybe one reason Charlie is so comfortable with Sam is that Sam's hands are big and strong and Sam never lets him slip. Or maybe the little monkey just likes all that Whee! business.

As I fix the coffee, I think of something's that been hovering in the back of my mind since yesterday—a question for Cindy. I pour two cups of coffee, put them on a tray with some chocolate chip cookies, and take them into the living room where she's sitting on the floor with Charlie.

"Cindy, I keep meaning to ask you. What about signing the papers? Will I have to go back to San Ramon to sign the offer?"

Sorting out colored blocks on the floor, she answers quickly. "No. I can handle that myself."

"Oh." I watch the two of them playing for a moment. "But I'll need to sign papers at some point, won't I? Loan applications or whatever? Or maybe you can just bring them back here for me to sign."

To my surprise, she doesn't answer right away, seemingly preoccupied with getting the blocks sorted. After a while, she says, "Diane, we were talking. The realtor, Marigold and I. It would simplify things a lot if I were to be the primary purchaser of this house." She looks up at me, eyes wide as if fearful of my response. "Don't misunderstand but it really complicates things to have more than one person on the house deed and mortgage, especially given we're not a married couple."

"What do you mean *primary* purchaser? That you'd be the sole purchaser?"

"Well, yes. In a way it is fair, Di-dee. I'm providing the money for the down payment and I'll be making the mortgage payments."

I feel I've been hit in the chest. "I thought I'd be helping with the monthly payments. And isn't some of that down payment my money?"

"Look, there's no question of you being squeezed out. I'm having an attorney draw up papers specifying the house belongs to you and Charlie in the event something were to happen to me." She smiles in a bright, determined manner. "It'll be okay, I promise. It's just cleaner this way. Oh, and I promise I won't use any of your savings in the down payment."

Too stunned to say anything, I chew a cookie and watch Cindy playing with Charlie.

She says, "The week is so long without the two of you. I can't wait for us to be living together again all the time." She underscores this sentiment by baby-talking with Charlie. "How I miss my little Charlie. Yes, I do."

At five o'clock, Cindy gets up to finish packing her bag. I carry the dishes into the kitchen and call out to her. "So I guess we'll see you next Saturday, noonish?"

She appears at the kitchen door. "That reminds me, next Saturday, I'll be a bit late getting here. Marigold—bless her heart—has decided our management team needs to hold a retreat. This is part of her plan to become a better people person." Cindy giggles.

"She needs to retreat all right. Into a hole in the ground...."

"Oh, Diane! Anyway, she's booked a room for the day in some conference center near Stinson Beach so all us managers can sit around and do some heavy duty bonding. But, no matter what, I'm going to try to get away by dinnertime. I should be here by seven at the latest."

I shriek, "Seven! That's the whole day shot. We see so little of you as it is. That damned woman!"

"I know, sweetie. It's a real pain. I did try my best to talk her out of it but we don't have time for this bonding stuff during the week. And, God knows, we have to do something. Morale is terrible." She looks anxiously at me. "Please, Di-dee, don't be mad. This should be such a joyous weekend for us, and all I've done today is make you mad."

She looks upset. I do my best to look *not*-mad.

At five-thirty, Cindy takes her bag out to the car. I go with her to help her remove Charlie's car seat from the back of her car where we usually keep it. We have to take the seat out because next weekend her car will be loaded with things for the retreat—easels and charts and stuff. Before leaving, she gives me an affectionate kiss. "Cheer up, sweetie. Next Sunday, we'll have another lovely day together, just like today."

But, as I walk back up the steps with the car seat, my feelings alternate between annoyed and alarmed. Annoyed because Cindy knows I like to grocery shop on Saturdays and it's hard for me to carry much home without her and the car. Annoyed that the horrible Marigold is eating into time Cindy should be spending with Charlie and me. Alarmed by the advice Marigold is giving Cindy about the house purchase. And alarmed that no matter how much she says it breaks her heart to be away from us, Cindy doesn't seem to be as bothered by any of this as I feel she should be.

• • •

The following Saturday morning I'm in a totally different mood. I sing as I clean the bathroom, change the bedding, vacuum the rugs.

As it happens, Cindy's abandonment of me today has worked out rather well. Sam called a couple of nights ago and said today is a really good day for him to come over for our farewell cup of tea. "Only why don't we make it lunch?" he suggested when he called. "We can go to the coffee shop again, then I'll take you grocery shopping, and then we'll go back to your place for a cup of your delicious tea."

"You know, Cindy will be here by seven. So we'd have to be back well before then."

"No problem."

Around ten o'clock, I'm flat on my face in the living room trying to rescue a ball that's rolled under the futon. The furniture is too heavy to move and I poke around underneath it with a straightened-out wire coat hanger. Charlie's on his stomach beside me watching with interest. "It's no good, Charlie," I mutter, "We'll have to say bye-bye to that one." The phone in the kitchen rings. I jump up and go to answer it.

It's Sam. "Diane, I'm afraid we can't have lunch at the coffee shop after all. My plumbing contractor just called and he wants me to meet him at the Mill Valley house at noon. He was supposed to come next week but he got his schedule messed up somehow."

"Oh." It's an understatement to say I'm disappointed.

Sam goes on. "When the kitchen was renovated, the piping to the sink wasn't connected. I have to get this work done before I can move in."

"Couldn't we have lunch after you get back?"

"I'm meeting him at noon so that might make it kind of late. But you know what I was thinking? If you and Charlie can be ready in an hour, I can take you with me. All I have to do is to let the contractor into the house and tell him what needs to be done. Then we can go get lunch. Somewhere nice—maybe a waterfront café in Sausalito."

I draw in a breath. "Would we still be back in time for Cindy?"

"No problem." Sam's favorite expression, it seems. "We should be back in the city by about three. That leaves plenty of time for your grocery shopping, and our cup of tea afterwards."

There's a long cord on this phone and it's fully extended now as I crane my neck into the living room to peek at Charlie. An outing for my baby with a person my baby enjoys. A drive over the Golden Gate Bridge to the lovely rolling hills of Marin County. Having a look at Sam's house— I just love looking at houses. Lunch by the bay. I picture an outdoor table with a big umbrella. It sounds marvelous.

And how fortuitous that Charlie's car seat is sitting in the kitchen and not in Cindy's car.

But I hesitate. I feel I'm starting down a road I ought not to be on at all. If I go, how will I explain it all to Cindy?

Sam says, "What do you think?"

I have to tell him something. What, I wonder, would Cindy say if she were faced with a similar dilemma? Well, that's easy.

"Sam, it sounds great. We'll be ready at eleven."

CHAPTER 14

"Sam, what made you decide to buy a house outside the city?" We're driving along Lombard Street on the way to the Golden Gate Bridge. I haven't crossed the Golden Gate in years and am looking forward to it.

He says, "Because this particular house was a fantastic buy. You know how ludicrous the price of property in the Bay Area is? I just couldn't pass up this opportunity. Big house with two wooded acres in a prestigious area at a bargain price. It's a great investment, if nothing else."

"So what's the catch? Isn't it true 'you gits what you pays for'?"

"Sure, that's generally true," he says. "But this is a special case. This house was owned by an old lady who'd lived there since she was a young bride. She died recently and stipulated in her will that I was to have first shot at buying the house. It never even went on the open market."

"How come? Was she a relative of yours?"

"No. She was one of my clients. I handled her account for years and we became good friends. When she got too infirm to travel to the city, I'd drive out to the house to go over her investments with her. Then, while I was there, she'd sometimes ask me to do little things for her—change a light bulb, take a package to the post office. That kind of thing."

He pauses to look over his shoulder as we merge with the parkway that approaches the bridge, and continues, "I really got to know the house well during my visits. She knew how much I liked it. That's why she wanted me to have it. She suggested the price. A ridiculously low price."

"Well, that's nice." I say. "I wonder if her heirs are as thrilled by this deal as you are."

"She doesn't have any heirs. She left the bulk of her estate to an animal shelter or something." Sam suddenly sounds sad. It dawns on me he must have been fond of the old lady.

Charlie, in the back seat, hasn't made a sound since we left home fifteen minutes ago. I turn to check on him, and smile. His eyes are huge as he watches the moving scene, turning his head to look from one side of the car to the other. He so enjoys going for a drive.

After a minute, I ask, "So your decision to move had nothing to do with breaking up with Roland?"

"Breaking up with Roland?" Sam sounds startled. "You make it sound like we were lovers or something."

"Weren't you?"

"Hell, no. When I got the house on Bayley Street, I was looking for someone to share the rent. The woman at the agency introduced me to Roland. It's always been a strictly business relationship."

H-mm! Curiouser and curiouser. Sam sees me looking at him and says, "Don't tell me you're disappointed I'm not gay?" He sounds indignant. Well, he's not the only one who's indignant right now.

"Sam Bradshawe," I say, "You may remember that Cindy and I were looking for a *gay* man to father our child? In fact, I asked you outright if you were gay. You said you were bisexual. I believed you mainly because I assumed you and

Roland were a couple. Now I'm beginning to wonder just what you are."

Sam gives a contemptuous snort but looks embarrassed. He hesitates, and then says, "You know, Diane, in all honesty, I don't feel comfortable discussing my sex life with you. You're...what shall I say? Maybe 'prudish' is too strong a word. But I do think of you as being a very proper, conventional type of person."

I look down at my lap and smile. Sam's words have rekindled the memory of the day I "came out" to my mother. I can't imagine *conventional* would be her adjective of choice to describe me.

Sam squirms a bit. He probably thinks he's offended me. He says, "Believe me, there's nothing wrong with being conventional. Deep down inside me, there's a pretty conventional guy who's going to take over one of these days. But the past few years I've been determined to kick over the traces of my conservative background and live as freewheeling a life as I could stomach. That's why I moved to the Castro District, as I told you before. I've done a lot of fooling around. A lot of experimenting in ways that I'm sure would shock you. Or maybe not." He's looking straight ahead, but I see the corners of his mouth turning up.

We've left the toll plaza behind and are in the middle of the bridge itself. I love the views from this bridge and lean toward the window in eager anticipation. It's a shame Charlie has to remain strapped into his seat; I'd like to be able to hold him up and show him the water.

But Sam hasn't really answered my question. I try again. "So you *are* bisexual?"

He says, "No, I'm straight. I've never been the slightest bit confused on that issue." Deliberately, I give an audible gasp and swing around to face him. Not that I'm really surprised at his reply, but I want to display shock that he so blatantly lied to Cindy and me. Sam says, "Okay, okay, I guess I shouldn't have lied to you, but frankly I couldn't see how my sexual orientation was any of your business. I mean, how does my being straight render my services any less valuable to you?"

At the moment, I can't think of an answer to that question, but that's not the point. The point is one should be honest and above-board in dealings with others. But who am I to be taking the moral high ground? I turn my back on him again to concentrate on the view.

Through the orange-brown rails of the bridge flashing by, I look out at the green waters of the bay and the city skyline beyond. It's choppy out there today with lots of little sailboats bobbing around in the water. Sam, following my glance, says, "I have a view of the bay from my house."

Because I'm still miffed at him, I don't respond right away. He talks on anyway about his house. "It's a great house. Four bedrooms, three bathrooms, living room, dining room, library, office, greenhouse." *Déjà vu.* Was it really only a week ago that Cindy and I were having a similar conversation on our way to San Ramon?

Finally, I can't be bothered to maintain my pique and comment, "Isn't that a lot of house for one person?"

"Oh, I'm planning to have plenty of company. It's a fantastic party house, as you'll see. Roomy and private."

Plenty of company! I can see it now. Bacchanalian revelry on two wooded acres. Wanton women running in and out of four bedrooms and the greenhouse. Which reminds me....

"Sam, do you still see that woman who was at Phyllis' party with you?"

He looks puzzled. "You mean Juanita?" We've crossed the bridge now and continue north on the highway.

"No. This was a tall blonde woman."

"Yes, that's Juanita." I look at him in astonishment. How could that strapping Germanic wench be called *Juanita*? A Juanita would be petite, black of hair and eye, gold hoop earrings. Sam catches my expression and misunderstands. He teases. "Why, Diane, I do believe you're jealous."

Quick as a flash, I retort, "Nah! She's not my type."

Sam finds this very funny. He puts his head back and lets loose with many loud, steering-wheel-slapping guffaws, startling Charlie into a frenzy of arm and leg waving. When Sam stops laughing, he says, "You're in good form today. So, tell me, Diane, just who is your type?"

There was a time I could have answered his question with ease. Now as I study his mischievous grin, all I can truthfully say is, "I really don't know."

To my surprise, he doesn't rib me about my uncertainty. He says, "I bet a lot of people couldn't answer that question. I sure couldn't."

After a short while, we leave the highway and drive westward into the town of Mill Valley, nestled in the shadow of Mount Tamalpais. We drive around a square of stores and cafés in the center of town and take a narrow street heading uphill. A mile or so further on, we turn onto a small, potholed lane, lined with trees and bougainvillea-covered fences. We bump along until the lane runs out in a bank of overgrown vegetation. Sam stops the car and I peer through the windshield. "There's a house here?"

Sam waves a hand. "It's in there somewhere."

We climb out and Sam gets Charlie from the back seat. I say, "Shouldn't we have brought machetes?"

I'm only partly joking. This is like some scene in a jungle movie. Long, tangled vines with pink and white sweet-smelling flowers envelop every bush and tree around the house, their tendrils crisscrossing the path leading to the front door. The vines have even attached themselves to the house itself. Gutters, window frames, everything that sticks out, are draped in tangled masses of vine.

Sam says, "It's jasmine. The damned stuff strangles everything if it's not kept in check. Next week, I'm having a gardener come in to chop it all out and also to cut the lawn." He indicates a field of knee-high weeds to our right. We battle our way to the front door, which Sam unlocks, and we go inside.

It's obvious no one has lived here for a while. The place is full of dust and cobwebs, with stained carpets and ratty odds and ends of furniture. Sam says, "You have to use your imagination to see the potential here. Like, for instance..." He leads me through the various rooms, explaining changes he plans to make. "In the living room I'll expand the fireplace—put in one of those big manor house things with a seat built around it. I'll knock down the wall between the living room and dining room. So there'll be one huge..." throwing out his free arm to illustrate. "...room stretching from front to back . Back there, I'll put in French doors."

I skip ahead of him into the kitchen. This room is a dramatic departure from the rest of the house. Everything is brand new—floors, cabinets, appliances. "Sam, what happened here?"

"The old lady got careless just before she died. She left a pot on the stove and there was a fire that gutted the kitchen. The insurance paid for all this. They didn't get around to hooking up the plumbing though." He points to a disconnected pipe poking out from under the sink. "That's why the plumber's coming today."

We go upstairs. Sam leads me into the master bedroom and takes me over to the big picture windows covering one wall. From here, we can see a distant view of the bay over the treetops.

The doorbell rings. "That must be the contractor." Still carrying Charlie, Sam sets off downstairs. I stand at the window for a few moments longer, looking down at the back of the property. There's another field of weeds—a second lawn presumably. There is also a dirty but solid-looking greenhouse, and the remnants of what probably was a vegetable garden: dead vines, trellises, a compost heap, a wheelbarrow.

It brings back a flood of memories. Memories of the two years we lived with my grandmother. As well as keeping chickens and pigs, Grandma grew corn, tomatoes, all our vegetables. My sister and mother weren't much interested but I really took to the soil. Grandma and I toiled away at digging and planting, watering and weeding. There are few thrills I've had since to equal that of seeing the first tomatoes sprouting on "my" plants. And, oh, the taste of those tomatoes, and the new radishes and lettuces and green onions, freshly gathered from the garden.

Male voices downstairs. I drag myself away from the window and go down to join them. Sam's taken the contractor into the kitchen and is giving instructions, waving his free arm around while holding onto Charlie with the other. The contractor—a fortyish, balding man in sport shirt and jeans—acknowledges my appearance at the door with a nod and a polite, "Mrs. Bradshawe." I open my mouth and close it again. Sam keeps talking.

As the two men continue to talk, I again wander through the downstairs rooms. I can't help chuckling at the contrast between Cindy's pristine townhouse and this place which looks as if it came straight from the fevered imagination of some Victorian novelist. Talk about the stuff of nightmares. But, to be fair, the stuff of dreams too.

In the dining room, I look around, trying to see it through Sam's eyes. I picture elegant French doors leading out onto a sweeping back lawn, the dirty chandelier transformed into sparkling crystal, parquet flooring gleaming where only dust is visible now. Also—now it's *my* imagination that's at work—perhaps a brightly colored Oriental rug in the middle of the room. Gorgeous!

My reveries are interrupted by the two men who've come to the doorway. The contractor says, "I'll just duck out to the truck and get my tools. Then I can get to work." He smiles at Charlie who is gurgling at him and says to Sam, "Handsome little guy you got there."

"Yeah." Sam beams. "He's the greatest."

Then the man asks, looking from Sam to me and back, "Your first?"

Sam's face is a picture. His expression freezes and he looks across at me as though appealing for help. It's a treat to see him so uncharacteristically flummoxed. He says, "Yes."

"There's nothing in the world like kids," the contractor assures us. "I have four of 'em. You folks were sure smart to pick up a place like this. It's a lot of work but well worth it. A great place to raise a family."

Sam mumbles something. I smile and say nothing.

There's an antique fair of sorts going on in Sausalito and the town is mobbed. However, we manage to find a restaurant near the water with an outdoor table. We have halibut and salad for lunch. People at adjoining tables smile at Charlie—who is a *very* cute baby—and comment on his cuteness. His Daddy swells with pride while his Mommy—well, she acts out this family charade as though born to the role.

As Sam predicted, we get back to the city a little after three. He takes me to Johanssen's, a big supermarket in the Twin Peaks area that I've been to once before with Cindy. I stock up on everything I can think of. Might as well take advantage of having both a vehicle *and* a muscular man at my disposal. Sam's trunk is full of junk related to house-moving, so he puts some grocery bags in the back seat with Charlie, and I hold one on my lap in the front. We set off for home.

"Sam, when we get back to my place, remind me to get your help in moving my futon. A ball of Charlie's got stuck under there and I can't get it out."

He says, "Sure." Then he returns to the topic that has dominated much of his conversation on the way home: his new house. "It's really solidly built," he tells me. "Just a few cosmetic changes will do wonders. Just you see—once I have the gardeners and house cleaners in, you won't recognize the place." He appears to have forgotten that today's get-together was supposed to be our farewell.

He goes on to tell me that our do-gooder friend Phyllis is trying to get him involved in a "Habitat for Humanity" project. Sam laughs. "I told her I'm going to be fully involved in a 'habitat for Sam' project." Talking of Phyllis reminds me of the party at her house where Blondie—excuse me, *Juanita!*—was frolicking on Sam's lap. And he never did tell me if he's still seeing her. Well, it really is none of my business.

As we near home, the aroma of French bread in the grocery bag I'm holding hits my nostrils. "Sam, this bread smells delicious. Shall we have a couple of slices with our tea?"

Sam doesn't reply. He's pulling up at the curb outside my place now and peers through the windshield, frowning. He says, "Isn't that Cindy's car?" Over the top of the grocery bag, I can just make out a white car like Cindy's parked in front of us.

"No, it can't be. She said she'd be here at seven. In Cindy-speak, that means between eight and nine. There're lots of cars that look like Cindy's."

He persists, "But it has that license plate."

Suddenly apprehensive, I push the bag aside and see the license plate just as Sam reads aloud, "*Hot2Trot*."

"Ohmygod! Sam, you can't park here. Keep going. Park in the next block."

But Sam has already shut off the engine and unbuckled his seat belt. He says, "Now why would I do that? Come on, Diane, I think Cindy and I can refrain from killing each other for a few minutes while I help you with the groceries."

"No, you don't understand. She doesn't know about you."

But he's out of the car already, looking up toward the front door. Then he leans down and grins at me. "Hey, Dragon Lady's on the porch already. What doesn't she know about me?"

I stare up at the house and, sure enough, there's Cindy on the porch, looking down at us. Sam closes his door and comes around to the curbside of the car to help me get Charlie out. In a low voice, I beg him, "Please, *please* let's tell her that I just met you in the supermarket and you were kind enough to offer us a ride home." He lifts his eyebrows in surprise, but there's no time to explain.

As I rush up the steps with Charlie in my arms and a welcoming smile on my face, I hear Sam behind me muttering, "That won't work, Diane." I ignore him. It has to work.

"Cindy, how nice. You got here early."

Cindy looks stunned. She says in a mesmerized sort of way, "I've been here for *hours*. I couldn't imagine where you'd gone." She's talking to me but her eyes are fixated beyond me—on Sam at the curb unloading groceries.

"But you said you wouldn't be here till seven."

Cindy explains in the same mesmerized way, "Only three people showed up for the retreat—out of eight who were invited. So Marigold ended the retreat right after lunch."

Sam has come up the steps now. "Hi, Cindy," he says, and marches past us through the open front door, down the hall and into the kitchen. Cindy and I follow. Sam dumps the bags onto the counter, and marches out again, saying, "I'll get the rest of the stuff."

I put Charlie in his infant seat and avoid Cindy's eye while I tell her about the great stroke of luck I've just had. "Sam was in the supermarket and he very kindly offered us a ride home. So I just went ahead and bought all this stuff…." I wave the loaf of bread in illustration.

Cindy is eyeing the grocery bags. Darn it, I was forgetting about the big store logo on the bags. She knows I wouldn't walk all the way to Johanssen's with Charlie. However, I reason, I could have taken the bus. There is one that stops only a block away that goes in that direction. I try to remember if it runs on Saturdays.

Sam returns with the rest of the groceries and Charlie's car seat. He holds up the car seat, "Where do you want this?" I indicate the floor near the door and he puts it down. "Now how about this couch you want moved?" Cindy and I stare at him. "The one with the ball stuck under it?"

"Oh, yes." I take him into the living room and he helps me recover the ball.

The wire coat hanger is still on the futon and Sam reproves me. "You shouldn't leave this coat hanger around. Charlie could poke his eye out." I mumble something and remove the coat hanger. I wonder how much of this dialog Cindy can hear.

Suddenly, Charlie starts to wail. We go back to the kitchen. Sam says, "Ah, wassa matter, little man?" He picks Charlie up—the wailing stops as if by magic—gives him a hug and a kiss and replaces him in the infant seat. More loud wails as Sam walks away. Again, I avoid looking at Cindy.

On our way to the front door, Sam mutters, "I suppose the tea party is off—*again!*" Our eyes meet, and his are so full of mirth I find it hard not to laugh out loud. Actually, I realize, Sam must be rather enjoying this little drama. After Cindy's meanness toward him, he must get a real kick out of seeing her upset. But it's really not funny. At the door, he whispers, "Call you later," and then bounds off down the steps.

Back in the kitchen, I see Cindy has found the bottle of white wine I always keep in the fridge for her, and poured herself a glass. Maybe that will keep her occupied while I get on with things. There's a lot to do. Charlie is still fussing. I have to put the groceries away, change Charlie, feed him, and then start fixing our dinner. Sorting through my purchases, I ask, "Cindy, what would you like to eat tonight? Chicken breasts or pork chops?"

Silence.

With a plastic-wrapped food offering in each hand, I turn to look at her. She takes a large swallow of wine and says in a voice of pure ice, "Okay, so what the hell's going on here?"

I stand stock still for a moment. "Well, I told you...."

"You told me you met Sam at Johanssen's. How many miles away is that? That's quite a feat, hiking all the way to Johanssen's by yourself, presumably dragging Charlie along behind you in his car seat." The car seat! My eyes turn to the incriminating seat, propped against the wall where Sam placed it. That must be why Sam said my explanation wouldn't work! Would I have taken the seat on the bus? No, of course not. I'm skewered.

"And then," Cindy goes on, "there's all this cozy domestic business about rescuing the ball from under the couch." She mimics, "'*Don't leave the coat hanger around, Diane, Charlie could get hurt.*' Don't tell me that big ape hasn't been in this apartment before—many, many times before. He seems to be getting ready to move in."

"Cindy, it's not like that. There's a perfectly innocent explanation." But her face is hard and she's gulping down the wine like crazy. No two ways about it. It's time to come clean. Cleaner, anyway.

Wine does nothing for me so I don't normally drink it. But, in times of crisis, anything is worth a try. I get a glass from the cupboard and sit down opposite Cindy. The bottle of wine is on the table between us. I top off her glass and pour one for myself. Here goes.

CHAPTER 15

My explanation doesn't take long. The growing decibel level of a hungry Charlie prods me into both raising my voice and speeding my pace. I tell Cindy about how I ran out of baby food the night Charlie was sick, the way Sam came to my rescue, how he begged to be allowed a brief visit with Charlie, his utter disappointment at not being able to see Charlie properly in the dark, and my suggestion he visit in the daylight.

Then I judiciously slide over some potentially troublesome details—after all, we are in a hurry here—to come to my plausible, if misleading, conclusion. "So he came over today, saw that I was going grocery shopping and drove us to Johanssen's."

Frankly, I'm rather pleased with my story. Not that I like deceiving Cindy but there's no way I could make some of the omitted details—a visit to Sam's new house, for Pete's sake!—palatable to her. Best to take things one step at a time.

By now, Charlie is throwing a full-fledged tantrum with kicking legs and arching back. "Cindy, I've got to take care of Charlie. We can talk more later." I stand up. The room lurches for a second as the wine kicks in. Cindy goes on sitting and sipping, her eyes staring into space.

• • •

A few hours later order has returned to our home. Charlie has been fed, bathed, and put to bed. Cindy and I have finished eating dinner. My explanation of Sam's presence may not have been as persuasive as I'd thought because Cindy has been in a sulk all evening. Probably what upset her so is the way Sam strode around the apartment as though he owned the place. But then, that's the way Sam is. Cindy should know that by now.

"Come on, Cindy," I say, "I've poured the coffee. Let's move into the living room and you tell me all about your day. Your partial retreat, or whatever it was." Cindy sighs heavily, but as we seat ourselves on the futon and sip our coffee, she does finally start talking.

"Well, the retreat was a joke. All we talked about was why so few people turned up. Marigold was really upset but she shouldn't have been surprised. She just can't seem to handle her subordinates. It seems every week or so we have yet another person threatening to quit."

As Cindy talks, her face brightens. "The good news is that Marigold is relying on *me* more and more to put herself in good standing with the bosses in New York. She keeps telling them she has this wonder-person to deal with things like employee relations."

My mind is starting to wander a bit as it often does when Cindy gets into shoptalk. But now she catches my attention by leaning forward and saying earnestly, "She means me, you know. The wonder person?"

I nod vigorously. "Yes, I know."

"In fact, during our trip to New York Marigold plans to get approval for a special position for me. Assistant Director."

Now I'm fully awake. "What trip to New York?"

Cindy says, "The one where I'll be meeting with Mr. J. and Mr. B. Our company founders. Remember, I told you about it last weekend when we were driving back from San Ramon? You probably weren't listening."

I probably wasn't—at least, I missed the New York part. I'm not too thrilled with the idea. Obviously, I'm not invited—not with Charlie in tow. But it's a relief to find Cindy in good humor again.

The rest of the evening passes in a civil enough fashion with more shoptalk from Cindy, followed by Charlie talk from me. But, at bedtime, it becomes clear that all is still not completely well. I go to the kitchen for a glass of water, and when I return to the living room I find Cindy has cleared off the futon and is folding it down.

"What are you doing?"

She looks embarrassed but her voice is firm. "I'm in a tossy-turny mode tonight. We'll both be better off if I sleep in here."

This is a first.

With glass in hand, I lean against the doorframe and try to sound sympathetic. "I understand. You've had a pretty harrowing day all round, what with the retreat getting messed up...."

She smiles. "That dumb retreat. But, you know, some things worked out pretty well. Like lunch. There were only three of us so we skipped the cold cuts buffet we were supposed to have at the conference center. Marigold treated us to lunch in Sausalito. It was mobbed because there was some antique fair going on, but we found a nice little restaurant by the bay."

A sip of water on its way down my throat sticks in mid-gulp. I swallow hard and try not to cough. For a moment, I'm convinced some horrible revelation from Cindy will follow. But she talks on, oblivious to my consternation. Evidently, she didn't see us in Sausalito, but what a near miss! Grandma was right: your lies often catch up with you when you least expect it. I resolve that from this point on I will be a reformed woman. No more lies, evasions, half-truths, creative explanations.

But as Cindy describes the salmon she had for her lunch, I find myself quite unwilling to talk about the halibut I had for mine. I guess I'll have to postpone my reformation until tomorrow.

On Sunday, Cindy is still not back to her normal self. She's in a strangely pensive mood, often seeming to retreat to some far-off place in her mind. And Charlie is uncharacteristically cranky today. He's probably teething.

After breakfast, I propose a visit to the park. "We can show Charlie the ducks. That should cheer him up a bit. I'll fix snacks for us to take." Cindy agrees and sits at the kitchen table bouncing Charlie on her knee while I prepare our picnic. I put a thermos of coffee in a canvas carryall along with some sweet rolls and apples and a bottle for Charlie. Later, there's an awkward moment when Cindy and I reinstall Charlie's car seat in the back of Cindy's Toyota. From this time on, I'll always feel guilty when I look at that car seat. We climb aboard and set off.

An hour or so later, Cindy and I are sitting on a bench by the duck pond in Golden Gate Park. Charlie is in his stroller and I rock him back and forth. His mood hasn't improved much. I guess he doesn't care for ducks. We're silent for a long time. My mind drifts to some minor argument I'm having at work with Lucinda about how to set the columns in our monthly financial reports.

Suddenly, Cindy says, "Did having Charlie turn out the way you expected?" I look at her in surprise. She says, "I don't mean giving birth to him. I mean having another person in your life. Has that turned out the way you expected?"

I'm not sure what she's getting at but don't want to irritate her by saying so. So I furrow my brow to indicate I'm considering her question, and then say, "Well, he's turned out to be a lot of work. Which we both *did* expect, of course. Er...also a lot more anxiety than I'd expected."

From Cindy's expression, I sense I'm not addressing her question. Does she feel now I have Charlie, I don't need her anymore? I try again. "Another person in my life? I suppose he is that. But, Cindy, he in no way replaces having an adult around. In fact, now I have Charlie, I more than ever feel the need for a caring *supportive* adult to help me raise him."

Cindy sucks her lips and stares morosely at the ducks. I guess my answer still wasn't what she wanted to hear. "Why do you ask?"

She says, "I always thought there'd be a few rough spots before everything got sorted out for us. I sure was right there, wasn't I?" She sounds dejected. "Remember that TV program we saw once on stress? Where they said that life events don't have to be negative to be stressful—even positive events can be stressful."

"That's right," I agree. "Like the new job and the new house and having a baby. They've all been stressful although they're positive things."

"Yes, but there've been some negative things too, haven't there?"

Like Marigold, I think.

Cindy says, "Like Sam."

"Sam? Why Sam?" I feel indignant on Sam's behalf. And dismayed. Why won't she accept my explanation of his presence yesterday?

Cindy asks slowly, "Did Sam tell you what I said to him when I phoned him? That time when you were in the hospital having Charlie?"

So that's it! She's feeling guilty about that call, worried that Sam has told me and wondering how to explain herself to me. This must have been on her mind ever since she saw him with me yesterday. Determined to set her mind at rest, I say, "Oh, sweetie, he did. I didn't bring it up before because I didn't want to upset you. Believe me, I do understand completely where you were coming from. There's no need...."

All at once Cindy appears overcome with despair. She gives a little cry, folds her arms around herself and rocks, forward and back. She moans, "After I phoned him that time, I was so sure he would never bother us again. Now, I have this horrible feeling we're never going to be free of him." She stops rocking and glares at me. "Especially since you keep encouraging him."

I open my mouth but she won't let me interrupt.

"How could you be *friendly* with him, for God's sake? You actually knew about my phone call, but still you encouraged him."

It's dawning on me that I've got this figured out all wrong. Cindy doesn't feel she owes me an apology. She feels I owe her one. I listen open-mouthed as she rants.

"Do you have any idea how rough things have been for me lately? I'm exhausted with the long hours I have to work, and all this driving back and forth to the city every weekend. I'm stressed up to gazoo worrying about how to come up with all the money for the house." She swings around to glare at me before continuing. "And I am the one who has to come up with the money, right? I mean, on your salary, we couldn't afford a shoebox."

I gasp at this. She says quickly, "Oh, I know you can't help it. But somehow it doesn't seem fair, Diane, because on top of everything else..." She stops again and gulps. The tears are welling up.

"Diane, I'm happy to do all of this for you, for all three of us, if only I felt my efforts were appreciated. But, no, all I ever get from you is an endless stream of complaints about how you hate your job, how hard it is to be alone with Charlie. Snide comments about how you're virtually a single mother. Constant nagging about how long it's taking to get the house." Now, the tears are pouring down her cheeks. "In fact, I think you actually *resent* me. You don't seem to have any idea how much I'm doing here. You say *you* need a supportive adult by your side. Well, I could write a book on that subject."

Her angry words astonish and frighten me. Ever since Cindy moved to San Ramon, it's seemed to me that I am the one who has been underappreciated. Bad enough that she put the house in her name—no doubt, with the active encouragement of that damned Marigold. But already she's forgotten that for the past five years I've been the one who has made sure we put away money every month for our "house fund."

But Cindy thinks she's the one who carries the brunt of the work and worry in our relationship. As for me…. In her eyes, apparently, I have it easy. Setting off for a mindless job every day, nothing to do in the evenings but take care of a small baby, while she slaves away. Is this really the way it's become for us?

By the time she falls silent, I'm too choked up to say anything. And Charlie just keeps on whining. What the hell's wrong with him today? Maybe he's picked up the tension. God knows, there's been enough around this weekend.

After a while, I pack up the remnants of our largely uneaten picnic. We make our way back to the car and drive home.

This evening I'd been planning to fix the pork chops. Cindy particularly likes a recipe of mine where I bake the chops with sage stuffing and slices of apple. But I need to feel energetic and loving to get geared up for a meal like that, and right now, I feel neither of those things. I put the chops in the freezer and heat a can of beef stew.

After dinner, we sit on the futon with our coffee. Charlie, quiet at last, is cradled in my arms with his bottle. I say, "Cindy, I'm sorry you're so unhappy with me and our relationship."

Right away, she puts down her coffee cup and turns to me. The tears start again. "No, that's not it at all. As I said, I'm perfectly happy to do everything I'm doing if only I thought you appreciated it. You make me feel I'm neglecting you. Otherwise, why would you turn to others? Like Sam."

"But Cindy," I protest, "of course, I appreciate it. And I explained about Sam. It was just an accident I ran into him. Surely, you understand. And I told you in another week or so he'll be moving out of town. It's unlikely we'll ever see him again. What else can I say to reassure you?"

Cindy pulls a tissue out of her pocket and blows her nose. She says, "You see, it's essential I be able to trust you. You'll have to keep living here in the city for at least a month or more while I get the loan approved and the house ready to move into. And then at some point I'll be taking that trip to New York. And that means I may have to be away for a whole weekend."

She snuffles. "Now I seriously wonder if I should just chuck it all in. Forget about New York and this assistant director thing. I thought you were as happy as I am about it all but maybe I'm just being selfish. I mean, if it's making life so unbearable for you...."

And now the tears are welling up in *my* eyes. I cry, "Oh, Cindy, of course not. Of course, I value everything you're doing for us. You mustn't even think about foregoing the New York trip. I feel horrible thinking you don't trust me."

With Charlie on my lap, it's awkward but Cindy manages to lean forward and put her arms around me. She sobs, "I've been under so much pressure lately. Of course, I trust you. I know I'm overreacting."

As we weep in each other's arms, I whisper, "Oh, my love, I'm the one who's been selfish. I can't believe I've been adding to your stress this way. From this day on, I'll have nothing more to do with Sam. I *promise*—cross my heart and hope to die. Please believe me."

She looks back at me with a tear-streaked smile. "I do believe you. Thank you, thank you, thank you." She intersperses each *thank you* with a little kiss.

After Cindy leaves to go back to San Ramon, I collapse on the couch. I think this is the first time I've ever been happy to have her leave. These emotional scenes are so draining. There've been so many of them lately. Showdown with Sam last week. Showdown with Cindy this week. To say nothing of mini-showdowns with Morales at work all the time. Come to think of it, I'd better watch my step with Morales from now on; it would be terrible to be fired at this stage of events. My stomach tightens at the thought.

Later in the evening, I give Charlie a bath and play with him for a while before putting him to bed. Poor little baby. I've felt so cross at his crankiness today and too stressed to find out what might be wrong. I sing to him. "*Sing a song of sixpence. A pocket full of rye...*"

These babyhood nursery rhymes are as soothing to me as they are to Charlie. They evoke feelings of safety and warmth extending back to the deepest reaches of my childhood. Are these fantasy memories? Or was there really once a tender, loving mother who was transformed by the disintegration of her marriage into the remote, indifferent woman whom Hazel and I have known for most of our lives?

So much for the past. After Charlie falls asleep, I switch my thoughts to the present.

It's clear that Sam has been a most welcome distraction for me the past few weeks. But I need to face one truth I've been sidestepping. That is, I'll be destroying my relationship with Cindy if I allow this distraction to continue. It's not only unfair to Cindy. It's also cruel to Sam and Charlie to allow them to become attached to each other when I know full well their relationship will soon be coming to a grinding halt.

Well, no good fretting about all this. It's clear what I have to do next.

I go to the phone.

Sam's voice lightens when he hears mine. "Hi there. How did it go with Dragon Lady?"

"Sam," I say, my words tumbling over one another other, "Cindy is extremely upset because you—and I—have been violating the terms of the contract we had with you. Remember, you solemnly promised you wouldn't have any more contact with me after the baby was born? Well, that promise has kind of gone by the board of late, hasn't it? And I know I'm as guilty as you are. But it's got to come to an end. I promised Cindy we won't contact each other any more."

I can hear his sharp intake of breath before his predictable reaction.

"For God's sake, this is all so silly. Tell me, what harm can it possibly do if I call in occasionally while you're still living in the city? Or, for that matter, to keep in contact even after you move? In fact, I have every intention of doing that. Does that silly b...—woman —think I'm trying to take Charlie away from her? Or is she afraid I'm trying to take *you* away from her?"

"Sam, there's no point in arguing. You understood our agreement right from the start."

There's a pause before he says in a steady voice, "Don't forget Charlie is my son. My flesh and blood. Legally, I'm entitled to...."

I cut him short. "No, Sam, it won't wash. I can't believe you're so conveniently forgetting what our arrangement has been all along. And I'm really sorry I've encouraged you of late. But we've got to get back on track. It just won't work for us to have three parents in this family."

"I see. And I get the short straw."

Hearing the disappointment in his voice, I feel a pang but then I remember Cindy's skeptical analysis of Sam's interest in Charlie. *All a matter of power and control.* Whether she's right or wrong, it's time for me to get out of my position in the middle of this push-pull situation.

As gently as I can, I say, "Sam, without Cindy I never would have had Charlie in the first place. I know, I know..." I forestall what I'm sure he'll say. "I could hardly have had him without you either. But Cindy came first. She still comes first."

A very long silence follows. Finally, Sam says, "Well, if you're sure this is what you really want...."

Of course, this isn't what I *want*. What I want is to have it all. I want to get back my old loving relationship with Cindy. I want her to be happy. I want the best for Charlie. I want to have Sam living close by to be a sort of uncle figure who comes around every day or so to toss Charlie in the air and make me laugh. Only Sam isn't an uncle. And there's the rub.

I say, "This is the way it's going to be."

Sam sighs. "Listen, I'm going to give you the phone number at my new house. I'll be moving in next weekend.

I won't contact you again, but if you ever want to talk to me, please call. Okay? Do you have a pencil and paper?"

"Yes."

He dictates the number to me. "Did you get that?"

"Yes."

But I haven't written the number down. I don't even have a pencil in my hand. I mustn't take his number down because I don't trust myself not to call him.

"Goodbye, Sam."

I hear his last words as I hang up. "Give Charlie a kiss from me."

For some time, I sit by the phone with my head in my hands. There are gallons of unshed tears in me, but somehow I hurt too much to shed any of them. What a difference twenty-four hours can make. Yesterday morning I was anticipating my upcoming outing with Sam, feeling excitement and a tantalizing tinge of guilt. Yesterday morning, Cindy hadn't yet spelled out her ultimatum—for *ultimatum* is what it is. Yesterday morning seems a very long time ago.

Now I've made a decision and have a solemn promise to keep.

CHAPTER 16

Two months go by. It's noon on a hot Friday in early September. My co-worker Kitty and I sit on a bench in the plaza outside our office building eating our lunch. Kitty asks, "Any more news about the house?"

"Yes. Everything's all set. Cindy's picking up the key today."

Kitty stops in mid-bite and looks at me, her eyes wide. "But that's *wonderful*, Diane. Isn't it?" She teases. "How come you're not jumping up and down and screaming with excitement?"

Good question. The truth is there have been so many false alarms with this wretched house business that I can't be bothered to get excited any more.

I say, "Well, for one thing, I won't be able to celebrate with Cindy this weekend. Remember, I told you she's off to New York again tomorrow with Marigold. In fact, Kitty, I was wondering if you could meet us in the park on Saturday or Sunday afternoon. Charlie so enjoys being with your two little ones."

Kitty's two boys are aged four and two and they're marvelous company for Charlie, who sees virtually no children in his daily life. Over the past several weeks, there've been a couple of weekends when Cindy has been out of town or otherwise too tied up to drive to the city. At such times, Kitty's willingness to keep us company has staved off madness for me. But now she says regretfully, "No, not this weekend. I'm so very sorry, Diane. George's family is having a big get-together on Sunday for his mother's birthday. We'll be cooking all day Saturday."

It's funny how people are. Kitty is a traditional Italian-Catholic girl, who I'm sure is privately appalled at my unorthodox lifestyle. Yet she has shown me so much kindness, especially in the last trying months. On the other hand, the people I thought were my good friends from our old neighborhood don't seem to want to know me anymore. My pleas for them to come visit usually end with a promise to call. But no one ever does.

Kitty and I are silent for a while as we eat and people-watch. There's an interesting assortment of characters in downtown San Francisco at noontime: some in business attire, even in today's heat; many in dress-down-Friday garb; tourists of various shapes and hues. A couple of hip-hop kids zoom in front of us on their skateboards. I glare indignantly, half-fearing and half maliciously hoping they'll fall flat on their faces.

Kitty nudges me and points her chin toward the revolving glass doors of our building. Our indomitable supervisor, Lucinda Morales, has just emerged, accompanied by a friend with whom she often lunches. We smirk as we watch the two of them bounce down the street like a couple of chattering butterballs.

"Kitty, that reminds me. The strangest thing happened this morning. I went to Lucinda's office to hand in my time card. And then...." I turn and look hard at Kitty to emphasize what I'm about to say. "Lucinda asked me if everything was all right with me and with the baby."

Kitty doesn't look as flabbergasted as I expected her to. "Kitty, did you hear me? I'm talking about *Morales* acting like a caring human. I nearly fell over with astonishment." I laugh, but Kitty doesn't laugh with me. Incidentally, I don't tell her that when Morales spoke to me with such unexpected concern in her voice, I was hard pressed to hold back tears. These days, that's not unusual. I seem to get weepy at the slightest provocation.

Kitty finishes a mouthful of sandwich and takes a sip of milk. She says, "The other day Morales came and asked *me* if you and Charlie were okay." I gape at her. Kitty turns to me and touches my arm. "Diane, I'm not sure I should tell you this but lately everyone in the office has been a bit concerned about you. You haven't been your usual self for so long now. Morales thought you or the baby might have some awful illness."

Her words astonish me. It's true I've had fits of the blues the past couple of months but I thought I was hiding them pretty well. I've been working hard to appear cheerful and patient with everyone, especially Cindy. But now, Kitty's gentle touch and kind eyes make me weepy. I take out a tissue and blow my nose.

Kitty says, "Don't get upset. It's no wonder you've been in the dumps what with Cindy's trips to New York and the house deal taking so long. But any day now all that will be settled. Right?"

Yeah, sure, I think. If nothing else comes up. It's been one thing after another. Cindy's first application for a home loan got turned down because she hadn't been in her job long enough or something. Then, when she was all set to sign the papers a couple of weeks ago, *Marigold* discovered a crack in the driveway. *Marigold* urged Cindy to hold off signing until the builder fixed the crack. Then *Marigold* arranged this second trip to New York and that's delaying things even more.

Marigold this, *Marigold* that, *Marigold* the other!

• • •

On Saturday morning after breakfast, I sit in the living room folding a stack of laundry. Charlie is playing on the floor near my feet. He's attempting to crawl these days. Watching him, I think about Kitty's words yesterday. Now that I think about it, I must try to snap out of the doldrums for his sake. But it's hard, especially during these weekends when I'm alone with him.

When I walk to the bedroom with the folded laundry, Charlie lets out a loud cry. This is something new for him—fussing whenever he's left alone for a second. "Okay, Charlie." I hurry back and pick him up, laughing at the cross little face. "We'll play bounce-a-baby." I walk around the room, jouncing him up and down. "*Sing a song of sixpence...*" But the old nursery rhyme doesn't comfort me today; in fact, I feel it's time I got a new repertoire.

Going by the window, I notice a battered gray station wagon cruising slowly along our side of the street. It passes our house, stops at the corner; then backs up to park by our steps. It looks familiar. I stand by the curtain and peer out. The driver's door opens and a large female figure struggles out. For heaven's sake, it's Phyllis! And just yesterday I was complaining to myself that no one from the old neighborhood ever came to visit.

Phyllis looks up at the steps and hesitates. They must seem formidable for someone so out-of-shape. Fearing she might give up and get back in her car, I hurry to the front door and throw it open. "Phyllis. How lovely to see you. Come on, those steps aren't that bad."

Although Phyllis is a kind and well-meaning person, I'm usually not that thrilled to see her. This is because she nearly always manages to extract some sort of cash or time commitment from you on behalf of one of her good causes—or leaves you feeling riddled with guilt if you had the fortitude to resist. Today, however, I'm delighted to have company.

She struggles up the steps, muttering. "Diane, I swear, if I get a heart attack it will be on your head." I laugh. It occurs to me that maybe Cindy has talked Phyllis into checking up on me during this lonely weekend. But apparently not. For after Phyllis labors up the steps, staggers panting into my living room, and collapses onto the futon—"My God, is there a slab of concrete under this thing?"—she looks around and asks, "Where's Cindy? Isn't she usually here at the weekend?"

As we talk, it becomes clear Phyllis hasn't spoken to Cindy in a long while. She knows about the San Ramon house though because she asks why we haven't moved yet. After I bring her up to date on the house-purchase delays, Cindy's success in her new job, the trips to New York the job entails, I go to the kitchen to fix some lemonade. Charlie gives a single loud cry as I leave the room, but quiets down when Phyllis clucks at him.

As I fill the glasses and put cookies on a plate, Phyllis calls out to me. "It must be very hard for you living alone in this unpleasant neighborhood. In this gloomy apartment." I walk back into the room with the drinks. Phyllis is sitting in a pool of sunshine. She adds hastily, "Well, it's depressing at night anyway. Or so I hear."

You certainly can't accuse Phyllis of mincing words. But how does she know what it's like here at night?

She catches my eye as she tackles her lemonade. Then she says, "Sam...you know, Sam Bradshawe? Anyway, he asked me to check up on you. He wasn't sure whether you'd moved to San Ramon yet."

Sam! My voice rises in a little squeak as I ask, "Are you in regular contact with Sam?"

"I don't know that you'd call it regular contact. Not any more. He used to help me with some of my charity work before he moved to Mill Valley. What was that—a couple of months ago? This morning, he called me out of the blue and asked if I'd stop by sometime to see if you were still here and if you were okay." She gulps down more lemonade. "It so happened I was coming this way today, so here I am. This stuff is delicious, dear. Is there any more perchance?"

After I get her a refill, Phyllis, to my great surprise, embarks on a sort of lecture on my living conditions. "It's not healthy," she tells me, "for a young woman like you to be alone with a baby so much of the time. I can't imagine what Cindy is thinking of leaving you stranded like this for so long. What you need is a good friend. Like Sam, for example."

She takes a gulp of lemonade. "Sam's a fine lad, Diane. He can be a wonderful source of support for you. If he offers you friendship, you should take it."

She means well, of course. I say, "Phyllis, it's not that good an idea for me to see too much of Sam. It would make Cindy really unhappy."

Then Phyllis surprises me even more by exploding, waving her arms around and leaning forward as she spits out the angry words. "Just who, pray tell, is Cindy to dictate to you who your friends may or may not be? You're a grown woman, for heaven's sakes."

Charlie, who's sitting at my feet, reaches for my legs in alarm. I pick him up and cradle him as Phyllis continues.

"Remember Jane?" she asks. Jane was her long time partner who died of cancer two years ago. "Jane and I had many friends in common, but also she had friends who were uniquely hers and I had friends who were uniquely mine. It's essential for partners to give each other space."

For a fleeting moment, I wonder if Phyllis understands the kind of relationship Sam has with us. Surely she does. Not that we'd gone around advertising the news of his services, but we hadn't kept it a secret either. Now I'm getting a sneaky suspicion there might be some collusion here between Sam and this good lady who is so earnestly huffing and puffing away.

Phyllis pauses in her tirade and looks hard into my face. "I know, my dear, you're probably thinking this is none of my business. But you look really tired to me. Quite peaky."

I smile at the *peaky*—my grandmother used to say that.

"No, Diane, it's not funny. Cindy is a beautiful woman and smart as all get out, but she's also all out for herself. You must be prepared to take care of yourself, especially now you have someone else to think about." She nods toward Charlie, who is staring at her with a mix of awe and apprehension. "Sam's a good lad, as I said. Possibly a bit on the wild side, as many young men are, but goodhearted. He sounded really concerned about you and Charlie."

There *is* some collusion here, I'm sure. Still, I'm touched. "Phyllis, I do appreciate your coming and I appreciate Sam's concern. Please tell him that when you next talk to him."

She says, "Tell him yourself. He says you have his number."

"Well...I guess I lost it."

"I have it somewhere." She fishes around in her voluminous skirts as though expecting the number to pop up out of a pocket. "No, I guess I left my book at home. What about directory assistance? That's easy enough, isn't it?"

Phyllis finishes the second glass of lemonade while Charlie and I watch. There's something I'm itching to ask her, although I know I shouldn't. I say, "By the way, Phyllis, do you remember that blonde woman who was at your party last year? I think her name is Juanita."

Phyllis grunts as she swallows. "Sam's friend, you mean? She's down in South America for a few months."

Oh, really? Phyllis needs no urging to tell me more. "She's gone off with a young doctor friend of hers. They're on a humanitarian mission of some kind in one of those countries where they kill everyone all the time." She mutters to herself, trying to recall the name of the country.

"So she's a doctor?"

"A medical technician or something. Anyway, I think Sam was a bit put out." Phyllis makes a face. "He said he was worried because she was going into danger. I think he was worried because she was going off with this doctor laddie. Anyway, enough of that." She looks at her watch. "Better make tracks. I have to be at a meeting downtown at eleven."

As she struggles to get up, she asks, "What were you saying about Juanita?" At this moment, Charlie creates a distraction. He's overwhelmed by the sight of Phyllis looming to her feet before us and clings to me making little *uh-uh* noises of distress. "Poor baby," Phyllis chortles. "It's like seeing a hippo rising out of the swamp, isn't it, pet?" I join her laughter. I don't answer her question.

A couple of minutes later, Charlie and I watch from the porch as Phyllis plods down the steps, clutching the handrail and making self-deprecating remarks about her weight and clumsiness.

"Please come again, Phyllis." It really was nice to see her.

About an hour after Phyllis leaves, I sit in the kitchen, making up a grocery list. Without a car, I can buy only a few things at a time but at least the frequent trips to the corner store get me out of the house. Charlie's in his high chair playing with some Cheerios on the tray in front of him. The phone rings. I pick up the receiver and say "Hullo." And suddenly I'm sure I know who this is.

A deadpan male voice intones, "Is this the woman who owes me seven dollars and seven cents? Plus innumerable cups of tea."

Playing along, I drone, "This is she. Please submit all complaints in writing." But then I can't hold back my delight. "Oh, Sam!"

It's wonderful to hear from him. Farthest from my mind is the fact that the last time we talked I told him never to contact me again. I say, "What a coincidence. Phyllis came to see me just a short time ago and she was talking about you."

"I know. She told me all about it."

"But I thought she was on her way to a meeting."

"She phoned me as soon as she arrived at her meeting place."

"She did?"

"Yeah. She told me you and Charlie have been abandoned this weekend and you desperately need to be rescued. I'm alone for the weekend too so I thought we might be able to work something out."

"That would be lovely." I am quite unprepared for the rush of happiness I suddenly feel. "You mean, like dinner?"

"Yeah." He sounds nonchalant. "Dinner. Breakfast. Whatever. I'll come get you and bring you over here. We can figure out the meals as we go along."

Now wait a minute. Is he talking about taking us to his house? Overnight? Sam says, "Listen, no strings attached, okay. Just food and talk and relaxation. No sex."

I continue to hesitate. I'm not sure what to say because I'm not sure what I ought to say. Or how I ought to feel.

Finally, he says, "I can tell you're bitterly disappointed. Well, we can have the sex if you insist." He guffaws in his silly Sam-like way. I snicker too. He's a nut, but such a mood-enhancing nut. And I'd love to see that wacky house again. But mundane obstacles bar the way.

"Sam, it's harder than it seems. Taking a baby away for the weekend is a major production. For one thing, it's illegal to take Charlie in a car unless he's in a car seat. And our car seat is in Cindy's car. In San Ramon."

"H-mm." Sam ponders this for a few moments. "You know what, one of my neighbors has young kids. She's sure to have a car seat. What other stuff will we need for him? High chair? One of those beds with high sides? I bet I can scrounge a whole bunch of stuff from her."

Not a bet I would make with confidence!

I say, "The most important thing is that car seat."

"I'll get it. No problem."

I stop worrying. If he says it's no problem, it probably isn't.

"How about I come by about four o'clock? Can you be ready by then?"

Without even looking at the clock, I reply, "Oh, sure." As I hang up, it occurs to me that something is missing. It's that *but-what-shall-I-tell-Cindy?* feeling that's missing. Thanks to Phyllis.

By four o'clock, I'm as ready as I'm going to be. I can't believe all the stuff I've packed into one small suitcase and two bags: clothing and toiletries for me, ditto for Charlie, diapers, handiwipes, bottles, formula, toys. I keep thinking of more things to take.

Charlie is in his playpen in the living room, all dressed to go. I'm a bit concerned about his reaction to Sam after all this time. Two months is a long time in a baby's life, and these days Charlie tends to be skittish with anyone who is not an everyday figure to him. Sam would be hurt to think Charlie didn't know him any more.

When Sam arrives, I open the door and we say "Hi." We smile at each other a little shyly. I consider hugging him, but that seems awkward somehow, so I just put out my hand and he holds it for a moment. Then we go into the living room.

Charlie peeks curiously at Sam. I say, "You know, Sam, he may be a bit unsure of you. He hasn't seen you for a while. Why don't you let me carry him until he figures you out?" I gather Charlie up in my arms and walk over to stand next to Sam. The two of them look at each other. Charlie looks uncertain, and Sam... The tenderness on Sam's face makes my throat tighten. A desire for power and control? I don't think so.

Maybe it's something to do with Phyllis' visit, maybe it's because I've become disillusioned by all these tedious weeks of fruitless waiting for something to happen. Who knows! But it's becoming very clear to me that nothing good can possibly come of trying to keep Sam and Charlie apart forever. How selfish of me to even think of denying my baby the love his father so wants to give him. I must find a way to make Cindy see this too.

I say, "Here, I'll hand him to you slowly, and I'll keep holding his hand so he'll feel safe." And that's how we walk to the door, where we stand and wait for Charlie to release my hand, which he soon does in order to explore a button on Sam's shirt. Then Sam and I between us pick up my assorted bags and go down to the car.

"Oh, you did get the car seat! How kind of your neighbor." We're strapping Charlie into what looks like a brand new car seat. "She sure keeps her things in pristine condition." Then I notice the label hanging down the back of the seat. "So pristine, in fact, she even leaves the price tag on."

"Whoops!" Sam grins and confesses, "She wasn't in when I called so I bought the car seat. I'm afraid I didn't have time to get anything else—the bed and stuff."

"Heavens, we can manage without all that. We're only talking about one night after all."

We embark on our journey. A cheerful Sam sings along to the radio. As for me, I think about Cindy. Phyllis had some great ideas. Cindy and I must forge a new kind of partnership. More space. More room for Sam. Charlie needs a father. It's understandable that Cindy feels insecure with Sam around but she's a loving, reasonable woman. It's up to me to get us past this sticking point. We'll work it out somehow. We must.

CHAPTER 17

At ten o'clock that Saturday evening, Sam and I are in his living room, each of us stretched out in a recliner chair. We're sipping hot milk spiked with chocolate syrup. Sam is reading the weekend paper; I'm browsing through a *Sunset* book on Western gardens. We couldn't get Charlie settled down in the bed upstairs by himself, so he's sleeping on the couch.

My eyes wander around the room. The whole house is considerably cleaner and tidier than it was at my last visit a couple of months ago, but most of it badly needs redecorating. I ask, "What color are you thinking of painting this room?"

Sam says, "I don't know. White, I suppose."

"*White?* Surely not. An old house like this just cries out for warm tones. You should do this room in cream. Or old rose. Or maybe you should use wall paper."

He says in his breezy way, "Well, I'm not doing anything until after my housewarming party next weekend. With the kind of friends I have we'll end up with beer and salsa plastered all over the walls. But after that I'll be happy to get your advice."

I purse my lips at the thought of such messy friends. But I must stop being such an interfering busybody. It's his house after all.

Charlie turns in his sleep, one arm flies out and the blanket rolls off him. Sam puts down his drink and reaches out to cover Charlie again. It's nice to have someone else do that while I remain indolently reclined. "You know, Sam," I say, "I just can't get over how good you are with Charlie. Didn't you once tell me you couldn't stand babies?"

Sam smiles fondly at Charlie. "Believe me, no one is more surprised than I am at the way I feel about this little guy. I've never had the slightest interest in kids nor the slightest desire to have one. I've never even thought about it."

"It's strange how people change," I muse. Then, half-teasing, I remind him, "But you did make that promise to your grandfather so the thought must have entered your mind at some point."

Sam looks blank. "What promise?"

"You promised your grandfather Alexander you'd name your first son after him."

"Oh, that's right."

I note his eyelids flicker and he lowers his gaze to concentrate again on his newspaper. I sip my milk and watch him while a tiny seed of suspicion grows. I say, "Let me guess. You don't even have a grandfather called Alexander."

Sam's head jerks up. "Oh, but I do—or did. He died a while ago." He's looking me in the eye now but has a shifty expression.

"How old were you when he died?"

The expression becomes even shiftier as Sam replies. "I can't really remember. Probably—oh, a few months old."

"My," I mock, "such a mature baby for conversations like this with your grandfather."

"M-mm, yes. I was extremely advanced for my age."

So this is the second time I've caught him out in a flat lie. My indignation grows as I speak. "Evidently, you find all this very amusing. Do you have any idea how upsetting it was for me when you insisted on getting involved in naming the baby? For heaven's sake, I'd only just given birth. I was about as emotionally fragile as I've ever been in my life." My voice catches at the remembrance of my past distress.

Sam says quickly, "I was sorry as soon as I saw how upset I made you. At the time, I was deliberately trying to annoy you because I was sort of pissed off at you and Cindy."

Hey, what's this? I put down my cup and lean forward. Sam goes on. "First off, Cindy ordered me not to come visit you in the hospital. She wouldn't even tell me where you were; I had to find out from Phyllis. Then, when Roland and I got there, *you* didn't look that thrilled to see us either."

Thinking back, I seem to recall I had in fact been glad to see him that evening, but my gladness may not have been that evident. After all, I was feeling tired and weak and sore. Sam says, "You didn't even thank me for the flowers."

Those gorgeous, exuberant flowers! "Oh, Sam, I'm so sorry. They were beautiful. I just wasn't myself. I had so much on my mind." He nods, looking injured, while I expand. "I just loved those flowers. The nurses did too. The night nurse said they made her think of a summer day."

"Yeah?" His tone is skeptical but he looks pleased. He tosses a section of the paper on the floor and selects another one. I return to my *Sunset* book. While I flip the pages, my mind wanders to other things that remind me of summer days. Sam's blue eyes, for instance. Such beguiling, blue eyes.

"Sam," I say, looking across at him, "You lied about being bisexual and you lied about your grandfather. Have you ever lied to me about anything else?"

He's silent at first, not even looking up from his paper, but I sense he's wondering how to answer my question.

Finally, he looks up and says, "No, not really. Except for that stupid résumé."

Résumé? The résumé wherein he listed his implausibly outstanding qualifications for fatherhood? The résumé that Cindy swallowed hook, line and sinker! Triumphantly, I straighten up in my seat. "I knew it! I just knew it. I *told* Cindy it was a pack of lies."

Sam is indignant. "Hey, wait a minute. Some of it was true. My job, my education—that was all true. Only the stuff about my family was sort of elaborated." He puts his head back, eyes half-closed. "Didn't it say my mother was a judge, or was that my father? And Roland invented something far-fetched for my brother. I forget what." His face is glowing as he remembers.

Roland? So the two of them were plotting together to deceive us. And here's Sam snickering away, remembering the fun they had. He looks at my unamused face. "Yeah, okay. I suppose you think I should be ashamed of myself. But, damn it, I'm not. You and Cindy were so all high and mighty in those days." He stops for a moment, folds his paper and puts it down on the table beside him. He says, "I'm not sure whether to tell you any more. You probably won't enjoy hearing it."

My stomach tenses. "I'm all ears."

He settles back in his chair as though to get comfortable for what's to follow. Then he tells me, "When I offered to father a child for you, I did so in all good faith. Frankly, I thought it would be a bit of a lark, but that's neither here nor there. The fact is I intended to carry out my side of the bargain in a perfectly serious and responsible way. Then, right off the bat, you and Cindy started to make a mockery of the whole thing."

Sam pauses to sip some milk. The injured look is back. "I was quite prepared to produce medical records, but a *résumé!* What was that all about?" I say nothing. He continues. "Anyway, I was so annoyed that at first I decided to forget the whole thing. But then Roland and I got to talking about it and decided it would be fun to string you girls along a bit." He grins. "You should see some of the versions of that résumé we came up with. Talk about obscene! But finally we produced what we thought was a half-way believable version."

"Not to me, it wasn't."

"Oh, no? It worked, didn't it? I managed to lure you into my hot little bed. Or rather into your hot little bed."

I should be seething at this point. But now it's my turn.

"You can take that smirk off your face, Sonny-boy, because I have something to tell you. Cindy and I were so indignant at the way you just assumed we'd be delighted to have you take Roland's place. We thought you were incredibly arrogant. We devised that whole résumé and interview routine to humiliate you. Our plan was to have you jump through all the hoops and *then* say, 'Sorry, you don't qualify.'"

Sam looks shocked. "Diane, I'd no idea you could be so mean." We both laugh—a bit uneasily. Sam looks over at our blissfully sleeping baby and says, "Charlie, you'll never know how close you came to not being here."

For a moment, we reflect on this sober thought.

Sam asks, "So what made you change your mind?"

If I had not been so intent on getting back at him for doctoring his résumé, I would have realized I was walking into this question. So how to respond?

"We-e-ell, I guess it was that the whole business of getting me pregnant was dragging on and we didn't seem to be getting any closer to a solution. After Roland turned us down, I didn't have the courage to approach anyone else."

He watches me in silence for a few seconds. "And then you thought, 'Oh, what the hell, it might as well be Sam.'"

"Not quite. In fact, you know something ironic? Cindy was the one responsible for things working out as they did. She was so impressed with your résumé, she suggested I ask you to be a sperm donor. Which is what I tried to do, as you know. But before I knew what had hit me..." I throw up my hands. "...we had a date for eight o'clock. And the rest is history."

He's smiling but the smile is tinged with what looks like disappointment. Had he really thought we had been enthusiastic about him? As I think about it, I can't help marveling at what a pair of wimps Cindy and I were. In retrospect, our actions seem incredibly lazy. Surely there must have been some alternative to Sam if we'd thought hard enough about it.

But, I remind myself, we did think about it, and there wasn't.

I say, "So what about you? When I asked you if you really wanted the job, you seemed sort of hesitant."

"I was taken aback because I hadn't expected you to say that. But the closer we got to the big day, the more I was looking forward to it. I really was curious about how it would be with..." he hesitates, "...with a lesbian. Anyhow, what red-blooded male would turn down an opportunity for sex?"

An amazing pair of confessions! As we look at each other across the room, I think what a wily manipulator he was. And yet I can't say I'm sorry about the way things worked out.

"So how was it," I ask, "having sex with a lesbian?"

Sam grins; he obviously remembers he'd asked me that first time how it was to have sex with a man. He says, "Well, the first time was kind of like trying to make out with

Mother Superior. But after that I thought it went pretty swimmingly. Didn't it?"

"Yes, it did."

"In fact, I have trouble thinking of you as a lesbian. Are you sure you really are?"

Now he's being presumptuous. "Sam, you're a kind, goodhearted person and I'm glad you're Charlie's father. But keep in mind I slept with you for a very specific reason. Certainly not because I'm attracted to you—at least, not in that way."

He scoffs. "I'll tell you something, ma'am. You certainly react to me as though you're attracted in *that way*."

I give an exasperated sigh and recall something Cindy and I have discussed more than once. "You must be one of those men who's convinced that lesbianism is a myth dreamed up by women who just can't get a man. Believe it or not, some women don't want a man; some women really want another woman."

"Hogwash!" he says. "You can't tell me any woman can satisfy you sexually as well as I can. After all, I have more *resources* at my disposal." This with an impudent snicker.

God, he's impossible! But I see his smile is warm in spite of the mocking tone. Increasingly, I'm aware of the tension between us—a friendly and pleasurable tension I'm not accustomed to. Could it be we're flirting with each other? But, back into the fray....

"Sam, more resources, as you so delicately put it, are not necessarily better. That's a thought only a male chauvinist could have, assuming I can guess what resources you have in mind. Believe it or not, what really turns me on is the gentle stuff—cuddling, kissing and the like."

He challenges me. "I can cuddle and kiss. I'm gentle, aren't I?"

In fact, he was very gentle and patient during those Charlie-begetting sessions. I say, "Yes, you are. But you'll always want more than cuddling. You know, all that acrobatic stuff."

"*Acrobatic stuff!*"

I knew this would set him off, and it does. But I'd forgotten about Charlie asleep on the couch, and quickly I beg, "Shush, not so loud. I wish you'd learn to laugh more *softly*." Of course, that doesn't help one bit. His attempts to suppress his hilarity are noisier than the laughter.

He finally quiets down, but his eyes are still laughing. He says, "Let's make a deal? How about two for one? I'll guarantee you two minutes of cuddling and kissing for every one minute of acrobatics you let me have? Pretty fair, huh?"

"I'm not making any deals with you, you big buffoon!" There's another burst of laughter from Sam, prompting me to look around for something to throw at him. I grab the sweater I'm wearing around my shoulders, ball it up and toss it across the room. It misses, landing on the floor beside his chair. Sam stretches his arms up and behind his head. From his smug expression, he seems to feel he's won this round.

Stymied for the moment, I go back to my *Sunset*. I'm getting a bit cold though and wish I had thrown the book at him instead. I decide I'll rescue my sweater as soon as he goes back to reading. Once or twice, I sneak a glance at him from under my eyelashes. But he continues to slouch in his chair, watching me and smirking. Well, I can't wait any more; I'm getting goose bumps. Mumbling something about getting a tissue, I stand up and saunter across the room. Once I get abreast of the sweater, I swoop down toward it....

Not quickly enough. So fast I hardly know what's happening, Sam reaches out, grabs hold of my arm and pulls me over toward him and down on top of him. I give an involuntary shriek and he chides, "Diane, I wish you'd learn to scream more softly." He wraps both arms around me, easing his body over to one side of the recliner and squeezing me in beside him. It's a tight fit.

I whisper, "Sam, you promised."

He whispers back, "This is the cuddling, the part you like." Well, he's about fifty times stronger than I am so after a token struggle, I relax and nestle my head into his shoulder. It's amazing how the very feel of him evokes everything that's warm and strong and safe. How can this playboy, who's barged into my life with all the aplomb of a circus barker, possibly make me feel like this?

While I snuggle, Sam runs his fingers through my hair, lifting up the strands. He says in a husky voice, "Your hair looks like spun gold with the light shining through it."

Compliments tend to embarrass me. I say, "Is there such a thing as *mousy* spun gold?"

He laughs. "Mousy! That's what you remind me of— a little mouse." One hand tips my chin up so he can look into my face. "Big brown eyes, pert little nose, sort of anxious expression...."

I interject, "Twitchy whiskers, skinny tail," but he taps my mouth with his hand to shush me.

"Understand this, Diane. I love mousies. When I was a boy I used to keep mice as pets." He ponders, "Also, hamsters, rats, snakes... but the mice were the cutest. I let them run up and down all over my body." With his fingers, he gives a gratuitous demonstration of "mousy feet" running down *my* body from chin to tummy, and I smack his hand.

It's a pity, but all too soon our snug position in the chair leads to severe cramping of the limbs. And it's bedtime anyhow. So we get disentangled and struggle to our feet. Sam takes the cups into the kitchen while I carry Charlie upstairs.

Charlie and I will be sharing a bed in a guest bedroom tonight.

Soon, Sam comes upstairs and peeks in the open door of my room. He says, "Is everything okay? I hope you'll be comfortable."

"We'll be fine." I smile at him. He smiles back in a slightly distracted way as though wondering whether to propose something. Like moving down the hall to spend the night with him in his bed? That wouldn't surprise me after all that sexually charged discussion tonight. Of course, yesterday, he did promise *no sex*, but….

He says, "Diane, I hope you didn't get annoyed or upset at the way I was acting tonight."

"No, of course not."

"I really do respect you and like you very much. You know that, don't you?" For answer, I walk over to him, put an arm around his neck and pull him down to me. He kisses my mouth very gently. Then, rather to my surprise, he says, "Goodnight, angel."

I say "Goodnight" too—and he goes down the hall to his room.

Later, when I'm in bed, I think back to the early days with Sam. How solemn and earnest we were in our baby-making efforts, like a couple of scientists working on some great breakthrough. Of course, sex with him now would be quite a different matter. For him, it would undoubtedly still be "a bit of a lark," something to distract him from the thought of Blondie charging around the Andes with her "doctor laddie." But for me…well, I'm afraid to think what it would be for me. Or for Cindy! No, it really is good that he kept his promise.

Sunday is a sunny, warm day. Sam suggests we drive into town for brunch, but first he takes me outside to admire some of his outdoor improvements. First, we view the newly mown front "lawn," which frankly looks just like a shorter version of the weedy field he had before. I'm not much interested in the lawn anyhow. I make a beeline for the back yard while Sam protests, "But I haven't done a thing to the back." I don't care; I just want to take a closer look at what I have mentally dubbed "the vegetable garden." And the greenhouse, of course. Sam lumbers along behind me, Charlie perched on his shoulders.

"Sam, it's so neat you have a greenhouse. I bet you could grow stuff all year round." In truth, I'm not at all sure what one would grow in a greenhouse, but it seems like a super-valuable thing to have. Sam mumbles something about thinking of tearing it down. I turn to him in horror. "No, you absolutely mustn't. We'll look in those Sunset books; they'll tell us what you can do with a greenhouse."

My eyes sweep across the area of earth adjoining the greenhouse. "And here," I enthuse, "you could have a marvelous vegetable garden. Just look at that soil. You could grow tomatoes, green beans, corn, squash, anything."

"You don't say." He sounds amused. "Too bad Cindy and I aren't better friends. Otherwise, I could hire you to be the garden manager and we could all have veggies coming out of our ears." He adds, "Ugh!" which I ignore.

He's being facetious, I know, about managing the garden but, even so, the fantasy grips me for a moment and I stare with longing at the rich, dark soil.

Charlie's getting restless on Sam's shoulders, so Sam swings him down into his arms. He says, "Enough of the grand tour. How about we go to breakfast." With great reluctance, I turn away from this patch of earth that so lures me. Even though I know full well it isn't my patch of earth.

• • •

We leave for the city about eight that evening. Charlie is bathed and dressed for bed. He's sure to fall asleep in the car on the way home. On the approach to the bridge, traffic is practically at a standstill. After he takes us home, Sam will have to return to his house and then tomorrow morning travel back to the city again. It's kind of him to go to all this trouble.

Sam asks, "So how do things stand with Cindy these days?"

"Oh, fine. We should be moving into the new house in a couple of weeks."

Sam says, "Yeah? That story sounds familiar."

"It's really not Cindy's fault. Getting the loan approved took longer than we expected. Then we've had various problems like this crack in the driveway."

Sam talks over me. "Does this mean the embargo will be back on again? No visits, no phone calls?"

"Oh, Sam, I hope not. I'm hoping I can get Cindy to loosen up." He glances at me. I expect he's puzzled. Given the history of the three of us, my hope seems a pretty futile one. But I don't want to discuss this with him right now. "So your party's next weekend? Hope it goes well."

Sam says, "You're quite welcome to come, you know."

"No, thank you. I get nervous when the salsa starts flying."

His inviting me implies there'll be women there as well as men. But not Juanita.

Back in my apartment, I tuck a sleeping Charlie into his crib. Except for some murmurs of protest as we transferred him out of the car, he's shown no sign of waking. He's been an angel all weekend. As I bend over Charlie, Sam sits down on my bed, which is alongside Charlie's. *Groan, squeak!* Sam says, "Now don't tell me this is the same awful bed you had in your last place?"

"The very same." I keep my voice low to encourage Sam to be quiet. But he bounces up and down a couple of times with the bed groaning loudly in response. "Sam, stop it. You'll wake him. Come on, let's get out of here."

He follows me into the living room. "Diane, did you hear that bed calling my name? Obviously, it misses me."

"I doubt that very much." But I just can't keep a stern expression and add affectionately, "You idiot!"

Sam puts his head down and touches his forehead to mine. "I really, really enjoyed having you over, little Mousy. I hope you come again."

"Oh, Sam, so do I."

The phone rings. He says, "Better get that. I'll let myself out." He holds my hand and walks with me into the hallway. Then he moves one way toward the front door and I move the other toward the kitchen phone until our fingers are no longer touching. He silently makes exaggerated kissing motions as he goes, like a fish in an aquarium, and I giggle like a silly kid. As soon as the door closes behind him, I answer the phone.

It's Cindy.

CHAPTER 18

"Cindy! It must be one in the morning there."

Cindy sounds breathless. "Sorry. Hope I didn't waken you. I've only just got back to the hotel. We've been sailing on Mr. B.'s yacht all day on Long Island Sound, and then we went to his house afterwards to eat." She adds, "I can't talk for long; we have an early morning meeting tomorrow. I just wanted to give you my room number here."

"Sailing? That sounds nice." I'm gathering my courage as we speak. She's bound to ask how I spent the weekend. And I'll tell her. No point in delaying our confrontation. But Cindy doesn't ask about my weekend.

"Oh, Di-dee, it's been frantic here. Last night, we went to this unbelievable restaurant in Oyster Bay. It's called The Yardstick, or something. It's supposed to be the latest, hottest place to dine on Long Island. Have you heard of it?" She doesn't wait for my reply. "Then today we went sailing, as I said. I was so scared when Mr. B first mentioned it. I had in mind some dinky little sailboat. But it was this monster yacht."

"Wow!"

"And get this," she lowers her voice in conspiratorial fashion. "Mr. B. kept dragging me aside and muttering to me about how much they appreciate having me on board. On board the company, that is. Honestly, Diane, it seems to me that between them Mr. J. and Mr. B. are getting disenchanted with Marigold."

She sounds pleased but I'm alarmed. "Cindy, is that a good thing? Marigold is your mentor, isn't she? Your advocate? She's trying to get this new position for you. If they're disenchanted with Marigold, where does that leave you?"

"Oh, sweetie, don't you see? They're not disenchanted with *me*. Quite the contrary. The future looks pretty bright at J&B for yours truly. Oh, Lord, just look at the time. I have so much more to tell you. I'll call you again tomorrow."

I've just about decided she is not, after all, going to inquire about Charlie's and my weekend. Then she says, "By the way, how is Baby-Boo? And you too, of course?"

Here's my opening. I've been holding onto my words for so long, I've almost forgotten them. I stumble a bit as I speak.

"We're both fine, Cindy. We had a really nice weekend. Charlie and I stayed with Sam at his house in Mill Valley."

A brief pause before she says, "You're kidding, right?" She doesn't sound angry. I guess she really does think I'm kidding.

"No, I'm not, Cindy. He called yesterday and suggested we go see his new place. He'd heard from someone that Charlie and I would be alone this weekend. It was very pleasant, actually. He has a charming old house on a big piece of land."

My heart pounds as I talk. I can just *feel* Cindy gathering her wits about her and trying to decide how best to react. The way I am so nonchalantly admitting this heinous crime must upset her as much as the crime itself.

"The house needs a lot of work," I gabble on. "But it has wonderful soil in the garden. That rich, dark stuff that's so great for growing vegetables. Remember, those fields we saw down near Watsonville? And there's this great greenhouse."

Finally, she attacks. "My, my, Diane, I'm so glad I decided I could trust you."

"Of course, you can," I retort, the spirit of Phyllis spurring me on. "Sam is just a *friend*—a good friend."

"I would say a very good friend," she agrees. "A very, *very* good friend."

But I'm on a roll. "Cindy, it's ridiculous that you keep trying to monitor who may and may not be my friend. You've got to give me *space*. Partners should always give each other lots of space."

Somehow this doesn't sound as compelling as when Phyllis said it. Cindy doesn't seem to find it compelling at all.

She screams, "Space? You want space? Every time I turn my back for a minute, I find you've been with Sam. It doesn't sound like it's space you want. Sounds to me like you want…."

At this point, Cindy shocks me to the core by voicing an obscenity. She doesn't usually go much beyond a *hell* or a *damn;* the wine must have been flowing in New York tonight. "Cindy, please stop that."

I take a deep breath and say, "You must admit I give *you* all the space in the world. For months now, you've lived most of the time away from me. I don't know what you're doing, who you're with. I never question you, do I?"

Cindy is silent. I add, "And, contrary to any conclusions you're jumping to, I did *not* sleep with Sam this weekend. I haven't had sex with him since I found out I was pregnant."

After a minute, Cindy says, "Maybe we should talk about this some other time. Right now, I'm exhausted."

By now, I'm trembling so hard I can hardly hold onto the phone. I mumble, "Yes, me too. Goodnight then."

The phone clicks as she hangs up. I realize she still hasn't given me her room number.

As I perform the usual evening chores, I continue to tremble. The adrenaline rush, I guess. Naturally, I'm upset because of our quarrel, but in a way I'm also rather proud of myself. The more I think about Phyllis' words, the more convinced I am that she was right. My relationship with Cindy has become smothering in a way I'd never ever thought would be possible.

Charlie coming into our lives has a lot to do with it, of course. It's obvious that Charlie would bond with me more strongly than with Cindy. I can see she must feel left out and is going overboard on this career thing to prove herself or boost her ego or whatever. Add Sam to this mix and fireworks are inevitable.

But, darn it, getting rid of Sam isn't the answer. He is Charlie's father, after all. And I might be imagining this but it seems that having him around does something for my mothering abilities too. Whatever. If Cindy and I are to survive as a couple—as a family with Charlie—we have to build a new relationship with more trust. More tolerance. More space.

At work on Monday, I still tremble when I recall our conversation last night. My first project this morning is a legal brief—long, boring, and dense. I'm glad all I have to do is type this stuff, not understand it. At one point, Kitty walks behind me on her way to the printer. She leans down and whispers, "How was your weekend? Did you get to the park after all?" I glance around and catch Lucinda's eagle eye roaming the room for signs of slacking. Lucinda runs a tight ship here.

"It was some weekend!" I mutter. "I'll tell you about it at lunch time."

It's a bit cool outside today, so at noon Kitty and I take our lunch to the cafeteria and find a corner table where we won't be disturbed.

"Well," I tell her, "this weekend was a total surprise. Sam called and somehow talked me into spending the weekend visiting him in his new Mill Valley house. Charlie too, of course."

Kitty gasps and her whole face lights up. I'm convinced the poor girl has hopes that one day I will see the light, go straight, find some man to make an honest woman of me, and all that kind of thing. She's never said as much but I often sense this during our cozy noontime talks. She says, "Tell me *everything*."

"Nothing much to tell really. He's had the house cleaned up a bit. It's still mainly a mess though." We both laugh. "We went out to eat on Saturday night. Also on Sunday for breakfast. He showed me his old greenhouse and the vegetable garden. Well, it could be a vegetable garden. It was just a very nice, comfortable weekend."

Of course, I don't say anything about Saturday evening's tussling and cuddling.

Kitty's face is still aglow, "Oh, Diane, I was so concerned about you being alone yet again for the whole weekend. But apparently you were having the most wonderful time!"

Yes, until Cindy called.

Kitty looks at me. "Weren't you?" I hesitate. I know I shouldn't discuss Cindy's call with anyone else. It was pretty personal after all. But that call is eating away at my insides. In fact, I'm starting to tremble again just thinking of it. And there's no one else to confide in.

"Well, things started to go wrong on Sunday evening after Sam took me home. Cindy called from New York."

Kitty stops eating for a moment, her partly eaten sandwich held aloft. "Oh, no. Don't tell me Sam answered the phone?"

"No, he'd left by then. But I told Cindy we'd been at his place over the weekend." Kitty looks stunned. I say, "Yes, I know that sounds foolhardy to the point of imbecility. But you see, Kitty, I've decided I must have this out with Cindy and get her to understand that her fierce hatred of Sam is... well, dysfunctional. It's poisoning our relationship. Apart from anything else, she should understand that it's so good for Charlie to have Sam around."

Kitty nods her head vigorously. "Absolutely. It's so important for boys to have a father in their lives. It's a tragedy when they don't...." Her voice trails off, no doubt remembering my original plans for Charlie did not include a father.

I go on. "Cindy and I must give each other more space. I've got to persuade her to trust me and let me have friends of my own—even the occasional male friend like Sam. For heaven's sakes, it's not as though I'm sleeping with him or anything." Kitty gulps—whether through surprise or relief, I'm not sure.

We go on eating for a while. Kitty seems deep in thought. Finally, she says, "Diane, do you honestly think Cindy will go along with you on this? I mean, she's been so negative about Sam all along. Why would she change her mind now? Don't you think if you won't stop seeing him, she'll just break up with you?"

"No, I don't think so." In spite of my inner turmoil, I'm sure Cindy wouldn't go that far. Looking into Kitty's kind but also somehow hopeful eyes, I explain, "We do love each other very much. And we have a pretty solemn contract."

"Contract?"

"Not a legal contract. But it's absolutely binding as far as I'm concerned. We both wanted to have a baby. I agreed to be the birth mother with the understanding the baby would belong equally to both of us. We didn't make this commitment lightly. She can't back away from it any more than I can."

Kitty says between bites of sandwich, "I had no idea Cindy was particularly interested in Charlie. It sure doesn't seem like it with her living apart from you for so long."

"That's only temporary, remember? Cindy just *adores* Charlie. She couldn't live without him."

"M-mm."

"Besides, on a more mundane note, with this new house we'll be taking on a big fat mortgage. Cindy won't be able to carry that by herself. At least not until she gets some of the raises they've promised her."

"That's right. She was arranging for you to work in her new company, wasn't she?"

"Shh!" I look around at the adjoining tables to make sure no coworkers are listening. "The budget isn't going to be approved till October. But I guess that's getting pretty close, isn't it?"

Kitty smiles and winks at me. She knows how much I'm looking forward to that Administrative Assistant position that's going to leapfrog me across the college degree divide. Out of Lawrence Jackman & Sons and away from Lucinda Morales. But the reminder doesn't lift my spirits because Cindy hasn't mentioned that job for such a long time.

Kitty looks at the remains of my lunch, which I've placed on the table. "Aren't you hungry today? I brought some brownies for us to share." Kitty knows I love her home-made brownies and I try to look enthusiastic as she pulls out a package of them from her tote bag and offers me one.

The trouble is, everything I've eaten this lunchtime is sitting in the pit of my stomach like a lump of lead. I'm feeling increasingly anxious. What if Kitty's right? What if Cindy flatly rejects my idea of including Sam more in our lives? In fact, the more I think about it, the less workable it seems. And why did I raise the issue last night on the phone—when Cindy was tired? I should have waited to speak to her in person.

Kitty is studying my face with concern. I try to laugh. "Oh, Kitty, don't worry about me. The worst that can happen is I'll end up a single mother? When you think about it, I'm half-way there already, aren't I?"

Kitty says, "Surely it won't come to that. Cindy isn't your only option, is she?"

"What do you mean?" Kitty blushes and turns away. "You're not suggesting I throw in my lot with Sam?"

She nods.

"No, Kitty. That's not an option. Mind you, Sam has a lot of good points. He's wonderful with Charlie. And I love his crazy old house. But Sam never signed on for any permanent responsibility for us. He's never even hinted he wants it."

In her soft voice, Kitty says, "You like him a lot, don't you?"

"That's irrelevant," I assure her. "Sam's a playboy at heart; he enjoys his friends and parties and freedom. Even this woman we know, Phyllis, who really likes and approves of Sam, describes him as kind of wild. I can't imagine putting Charlie's and my well-being in the hands of someone like that."

Kitty looks disappointed. She says, "No, you're quite right. That doesn't sound good at all." I wipe brownie crumbs off my face and fingers and tell myself to stop feeling annoyed at Kitty for agreeing with me.

• • •

It's not surprising I don't hear from Cindy all week. She needs a few days to sulk it off. On Saturday, I stay in all day so I won't miss her call. She doesn't call. On Sunday, it's a lovely day so I take Charlie for a couple of little walks in his stroller. Just around the block.

By Sunday afternoon, the strain of not hearing is getting me down. I worry that maybe Cindy tried to call while we were out walking. At times like this, I wish I had invested in an answering machine. I opted against getting one because it didn't seem worth while for what I've kept telling myself would be "only a couple of weeks."

Shortly after four, I dial Marigold's number. I hate to do this because I hate to talk to Marigold. But there's no other way to reach Cindy. Marigold answers in her usual gruff voice. I say, "May I please speak with Cindy."

Even though I don't identify myself, she responds, "Oh, hullo, Diane. Cindy's not here, I'm afraid. She's over at her house, fiddling around with something or other."

Pause. I say, "I was just calling to make sure she got back safely from New York."

"We got back Thursday night. Hasn't she called you yet?"

Marigold sounds genuinely surprised and I'm angry at myself for having made this call and have Marigold be a witness to my humiliation. Brusquely, I say, "Would you please ask her to call me when she gets back."

"Of course, I will." And what I'm sure is a tinge of pity in her voice makes me feel angrier still.

Cindy doesn't call back. No matter, I think. I'll call her every day this week if need be. If she won't answer my calls, then next weekend, I'll find a way to transport Charlie and myself to San Ramon and make her confront me. We must heal this breach that's opened up between us. We *have* to talk things through.

· · ·

The next evening, Monday, I pick up Charlie at Mrs. Z.'s at six as usual and wheel him home in the stroller. The days are already getting shorter and when daylight savings ends next month, it will be dark at this time of night. Tonight, Mrs. Z. gave me something else to worry about. She hinted she hopes I won't need her services for much longer. Not that she's rushing me, she said, but she had expected us to move to the East Bay some time ago. Charlie's getting more active and she's getting tired.

At the bottom of our steps, I embark on my two-stage process of getting us into the apartment. First, I take Charlie out of the stroller, carry him up the steps, open the door—the door sticks tonight for some reason—put Charlie in his playpen. Next, back down the steps to collect the stroller.

On my way back out to get the stroller, I see why the door was sticking. The mailman has pushed the mail through the slot in the door and a large advertising supplement has caught under the mat. I drag out the advertisement with my other mail folded up inside it and dump the lot on the coffee table. After retrieving the stroller, I look in on Charlie who is happily checking out the good stuff in his playpen he hasn't seen since yesterday. I leave him there and go into the kitchen to get dinner.

Tonight, I'm fixing a frozen dinner for myself so first I put that in the oven to heat while I get Charlie's food ready. These days, he gets "solid," which is to say "mushy," food out of a jar. Mashed peas tonight. When I go to lift him out of his playpen, I note the folded advertisement on the coffee table has fallen open and there's a letter in amongst the usual junk mail. I pick it up. It's a real letter—addressed in real handwriting. Cindy's handwriting!

Charlie is getting very heavy these days. He energetically bounces in my arms as we head to the nightly feeding fiasco, which he seems to find most entertaining, if not particularly nourishing. It's hard to hold him and I wonder how I'll manage when he gets really big. I also wonder why Cindy is writing to me. I don't think she's ever written me a letter before.

In the kitchen, I put the letter on the table and Charlie in his high chair. Then I get a washcloth to clean off his face and hands, an indignity he always resists. Then I sit down beside Charlie, open the envelope and take out the two sheets of paper inside. With one hand and eye, I start to spoon food into Charlie's mouth. With the other hand and eye, I tackle the letter. It's dated Thursday and starts,

Dear Diane...

> *Please forgive this formal method of communication but I can't really trust myself to talk to you about this. I can write so much more calmly and rationally than I can speak, I guess.*

Charlie gives one of his mini-yells. As I look up, he grins to indicate he's just kidding, but it's a hint I'm not paying enough attention. "Okay, Charlie." I turn to face him fully as I continue to spoon out the peas. I ought to save the letter for later. But my eyes are drawn back to it.

> *As you can imagine, I was extremely upset by our conversation the other night. I really don't know what to think, or do, about it. It feels to me as though our entire relationship is on a very shaky footing right now. This is such a shame, Diane, you have no idea. I am so close to getting where I've always longed to be, career-wise, and that means life can be so good for all three of us.*

Triumphant cooing interrupts my concentration and I look around. Some food has dropped on Charlie's tray and he has smeared the green stuff all over himself. I get him back on track.

I honestly don't know what's in your heart right now, but it does seem a good idea for us to take a "time out," so both of us can try to figure out where we are and where we want to go. Naturally, we must have a good long talk in person at some point, but I don't think right now is the time.

Well, it feels to me as though that "time out" has been going on ever since Cindy moved to San Ramon. But why isn't this the time to talk? My stomach tightens as I read on.

Actually, this is probably as good a time as any to take a break from each other. As you know, I was worried about meeting the mortgage payments over the next few months. Well, Marigold—bless her heart!—has saved the day for me again. She was so excited about my house-buying venture she has decided to buy a house herself.

I can't stand this. What on earth is coming next? I put down the spoon and jar and turn to focus on the letter. A happy whoop at my elbow. Charlie's grabbed the jar and is about to engage on another new love of his—throwing everything on the floor. "No, Charlie. Now please behave yourself."

In the meantime, seeing she's given me a roof over my head for the past few months, it seems only fair to repay the favor. So she'll be moving into my spare room until she finds a place of her own. This will be a tremendous help to me because she insists on paying me rent— even though she didn't collect any from me, as you know. So now I won't have to worry about how to meet the mortgage payments every month.

The letter ends with a couple more sentences that say something about hoping I agree with her, how is Charlie... blah, blah. But I can't concentrate any more. I can't do anything any more. I turn to the only other human being in the room and clutch his surprised green face in my two hands, howling—quite literally, howling—"Charlie, she doesn't need me any more. She doesn't even need my money."

I say it over and over. *She doesn't need me...she doesn't need me.* No wonder Marigold sounded pitying.

That night, I come closer to totally falling to pieces than I ever have before in my life. The next day, Tuesday, I wake with a heavy gray feeling pressing down on my temples. It's like the day after Dad left us for good: waking up and praying it was all a nightmare.

Thinking back to last night, I can't remember how I got through the hours. Did I take my dinner out of the oven? Did I finish feeding Charlie? Did I bathe him, play with him, put him to bed? I must have, I guess. All I do remember is agonizing over that letter and constantly rereading it, hoping somehow that I'd misinterpreted something.

Today, I'm supposed to go to work. Well, there are times in your life you have to put yourself first, and this is one of them. I get Charlie out of bed, dress and feed him, get dressed myself, and off we go to the Ziebowskis' house. I tell a concerned Mrs. Z. I'm too sick to go to work and will be resting at home all day.

Back at the apartment, I call the office to say I won't be in, then fix myself some tea and climb back into bed to reread the letter and agonize some more. At times, I think I'm overreacting. Cindy needs money for the mortgage payments; renting a room to Marigold is the easiest way to get it. It makes sense. She's proposed a time-out, not a breakup. But at other times I tell myself to face reality. Her letter has *drop dead* written on every line.

By three o'clock in the afternoon, I'm just about agonized-out. I take the wretched letter to my bureau to toss it in the top drawer where I keep all manner of odd documents I have no other place for. And when I pull open the drawer I burst out laughing. Because the first thing I see in there is Sam's résumé!

His business card is clipped to the top page and I remember the time I phoned him at work to tell him I was pregnant. On an impulse, I take the card and go to the phone. When the switchboard responds, I ask for Sam Bradshawe, expecting to hear his snippy secretary come on the line next. But then Sam's voice says, "Bradshawe speaking." He sounds so very nice, businesslike but approachable. If I had a broker, I would like it to be someone who sounded just like that.

I haven't even thought about what to say. What I do say is, "Would you like to come over for a cup of tea?" There's a moment of silence before he starts laughing.

"You mean, right now?"

"Anytime you like." Already, I can feel myself healing, just being connected to him. I explain, "I stayed home from work today. Sick. Charlie is at Mrs. Z.'s."

"Well, as it so happens, things are pretty quiet in the office and I was planning to leave early. Besides, they owe me a ton of comp time. So-o-o…if you're serious, I can be there in about half an hour."

"That's fine."

He says, "I'm sorry you're sick. Am I likely to catch anything?"

"No, I don't think so."

I know all Sam is likely to catch is me.

CHAPTER 19

After hanging up, I look around in mild panic. What made me say I could be ready in half an hour? For the next ten minutes, I whirl through the kitchen and living room picking up dirty dishes, toys, discarded clothing, magazines. But when I get to the bathroom, the disheveled tear-streaked mess staring back at me in the mirror reminds me I'd better get going on the biggest cleanup job of all. Me.

A bit later, after brushing my teeth and showering, I pause to take stock. All that's left is to get dressed, brush my hair, put on makeup. But while I'm rooting through my dresser drawer for clean underwear, the doorbell rings. Wouldn't you know he'd be on time! I grab my bathrobe and fasten it around me as I hurry down the hall.

An amused Sam looks me up and down when I open the door. "Well," he says, "You didn't tell me you were dressing up." But there's no time for levity. I can see beyond him through the open door to the sidewalk. And there are people walking by who, I'm sure, are looking up at us. Heaven knows what sort of establishment they'll think I'm running here! Quickly, I grab Sam's arm, drag him inside, and close the door.

Of course, as I do this, I inadvertently pull him up against me. Then, it feels quite natural to put my arms around his neck. Then Sam puts his arms around me and starts kissing me. He kisses me as I have never been kissed before. He kisses my mouth and hair and eyes and nose and ears and neck. His kisses are tender, passionate, playful, earnest, vigorous, dreamy.

And what do I do during this display of oscular ardor? Why, I kiss him back. I kiss him as I have never kissed anyone before. Fervently, I kiss his mouth and hair and eyes and nose—everything! And to think Mother used to warn us girls not to let boys find us too "easy." A warning that until now has never had the slightest relevance for me.

After a time, we come up for air. Sam moves his face back a little way from mine and whispers mischievously, "Let's see, how many minutes was that?"

He's referring, I assume, to his "two-for-one" proposal. What nerve! I say, "Now don't get ideas just because I greet you in a bathrobe. You see, I...." But he won't let me explain and starts kissing me again even as I pull away and lead him into the living room.

In front of the futon, I stand facing him while he holds my hands and smiles down at me. He's waiting for me to take the next step and I'm not sure what that should be. Although I'm often confused as to what motivates my behavior, I'm pretty certain I know why I invited him over this afternoon. But I feel a bit guilty. Sam doesn't know about the void that's opened up in my life and my resulting desperation to have someone comfort and reassure me. I feel I'm being underhanded here, just using him to give me solace. And that's wrong.

So I say, "Shall I make the tea?" Well, Sam starts laughing so hard that he gets me started too. And then I think the heck with it; I'm through with playing games. I take his hand and pull him after me into the bedroom. The bed is still unmade. "Oh, Sam, you must think me a real slob."

Sam doesn't comment; he just walks over to the bed and sits down heavily. *Groan*!

He says, "I told you it misses me."

And I, shameless hussy that I've become, lean toward him, slide my fingers through his thick dark hair, and whisper, "It sure does. That makes two of us." Sam's face lights up and he wraps his wonderful, warm arms around me. As we sink back onto my creaking bed, I forget completely about such stuff as the void in my life and my urgent need for solace. All I can think of is how very much I want him.

After the lovemaking, we lie in bed for a time, cuddling and chatting. I tell Sam about life with Charlie over the past ten days.

"You know, yesterday Charlie said what sounded like 'Da-da'. That wouldn't be his first word, would it? I thought a baby's first word was always 'Ma-ma.'"

Sam chuckles and strokes my hair. I lift my head a little, rubbing it back and forth under his chin. And then I get a glimpse of the clock. "Oh, no, it's past five-thirty already. I've got to pick up Charlie by six."

At first, Sam continues to lounge in bed while I jump up and dash to the bathroom. He calls out after me, "Hey, you promised me tea."

"No time for that now. Come on, hurry up. Mrs. Z. knows I was sick today. If I don't turn up in time, she's likely to send for the paramedics."

Sam grumbles facetiously as he gets dressed. "And I was so looking forward to that tea. That's the whole reason I rushed over here from work." He throws up his hands in a gesture of disgust. "And look what I got instead!"

I joke and fool around too. But somehow we're both ready to leave shortly before six.

As we're walking out the front door, Sam says, "Diane, it might seem kind of crass to bring this up right now, but does—er—our rendezvous this afternoon mean your moving date has been postponed again?"

My hand freezes in mid-air on its way to the doorknob. Of course, I must tell him about Cindy's letter. But not now. I say, "Yes, it has." I close and lock the door behind us. "It's a bit complicated. I'll tell you about it later."

It's cool out this evening. We've decided to walk to Mrs. Z.'s because Sam doesn't have Charlie's seat in his car. We walk along at a brisk pace, hand in hand. Sam asks, "So does this mean you'll be able to come visit me again? This weekend maybe?"

"Well, yes, I think that would work out really well."

"That's great."

He chatters on as we walk. "You know, I got hold of that neighbor of mine. The one with the baby furniture? She's willing to lend me a whole ton of things: playpen, high chair, baby bed. So when you come again you won't have to share a bed with Charlie." His mouth turns up at the corners as he glances sideways at me and squeezes my hand. "That will leave you free to share a bed with more deserving people."

Well, I knew all along once I'd stepped over that line, there was no turning back. I return his squeeze.

All three of us have a pleasant evening. While I feed Charlie, Sam drives to our local Kentucky Fried Chicken and brings home dinner for the grownups. It's the first time I've been enthusiastic about food since this latest round of Cindy trouble started. Charlie, of course, is excited to have Sam here and that does cause a problem at bedtime. The little monkey doesn't want us to leave him alone in the bedroom. It's past ten o'clock by the time he finally falls asleep and Sam and I tiptoe to the kitchen. I look at the clock. "I guess it's too late for tea."

But Sam scoffs, "Not on your life." So I put the kettle on. Waiting for the water to boil, I start washing Charlie's bottles for tomorrow. Sam sits at the table and watches. After a minute, he says, "You still haven't told me what's happening with the house-moving. Does Cindy have to take another trip?"

Some instinct tells me to be careful in what I say and how I say it. I don't want to present myself as an object of pity—no matter how close to the mark that may be! It would be best to sound matter-of-fact. Disappointed, but stoically resigned.

I start, "Well, Cindy will most likely move into the new house this week." I clatter things around as I speak so as to disguise any trace of hysteria that might creep into my voice. "But Charlie and I won't be moving in yet because, you see, Cindy will have trouble meeting her mortgage payments over the next few months." Rattle, clank, go Charlie's bottles as I place them on the draining board. I take the teapot out of the cupboard, put in tea, and pour in the boiling water. It occurs to me I'm not making much sense.

Sam says, "I don't understand."

"Well, she doesn't make enough money yet. Not until she gets her next raise. Which won't be for a few months."

Sam says, "And she's only just realized that?"

With more clatter, I get cups out of the cupboard and the sugar bowl and spoons. "No, of course not. The original idea was that when I moved in I'd be working and would contribute to the mortgage payments. So then she *would* be able to afford it."

I glance at Sam. He's resting an elbow on the table and his face is cocked to one side with a puzzled half-smile as though he's expecting a humorous punch line. I go on. "But Cindy's decided it will be best to have Marigold move in with her for a while and have Marigold share the expenses instead of me...."

I'm not sure how much longer I can keep my voice steady. I pour out two mugs of tea and carry them over to the table, watching them carefully to make sure they don't spill. I notice Sam has stopped smiling. In a mighty rush, I conclude, "Which makes good sense because Marigold makes far more money than I do so she can contribute more."

Sam's incredulous, *"Are you serious?"* is too much for me and I burst into tears. He leans forward to take the cups from me and places them on the table. Then he pulls me down onto his lap and hugs me. He says, "That goddamned woman is an insensitive bitch! What the hell's wrong with her?"

"You don't understand," I sob into his shoulder. "It's my fault too. Really, it was mainly my fault. In fact, it was all my fault."

"Shush. It's okay, it's okay." He keeps repeating this, rocking me in his arms. Finally, I force myself to stop crying and sit upright. I reach for my tea and hand Sam his cup. We sip for a few moments. Sam says, "This Marigold? Do you think something's going on there?"

"Between Cindy and Marigold? Oh, no." Sam looks dubious and I assure him, "If you'd ever met Marigold, you wouldn't think that for a second. She's a *gruesome* woman. But she's Cindy's boss so Cindy has to put up with her."

Sam still looks dubious. He says, "Well, you know what they say—one man's meat...." But his face relaxes as I burst out laughing at the very idea of Cindy being in love with that bombastic creature.

Of course, I'm fully aware that the reverse is probably true. I'm sure Marigold's "kindnesses" to Cindy originate in personal attraction. But I'm used to this. People are always being attracted to Cindy.

My eyes fill again. I try to hide my face from Sam but he's watching and brushes a tear off my cheek with his finger. He asks, "Diane, does any of this have anything to do with me?"

After hesitating a long moment, I say, "Yes, it does. Let me show you the letter she wrote." I put down my cup, climb off his lap, and go to the bedroom to find Cindy's letter in the bureau. When I return to the kitchen, Sam pulls me back onto his lap and reads the letter.

He asks, "What's this phone conversation that has her so upset?"

"Oh, poor Cindy. You see, she had no idea I was going to your house that weekend but she phoned on Sunday night and I came right out and told her. I had—I don't know—some dumb idea of trying to get her to soften up in her attitude toward you. To agree to let us see you more often because..."

I gulp and pull out a Kleenex to dab at my face. "Oh, Sam, because I so very much want you to be part of Charlie's life. But I made a real mess of it, the heartless way I talked to her, and I'm sure that triggered her decision to invite Marigold to move in with her. If I'd kept my mouth shut that night, I'd probably be packing to move right now."

Sam leans his head back and looks at me. I sit on his lap, one arm around his shoulders for balance, and study his face. I'm struck by his expression—sympathetic but also awkward, as though he's distinctly uncomfortable about all this. As well he might be.

It's now clear to me why I've felt hesitant to tell Sam about Cindy's withdrawal from the field, as it were.

Because Cindy's hostility toward Sam has acted not only as a barrier to keep me away from him but also as a shield for Sam. An excuse for avoiding too much involvement— or for retreating altogether. Without that shield, Sam will have to face decisions that until now he probably never realized he'd ever have to face: decisions about me and Charlie and how he wants us to fit into his life.

Now, looking at his thoughtful face, I can guess he honestly doesn't know where to go from here.

A few minutes later, Sam drains his cup. He declines when I offer him more tea and says, "I really should get going." He folds up Cindy's letter and puts it back into the envelope. "You know, she hasn't completely shut the door, has she?" He sounds hopeful.

Trying to sound chipper, I say, "No, of course not. I'll be fine. I'm sorry I got so emotional, but that's me."

As we walk down the hall, Sam talks about the weekend. "I'll pick you up on Friday night so we can spend two nights at my house. Okay?" At the door, he gives me the briefest of kisses. "I'm really looking forward to it." Then he stands and stares down at his feet for a while, seeming lost in his thoughts. Finally, he looks up and says, "You know, Diane, we won't be able to do this *every* weekend. I have various other things planned with friends over the next couple of months. But I'd love you to visit any time we can work it out."

So I was right. Already, he's feeling the need to be wary without Cindy's protective barrier. "Oh, Sam, don't worry about it. Things always work out in the end." *What inane words*, I chide myself. I don't know if they'll comfort him but they sure aren't much comfort to me.

He nods and sets off across the porch and down the steps. What a short time ago it was I told Kitty I couldn't imagine putting my happiness in his hands. And isn't that exactly what I'm doing now? But what alternative do I have now that Cindy has abandoned me? At the thought, an aching wellspring of tears opens up inside my stomach. But then, partway down the steps, Sam suddenly stops and turns. He flashes his familiar impish grin and says, "By the way, thanks for the tea."

My whole body relaxes. "Anytime." And with a sudden burst of optimism that surely everything will indeed be all right, I add, "Now come back here and give me a *real* kiss." He does.

On Friday, a card comes from Cindy. It's one of those eight-to-a-packet *New Address* cards. She's written in the address of the San Ramon house and her new phone number. No other message. I put the card in my bureau drawer with her letter and Sam's résumé.

CHAPTER 20

Five weeks go by. It's now the middle of October. I haven't heard anything from Cindy, nor have I attempted to contact her. Charlie and I have spent at least part of the past four weekends at Sam's house. Sam picks us up either Friday night or Saturday, depending on his schedule, and drives us back on Sunday evenings.

Tonight, the Friday of our fifth weekend in a row, Sam is already waiting outside when I arrive home with Charlie. As he carries the stroller in for me, Sam says, "It's getting darker in the evenings now, isn't it? Will you be nervous walking home after dark?"

"It's only a couple of blocks but I can't say I'm looking forward to it."

"H-mm," he says.

We go into the kitchen and Sam takes over Charlie's solid food feeding while I finish packing stuff to take with us. This feeding is great fun for both of them because they both seem to enjoy making a mess. Standing at the sink, washing Charlie's bottles, I have to smile at the shrieks and chortles coming from behind me.

When Sam tells me they're through, I get a washcloth to clean Charlie's face and hands. Then I rinse out the cloth and pretend to do the same for Sam, dabbing at his face and hands while he screws up his face and makes

Charlie-type protestations. All for the benefit of Charlie, of course, who noisily expresses his appreciation of Sam's performance.

I declare, "Hopeless reprobates, both of you," and give each of them a kiss on the nose. My heart thumps as Sam puts up his mouth to be kissed too. At times like this, it really hits home how much I rely on this man to keep me emotionally afloat.

We don't linger over a cup of tea tonight because Sam is in a hurry to get home and relax. He says he's had an extremely tiring day. So he helps me get my things together and soon we're on our way.

The traffic is particularly heavy tonight. On the bridge approach, we come to a complete standstill. A frustrated Sam says, "Oh, for God's sake, it seems it's like this night after night. I've decided commuting by car is for the birds." He glances at me. "Did I tell you, lately I've been taking the bus to work?"

A warning bell sounds in my brain. I look at him. He says, "I guess I didn't tell you. There's an express bus that runs from the plaza close to my house to within a block of the office. It's great. I can read or nap and let the driver deal with all this." After a minute, he adds, "Of course, some days I *have* to drive."

Yes, he has to drive every time he comes to get Charlie and me. My stomach tenses. I didn't eat much lunch today and feel hungry in a sick kind of way.

The traffic moves forward, but after only a few yards we stop again and I sigh. Sam says, "You know, Diane, it would make life a lot simpler for both of us if you and Charlie were to move in with me. It would cut out my having to pick you up and take you home every weekend. My express bus would work for you too; it goes right by the block where you work."

Now, I'm speechless. He's never before even hinted he had any such idea in mind. He says, "You'd like to move out of that crummy apartment, wouldn't you? Especially when it starts getting dark in the evenings." The traffic starts to move. He says, "What do you think?"

What do I think? I'm both thrilled and terrified. Thrilled because moving in with Sam would make life so much easier; no more holding my breath as Friday approaches, afraid that this weekend he might not call. Terrified because if I move in with him, I'd be burning a major bridge behind me. Or is there any longer a bridge there?

I say, "I'd need a sitter for Charlie."

"No problem. There's a woman who lives a couple of blocks from me who takes care of kids in her home. My neighbors say she's really good. She's looking after one little boy right now and would be delighted to take on Charlie as well."

"How do you know that?"

"I asked her." Sam sounds surprised at my question. I'm surprised too; he's obviously done some thinking about this. He says, "There'll be various details to work out, but we'll deal with them as they come up."

One detail is staring me in the face as he speaks. I choose my words with care. "Sam, are you sure you wouldn't feel too tied down with such an arrangement? I mean, I know you like the freedom to party with your friends…."

"Look, all I'm suggesting is a housing arrangement, not a jail sentence." He goes on, sounding defensive. "I'm sorry if you misunderstood but I'm not proposing marriage or anything. Basically, you'd just be renting space in my house."

This last sentence makes me reel. Mentally, I struggle to understand just what he *is* suggesting. He says, "Obviously we'd do a lot of things together, the way we do now at weekends. But I'd continue to see my friends and enjoy my current social life. And, of course, I'd expect you to do the same."

"Oh!"

Suddenly, I have visions of being left alone with Charlie in the Mill Valley house for hours—or days—on end while Sam is living it up elsewhere. Or, even worse, of skulking miserably in a corner while Sam entertains at home. The thought of male guests doesn't bother me, but I couldn't stand to think of him being with other women. Does a "housing arrangement only" leave him free to alley-cat around whenever he feels like it? As it is now, I have no idea what he does when he isn't with me and always refuse to think about it. But if I lived with him....

As for expecting me to "do the same," he surely realizes that apart from him my social life is zilch.

We're on the bridge finally, moving along at a steady clip. Sam says, "Soon be home!" He reaches out to touch my hand. "You know, Diane, there's another thing. If you move in with me, we'll have to get you a car. It's important you be able to get around, independent of me."

"I let my license lapse."

"No problem. Apply for another one. We'll get you a couple of lessons if need be."

Gloomily, I stare out the window. He's right, I guess, about the car. But who does he think is going to pay for it? And if he's offering to pay, how can I be independent of him? I'd be more independent living where I am. But if I refuse his offer, these weekends with him may come to an end.

Finally, I say, "I'll have to think about it."

"Fine." He sounds unconcerned.

As we finish our journey, I continue to brood. This is not a good time for me to have worrisome decisions dumped on my plate. The past week or so, I've been feeling quite unwell. The smell of food, coffee especially, sets off waves of nausea. An ominously familiar nausea. And there are other signs too. At first, I was in vehement denial. But earlier this week I finally broke down and bought a home pregnancy test kit. The result was most unsettling and I've made an appointment with the doctor for Monday after work. I'm hoping against hope she'll tell me the test kit was faulty somehow.

On Sunday afternoon, I stand at the kitchen sink, peeling potatoes for dinner, looking out the window at the freshly turned earth in the vegetable garden. Sam rototilled it yesterday. Sam and Charlie are in the living room, playing some noisy game or other.

In my previous weekends here, I've been able to push all the uncertainties of my current life to the back of my mind and just relax. Sam is easy to get along with and really helpful with the baby. He shares in Charlie's feeding, bathing, and playing in a lighthearted manner that lifts my spirits too. And, more and more, I've grown fond of this rambling old house with its unexpected nooks and crannies. Its sheer spaciousness fills me with a kind of euphoria. Probably because I've spent so much of my life cooped up in *little* places.

But this weekend it's hard to relax with so much on my mind. As I peel and rinse, I keep thinking about Sam's offer, which I suppose he'll expect me to respond to pretty soon. On the one hand, I feel hurt that he would even want to limit my role in his life to "someone who rents space." Of course, he might back down from that view—but in my confused state of mind I don't know that I want him to back down.

Why hasn't Cindy called? Isn't she even curious about Charlie? She's waiting, I suppose, for me to call her.

We're having poached salmon tonight. After I cut up the potatoes and put them in a pan with cold water, I take the fish out of the fridge and look at it. The sight of the slimy pink stuff nauseates me and I hastily put it away.

Sam comes to the kitchen door. "Hey, Mommy, us guys need a drink." As he walks by me on his way to the cupboard, he pats my head and says, "You look a bit pale, angel. Come take a juice break with us. And see the new game we're playing." I help him get the juice and take it into the living room.

Their new game is loading wooden rings onto a pole. This is somewhat beyond Charlie's current abilities, but he gazes at Sam with adoration as Sam instructs him. "See, you put the big yellow one on first." I resist the urge to laugh. They are so sweet together.

Somehow, I hold the queasiness at bay long enough to get the salmon poached, the potatoes boiled and mashed, green beans prepared. I warm up French bread to serve with the meal. Thank goodness for the bread. It's about all I can manage to eat. Sam frowns at my uneaten meal, and I quickly say, "We went to this Mexican place on Friday for someone's birthday. I've been feeling queasy ever since."

There's no way I'm going to share my suspicions with Sam. With his edginess about getting tied down, he'd probably be furious. But nowhere near as furious as Cindy. If she finds out, I'll be cut off from her forever.

I've concluded there is only one thing I can do if I am, in fact, pregnant. And I won't tell him about it.

That evening, as Sam drives us back to the apartment, the traffic is terrible again. He grumbles, "This is a real drag. I can't wait for you to move in." He glances at me. "Have you come to a decision about that yet?"

Cautiously, I say, "Sam, it's really sweet of you to offer. And you know how much we both love spending these weekends with you." Sam frowns, no doubt waiting for the *but*. I continue, "But I'm worried about Charlie. He's becoming so attached to you."

"Which means it would be good for you to move in, right?"

"The trouble is if we live with you all the time, Charlie will become even more attached. And then, if you decide you no longer want us living with you, it would be simply devastating...."

"Wait a minute." Sam sounds disbelieving. "You think one day I'll just toss you out into the street? You must think I'm quite a guy!"

"But you said yourself it would just be a housing arrangement. Just renting space. And housing arrangements aren't binding, are they?"

"Oh, you want a *binding* commitment? A written guarantee of a home for life?" I've never heard him sound so angry. My stomach churns and I reach in the door pocket for a paper bag I'd stashed there just for this purpose. Please, God, don't let me throw up.

Sam swears as another driver cuts in front of him. I unfold the bag and plead, "We shouldn't argue while you're trying to drive."

"*Trying* to drive? So I'm a lousy driver too."

In spite of the nausea, I lose my patience. "Look, Sam, I know you enjoy playing Daddy to Charlie. But you said you want more than that. You don't want to let go of your bachelor life which I assume means you want to keep up the—what did you call it?—the experimenting and partying and women."

"The women!" he mimics. "Of course, I couldn't give them up, could I? Honestly, Diane, do you think I'm that promiscuous?"

I shrill. "How do I know how promiscuous you are? But if I move in with you I'll find out pretty quick, won't I?"

Charlie, who was asleep in the back seat, wakes with a little cry. I turn to soothe him. As I turn, I get a glimpse of Sam's face; his lips are moving as though he's trying to formulate words. Maybe I'm being too harsh. I feel so sick. I take a few deep breaths and force myself to speak quietly. "Sam, you must see I'm thinking about you as well as Charlie. Really, you don't owe us anything. I'm not asking you to give up your freedom. It's just that I don't think I can handle...."

My voice trails off. What's the use? Sam's not listening; he's staring straight ahead and his mouth is set in a hard, angry line.

Charlie goes back to sleep. The nausea passes and I fold up the paper bag. Sam's eyes flicker to the bag as I put it away and I mutter something about Mexican food. He doesn't respond and we drive the rest of the way in silence.

Back at my apartment, Sam helps me unload everything, as usual. I put a sleeping Charlie into his bed, and then follow Sam to the front door. He stands for a moment, his hand on the knob; then says, "I'm sorry you feel the way you do. I really think things would have worked out."

My eyes are blurry with tears—but not too blurry to see he has tears in his eyes too. Unexpectedly, he says, "Maybe you should see a doctor. For your sickness."

"As it happens, I have an appointment tomorrow. Just for a checkup. I'll ask about the nausea too."

He nods. "I'll call you."

For a moment, I think he isn't going to kiss me good-night—then he does. But his body is very tense. After I close the door, I go to the living room window and watch him get into his car. He doesn't leave right away and I think maybe he'll come back. But after a minute, he starts the engine and drives off.

On Monday night, Mrs. Z. keeps Charlie late for me while I'm at the doctor's, and it's past seven by the time I pick him up. Then—wonder of wonders!—Mr. Z. drives us home because of the late hour. When I get home, I prepare our dinner: cereal and peaches for Charlie, vegetable soup and crackers for me.

Charlie won't eat his food. I think Mrs. Z. was smuggling him treats because I was so late picking him up. Finally, I give up on the cereal and put some Cheerios on his tray for him to throw around while I get on with my soup.

It didn't go at all well with the doctor tonight. She does think I'm pregnant and is doing a blood test to confirm it. However, the real shocker came when I told her that if the results were positive I planned to have an abortion. She acted *scandalized*, which seems quite inappropriate for a doctor. She muttered that she approves of abortion only in the case of rape or when the mother's health is in jeopardy, or "maybe in the case of a young unmarried woman." But when I reminded her I *am* unmarried, she seemed more disgusted than ever—as though I should have known better. In the end, she referred me to Planned Parenthood. I left her office feeling like a criminal!

Later that evening, after I get Charlie to sleep, I sit down at the kitchen table, staring at the Cheerio-strewn floor and wondering whether to call Sam. I've been really miserable since our argument yesterday. It was inexcusable of him not to make any attempt to see things through my eyes. We couldn't even discuss anything because every time I opened my mouth he'd come out with some sarcastic blast. But I'm longing to hear his voice.

The phone rings. I pick it up and say "Hullo."

"Hi," he says. "I want to apologize for my grouchiness yesterday."

Grouchiness, he calls it! Relieved though I am at his call, I keep in mind we have a lot of unresolved business to deal with. I say, "I apologize too for upsetting you. But I really do think we need to talk things through. In a calm, not angry, way."

"I agree. I was being quite unreasonable. I'm sorry."

"Sam, please don't get mad at me for saying this but I really don't know if I could stand living with you while you continue living a bachelor life. I suppose in theory that should work just fine, but I guess I'm too... insecure. Or something."

He doesn't get angry. He says, "Yes, I'll have to do more thinking about that. By the way, did you see the doctor?"

The sudden change of subject catches me off guard. I answer, "Yes," and add, with a little laugh, "She thinks I'll live."

Sam says, "Ah, but does she think you're pregnant?"

I'm surprised again. Astounded, in fact! What on earth put that idea into his head? Although I didn't want him to know about it, I can hardly lie in the face of such a direct question. I say, "She thinks I am. But, Sam, you don't have to worry about this."

"What makes you think I'm worried?"

"Well, I sure was worried for a while. But now I've made up my mind. If the test turns out positive, I'll take a trip to Planned Parenthood and have it taken care of."

Sam, I know, is ardently pro-choice so I don't anticipate any scandalized reaction here. But he says, *Taken care of?* You're not talking about an abortion, are you?" He sounds as horrified as the doctor. What is the matter with every-one all of a sudden?

With a loud sigh, I say, "Sam, just use your imagination. Do you have any idea how terribly vulnerable and alone I feel being responsible for even one baby? Having two would be...." The words stick in my throat. I croak, "No, it's no good. I just couldn't go through with it."

"But you're *not* alone. Not unless you choose to be. These are my babies too. See, this is even more reason for you to move in with me. I'd be there every day to help out with Charlie and take care of you."

I'm not sure what to say. Then Sam says, "Look, Diane, please don't worry that I'll be out partying and womanizing all over the place. That just won't happen."

"Oh? But isn't that the freedom you were talking about wanting?"

He says, "Forget that stuff I said yesterday. I've done a lot of growing up since yesterday."

Here's a turnaround. I wonder if it's only the news of the baby that's brought about this "growing up." Which reminds me....

"Sam, how did you guess I might be pregnant?"

"Well...to tell the truth, it's been on my mind somewhat ever since that time you invited me over for tea. Tea is about all I was prepared for that afternoon." He laughs. "I didn't worry too much though because it seemed so unlikely that just that once.... But you were feeling queasy this weekend and then you said you already had an appointment with the doctor. So I sort of put two and two together."

He sounds quite cheerful; I wonder if he thinks he's talked me out of an abortion. I say, "You know, Sam, I really don't think I should have this baby." To my annoyance, this comes out sounding more like a question than a statement.

He's silent for a time. Then he says, "I know it's your body. I know that no matter how much I try to help, most of the burden will be on you. So it really is your choice. But I wish you would reconsider."

"Why?"

"Because it would be nice for Charlie to have a brother or sister. And because it seems a shame to abort a child who would be so loved and cared for."

"Loved and cared for by whom? By you, Sam?"

"Certainly, by me. And you too, of course."

For a second, I hold my breath. Does he understand what kind of commitment his words imply? Sam's quiet for a moment. Then he says, "Look, I can understand you want to think carefully about all this. How about I come over tomorrow night and we'll talk everything through? In a nice, quiet, civilized way."

"Okay."

After we say goodnight and I hang up, I continue sitting in the kitchen by the phone. My eyes glaze over the littered floor. I'll have to sweep up this mess before I go to bed; the other night, I saw what I'm sure was a cockroach scuttling away behind the stove. A long time passes. Tired, I stretch back in my chair and look up. My eyes scan the hideous ceiling with its chocolate-brown pipes. Like a heap of manure just waiting to fall, as Cindy once said.

What on earth am I waiting for?

I reach for the phone. "Sam, I've decided. I want to move in with you."

"Great!" he exclaims. "Oh, baby, I'm so glad. I swear you won't regret it. Everything's going to work out, you'll see. Hey, you know what? I can't wait. How about we move you in this weekend?"

"Sounds perfect." And suddenly I really mean this. I'm truly fed up with the uncertainty that's been weighing me down for so long. Waiting for a lover who is keeping me in suspense in an innards-wrenching purgatory. To heck with her. Charlie and I will move in with Sam. Charlie will have a daddy. I'll have an adult companion to talk and laugh and play with. I'll have a proper home, a car. I'll be safe. So what if it isn't guaranteed for life. After all, what is?

My excitement grows as Sam keeps talking in what I've come to think of as his "Bradshawe-speaking" voice. He explains how he plans to rent a truck for Saturday, find a friend to help him with the moving, contact the new sitter. He tells me what I should be doing. "Give that crazy landlord two weeks' rent in lieu of notice. Okay? Oh, and figure out what furniture you want to take. You oughta dump a lot of it—like that Godawful bed."

The bed? I open my mouth to protest but he's still talking. He wouldn't understand about the bed anyway.

Later that evening, I take stock of my possessions. There's not much to pack really. Many of my things are still in boxes from my move from our home on Bayley Street. As to the furniture, there's nothing here I care a fig for. Except for the "Godawful" bed.

Shortly after moving into our house on Bayley Street, Cindy and I were scouting around the second-hand shops for treasures we could use to furnish our new home. With a whoop of glee, she pounced on a tangle of metal in a corner. "Di-dee, look, a brass bed!"

"That scrungy mess! Looks ready for the dump."

"No, no, Diane. These rails are solid brass. They'll clean up beautifully. Of course, we'll replace the frame and springs." It ended up she was right. The glow of the polished brass transformed our nondescript bedroom into a cosy, golden boudoir. We never did replace the springs. In fact, after a time, we even found the squeak charming.

• • •

Now, I slide my hand along the headboard and remember. I remember my joy at seeing the transformation in that piece of furniture and my marveling at how Cindy could make just about anything she touched look beautiful. On an impulse, I phone Sam again.

"Sam, I know this is crazy of me but I'd really like to take the bed with me. You know, the brass is beautiful. It's probably quite valuable."

He laughs, "Like all of ten bucks worth? No, I know why you really want to keep it."

"You do?"

"It's where we first made love, right?" He's right!

"We'll find somewhere for it," he says. "Just don't make me sleep in it."

Talk about not being able to hold onto a secret! On Monday evening, I decide I won't tell anyone about my move until it's a done deal. But at work on Tuesday I blurt out the news to all and sundry, even embellishing things somewhat as I enthuse about the "marvelous Victorian mansion with stately grounds."

At lunchtime, I buy some change of address cards. I'll get them written over the next few evenings and mail them this weekend. I'll send them to people I don't speak to much in person—my mother, my sister, a couple of school friends I'm still in contact with, a few people in the old neighborhood.

And Cindy.

CHAPTER 21

Charlie and I move into Sam's house in Mill Valley on a Saturday in late October. I take a couple of days' vacation from work to help us get adjusted to our new home. Charlie will soon be nine months old. He's highly mobile these days, crawling on all fours or scooting around on his seat, and can pull himself upright in his playpen. I'm thrilled at his progress but wish I had eyes that swivel three hundred and sixty degrees.

Wednesday is my first day back at work after the move. Everyone, even Lucinda Morales, asks if I'm enjoying my new home.

At noon, Kitty and I set off together for lunch. It's a warm day and we go to our favorite bench outdoors in the plaza. Kitty says, "So how did Charlie take to the new sitter?"

"Well, there were a few tears this morning. But when the other little boy arrived, Charlie was so intrigued! I think he barely noticed us leave after that."

In fact, although I'd been a bit anxious anticipating this first day with the new sitter, I can't pretend I'm sorry to see Charlie out of Mrs. Z.'s place. Sweet though she was, her house was as gloomy as my apartment. The new sitter's place is bright and airy and she has a big back yard with trees and shrubs and a lawn where the children can play in fine weather.

As Kitty and I eat, I do most of the talking. "Sam is so handy around the house," I enthuse. "He's already installed those neat little baby gates at the top and bottom of the staircase. And we're planning the decorating. Like in the dining room..." Kitty nods and listens as I chatter on. At one point, our eyes meet. Hers are sparkling. I ask, "What?"

"Oh, Diane, I'm so glad things are finally working out for you."

It occurs to me she doesn't yet know about the new baby. I know now for sure there will be a new baby, due next June.

"Kitty, there's something I want to tell you but promise you'll keep it to yourself for now."

"You're pregnant?"

I give a frustrated gasp. Another person who's guessed! She says, "I don't know why but I had a feeling about that. You have a sort of glow to you, the way pregnant women often do." Then she laughs. "Remember, the first time you stayed at Sam's house, you told me you weren't sleeping with him? I told George what you said and he said, 'I bet *that* won't last.'"

My face gets warm thinking of Kitty discussing me with her husband. Also, there's a *gotcha* quality to her tone that makes me feel foolish as though I'd been trying to deceive her. Which wasn't the case at all. Well, I don't think so anyway.

After we finish our sandwiches, we lean back against the bench and bask in the soothing warmth of this fall day. The sun is making me drowsy. Kitty says something but her words come from afar and it takes a while to dawn on me she's waiting for the answer to a question. I shake myself awake. "Sorry. What did you say?"

But now she's reluctant to repeat it. When I look at her, she blushes and fumbles with her lunch bag. "Oh, Diane, it's none of my business. But we've become such good friends of late and I can't help wondering." She looks at me apprehensively. Finally, she gets it out. "All this has been such a huge turnaround for you. Did you find it very hard?"

"You mean, moving in with Sam? No, not at all. You know, it isn't much fun raising a child on your own. It's wonderful to have Sam available to take care of Charlie while I get other stuff done. They get along so well with each other."

Kitty shuffles a bit. She says, "But it's more than just a question of being practical, isn't it? You really do *like* Sam, don't you? I mean, you're having another baby and…." This conversation suddenly seems too much for her. She stands, gathers up her lunch things, and waves a hand. "Oh, never mind."

But *now* I think I know what she's getting at. "Kitty, are you wondering if living with Sam means I'm no longer a lesbian? Is that the turnaround you're talking about?" Kitty's never managed to hide her unease with the non-heterosexual scene. She mutters something about this not being her business but I say, "No, I don't mind talking about it." I pat the seat beside me and she sits down again.

"You know," I tell her, "the strange thing is I don't feel that I *have* changed in any significant way by moving in with Sam. Remember how one time you and I discussed how having a child adds a completely new dimension to your life? It's like a door opens to a whole new world. But then over time that new world merges into your existing world."

Kitty nods. I say, "Well, for me, relating to a man for the first time is sort of like that. A whole new world has opened up for me. But it's something I'm *adding* to my life; it doesn't take away from anything that was there before."

She looks perplexed for a moment, then says, "In other words, you've discovered you're bisexual."

This isn't a question; she speaks with finality as though the issue is now resolved. It makes me feel sad to think Kitty would be so quick to label me like this. She evidently had me in a box marked *Gay* and has moved me to a box marked *Bisexual*.

"Oh, Kitty, these arbitrary classifications sort of bother me. I'm the same person I always was."

"I'm not talking about classifications," she flashes back. "I'm talking about feelings." I'm not sure what to say to this.

She stands up again. "It's getting late. We'd better be getting back."

As we move across the plaza, through the lobby and up the stairs to the office, I'm deep in thought. Moving in with Sam was a breeze. Like donning a new but comfortable suit of clothes. It's the breakup with Cindy that has so shattered me. Shedding her has felt like shedding my skin. I feel raw all over whenever I allow myself to think about it.

Cindy and I have both been so foolish during these past months. People's feelings toward one another, their relationships, change and evolve all the time. Everyone knows that. My relationship with Cindy couldn't possibly stay the same with all that's been happening: my preoccupation with Charlie, Cindy's preoccupation with her career, our physical separation, Marigold.

And Sam, of course—steadily moving into the widening gap between Cindy and myself. Both Cindy and I should have had the sense to realize that our relationship, like all relationships, need to be nurtured to survive. We had something wonderful going and we let it fall apart.

• • •

A couple of weeks later, on a Saturday afternoon, I'm in the kitchen preparing a chicken potpie for dinner. With this pregnancy, my sick spells aren't as debilitating as they were with Charlie—not as frequent either since I moved in with Sam. As I assemble the ingredients, I reflect on the fact that my cooking prowess doesn't provide me with quite the same ego boost it used to with Cindy. I always prized her compliments on my meals because I knew she was a discriminating eater. Sam shows great enthusiasm for my meals too, but sometimes I feel he'd be equally enthusiastic no matter what garbage I were to dish up.

This afternoon, Sam is at the hardware store buying new drawer pulls for a chest of drawers he's refinishing. We bought the chest last weekend in a garage sale. It's for the "new baby."

Sam has taken Charlie with him this afternoon; Charlie goes with Sam almost everywhere. That suits me. Much as I love Charlie, I also love taking a break from him. When the phone rings, I jump. Shoot! I have flour up to my wrists. It would make sense to let the answering machine get it. But I wipe my hands on a paper towel and pick up the receiver.

"Diane? It's Cindy."

Hearing her voice knocks the breath out of me. I gulp, "Oh."

"I got your change of address card. So how have you been?"

My heart is pounding somewhere in the vicinity of my throat and it's a struggle to find my voice. "Fine, thanks. How are you?"

"I'm fine too. How about Charlie? How is he?"

"He's fine too." We both giggle at the banality of this conversation. "He crawls a lot these days. In fact, he can almost stand."

"My, he's growing up so fast, isn't he? I really miss him."
I say nothing. There's a pause. Cindy says, "The reason I'm calling is I'm going to be in the city next week. We're opening a new sales office. I was wondering whether you'd be free for lunch one day. Say, Thursday?"

She's caught me so much by surprise that I speak without thinking. "Yes, I think so."

"Wonderful. I can come pick you up outside your building at noon and we'll make sure we get through by one so the old battle-ax doesn't get on your case." Another pause. Cindy says, "You are working at the same place, right? With the same battle-ax?" She laughs.

"Yes." I'm too stunned to laugh with her.

"I'll see you then."

As I'm hanging up, Sam comes in the door with Charlie. "That was Cindy on the phone," I say. "She asked me to have lunch with her on Thursday."

Sam busies himself with Charlie, putting him in the high chair, taking off his jacket. He says, "Does she know you're living with me?"

"Well, I didn't specifically tell her that but she's surely guessed from the Mill Valley address."

Sam's silent a while. He gets a bottle of beer out of the fridge for himself and pours apple juice for Charlie and me. Then he pats Charlie on the head. "Guess what this little devil did in the store. He leaned out of the shopping cart and knocked over a whole bunch of cards and folders they had on the counter. I think it made his day." Sam laughs. "Of course, the people in the store didn't exactly set him straight. Everyone was fussing and cooing over him and saying how cute he is. No discipline, that's his problem." He gives the object of his disapproval an affectionate smile. I smile too and roll out the pastry.

After a while, Sam says, "Why does she want to have lunch with you?"

"I imagine she's just curious. I was so surprised at her call, I basically didn't say anything except 'Yes.'"

"You're going? Why?"

We look at each other for a moment. "She caught me off guard, Sam. Do you think I should cancel?"

Sam doesn't reply right away. He goes over to the sink and looks out the window, taking swigs of beer from the bottle. Finally, he says, "It's up to you. You do what you want. But don't..." He turns to face me, waving the beer bottle around for emphasis. "Don't let that damned woman upset you. Okay?"

"Okay." I turn away to hide my smile. His fierceness is touching. I hope it's unwarranted.

On Thursday, it's cool and rainy. Just before noon, I put on my raincoat and make my way downstairs to meet Cindy. Ever since she called me, I've been wondering how I'll feel when I see her again: nervous, defensive, hostile?

She's already in the lobby, waiting. I'm surprised at the instant burst of warmth that comes over me at the sight of her. We hug each other with deep affection. It's been so long.

We walk to the corner deli, which is about the quickest place to eat around here. Inside, we order our food at the counter—"Now this is my treat, Diane"—and sit at a tiny table by the window. They'll call our number when the food is ready.

While we wait, Cindy chats about the dreary weather. I look her over as unobtrusively as I can. She's the same lovely Cindy, today wearing what looks like a new all-weather coat, beige with a moss-green lining. She takes it off to slide it over the back of her chair, revealing an elegant cream-color suit and a silk scarf in shades of gold and green.

She watches me as I take off my raincoat too, and says, "You're looking extremely well."

"Thank you. So are you." But, as I speak, I see this isn't completely true. Cindy looks older to me and tired. There are lines around her mouth I haven't noticed before, and her eyes look a bit puffy. Well, I guess times have been stressful for her too.

Our number is called and Cindy jumps up to get the food. She's ordered Caesar salad and a glass of white wine. I'm sticking with vegetable soup, crackers, and milk. She smiles as she puts my food in front of me. "Looks like a healthy meal, Diane." I smile back.

We eat and talk. At least, Cindy talks and I respond. "So how's Charlie? What's he up to these days?"

"Well, as I told you, he's very mobile these days, crawling all over the place. Oh, and a couple of times he's stood up. Holding onto furniture, of course."

Cindy nods in a distracted sort of way. "Bless his little heart. I can't wait to see him again. And how about you? You and Miz Loose Morales?" She giggles at the old joke.

"You know…same-ole, same-ole."

She doesn't ask about my new home. I should be inquiring about her life, but knowing Cindy she's bound to get around to that herself before long. Sure enough, after some more small talk, she says, "You're probably wondering about my job. Well, I have big news. A huge promotion!" She puts down her fork and leans toward me, one elbow on the table. "Starting this week, I am the director of Northern California operations for J&B Systems." From her face—wide eyes, half-open mouth—it's clear she expects an excited reaction to this news.

"Wow!" I exclaim. "That's really something. Congratulations!" I sip my milk. "I thought *assistant* director was the job they had in mind for you. Isn't Marigold the director?"

Cindy nods. In a sort of delighted hush and with a faint tremor in her voice, she says, "That's right. This is Marigold's former job. That's why I said it's a huge promotion. Remember I told you the folks at head office were really impressed with me? I didn't want to tell you any more until everything was settled."

"That's really exciting, Cindy." She smiles proudly and picks up her fork to spear some more salad. "So what's happened to Marigold? Have they promoted her to some other job?"

Between mouthfuls, Cindy mumbles, "I'm not sure what Marigold's plans are. She's left the company."

Whoa!

"Is she still living with you?"

Cindy gives a terse laugh. "Oh, dear God, no. She was infuriated when they gave me her job." She catches my eye and adds, "Well, Diane, the woman was hopeless. All the key people in our branch were ready to quit. When we were in New York, Mr. B. told me he'd been dissatisfied with her for a long time. She did a good job of setting up the branch; she has great marketing skills. But Marigold's no good at managing people. She can't delegate. She wants to micro-manage. And that drives everyone crazy."

Cindy finishes off her salad and looks at my empty bowl. She says, "That soup didn't look very substantial, Diane. Would you like anything else? How about a cup of coffee? I'm getting one myself."

Coffee! Ugh!

"No, thanks."

As she walks across to the counter to get her coffee, I watch her and reflect on Marigold. Marigold who was such a wonderful mentor and was so eager to introduce Cindy to the people at head office. Marigold fighting to create a new position for Cindy. While Cindy and Mr. B. yachted and plotted around Long Island Sound. Well, well, well....

Another thought comes to mind. With Marigold gone, Cindy has no one to share in her house expenses. Cindy comes back and settles down again in the chair opposite me. I say, "So you're living alone now?"

Cindy says, "That's just what I wanted to talk with you about." But now she starts to make a production about getting sugar for her coffee. They only have those blue packets on our table and Cindy searches around adjoining tables for "the real stuff." Finally, she finds a couple of packets, rips them open, and stirs the sugar into her cup. I glance at my watch.

She says, "I know, you have to get back to work so I'll make it brief. The thing is, Diane, with this promotion I'm now making a lot more money. And I do mean a lot more. More than I'd ever dreamed of." She speaks quietly but with that same tremor of excitement I'd noted earlier. "I can carry the mortgage all by myself."

She reaches across the table to put one hand on my arm and looks into my face. "Diane, I now have all I've ever dreamed of—a marvelous job, a darling house. I've got some great furniture, incidentally, and the landscaping is really starting to shape up. But I can't enjoy all this without you. I'm asking you to please come back to me. You and Charlie."

I can't believe what I'm hearing! Too astonished to do anything else, I just stare at her. For the first time, Cindy looks uncomfortable. She strokes my arm. "Yes, I know. It hasn't been going well between us for a while. And I know much of that has been my fault—well, probably most of it. But I've been so obsessed with this job. I could see the potential almost as soon as I started with J&B. From now on though, things will be different."

Her anxious eyes move around my face, waiting for me to say something. She says, "Di-dee, remember how we discussed your taking time off to stay home with Charlie? Well, you can do that now for as long as you like. No worrying about finding babysitters. No...."

Finally, I find my voice. "Cindy, I thought you would have guessed from my new address. I'm living with Sam now."

She says quickly, "Yes, I figured that was the case. And I don't blame you. I know you were really fed up with that dingy apartment. But you haven't been with him for long, have you? And I'm sure Sam would understand." She chuckles. "In fact, knowing Sam, he'll probably be highly relieved to have you move on. It must really cramp his style having a mother and child living with him."

I pull my arm out from under her hand and lean back, away from her. "What do you mean, *knowing Sam*. Since when did you know Sam?"

She looks surprised. "Well, of course, I don't know him that well but I know a lot of people who do know him. I think even you'll agree there's general consensus that he's not exactly the domestic type."

"People change, you know. And aren't you forgetting something? He's Charlie's father. Furthermore, he's a very good father. He's very attached to Charlie. Do you really expect him to give up his baby, just like that?"

Cindy's expression changes. Her mouth is set in a hard line. "And aren't *you* forgetting something, Diane? Charlie is my baby too, remember? Sam was supposed to just make you pregnant and walk away. Remember? How do you think I feel having my darling baby being virtually kidnapped from me?"

"What? You walked out on us."

"I did not."

I'm uncomfortably aware that our raised voices have attracted attention from the couple at the next table. I aim a glare in their direction and they look away. Cindy hisses, "A time-out is what I proposed. Not a time for you to skip town with Cro-Magnon Man. It didn't take you long, did it?"

She's almost in tears. And worst of all, I can hear the Ferry Building clock striking one. I must leave. Now. I reach behind me for my raincoat and plead, "Cindy, please don't. We have to talk about all this again later. But I can't stay now. Morales will eat me alive. She makes such a fuss about tardiness."

Cindy keeps talking. "Diane, I don't want to fight. Look, I know my faults. I know I've been down on Sam, because frankly I was jealous. But he obviously has a very decent side to him and I do think Charlie would benefit from having a male role model, or whatever, in his life."

I'm trying to get my raincoat on but can't seem to find one sleeve. Cindy says, a bit desperately, "We can arrange for him to visit from time to time. That's what you wanted, isn't it?"

"Cindy, there's something I have to tell you. I'm expecting another baby."

This comes out sounding a lot more offhand than I'd intended, mainly because of my search for the elusive sleeve. I mutter, "What on earth's going on? Oh, for heaven's sake, I'd pulled the lining inside out. That's why I couldn't get my arm in." Triumphant, I look up, right into Cindy's horror-struck face.

She squeals, "But you said you weren't sleeping with him." The adjoining couple stop pretending not to listen and turn their heads toward us again. Cindy lowers her voice and repeats, "You said you weren't sleeping with him." Her face has turned bright red.

"Well," I struggle to remember what I'd said and when. "I believe when I said that it was true." Cindy's hand shakes as she lifts her coffee cup. "Cindy, I'm so sorry but I really must go now. If I'm late, Morales will make me stay after five and I'll miss my bus." She puts down her cup and gets her coat on too.

Outside, it's drizzling. Cindy produces a smart little umbrella that was clipped to the outside of her purse. I put on my plastic rain hat. We stand under the awning of the deli, and look at each other. "Look," I say, "obviously we can't leave it like this. I'll call you. Okay?"

She pulls a tissue out of her pocket and wipes her eyes. "Diane, you're making a terrible mistake. Having another baby is just plain stupid. And irresponsible. You surely can't believe Sam will stick around forever. Ask Phyllis. She knows him. Ask those people who lived next door to him."

Oh, shut up, Cindy. I'm wondering whether she intends to walk me back to my building, but she stands with her body turned in the opposite direction. I say, "Thank you for the lunch."

She points her smart little umbrella into the air, presses a button and it shoots open—bright stripes of red and black. She says, "I bet he's never suggested marriage, has he?" I say nothing. She looks hard at me. "No, I thought not. Men like him simply aren't into commitment." There's no spite in her voice. In fact, she's close to tears again.

Suddenly, it starts to pour. I say, "I'm going to make a run for it."

As I step off the curb, she calls out, "Diane, please think carefully about what you're doing. Believe me, one day you're going to end up with nothing and no one."

Shut up, shut up, shut up. I leave her there and hurry back to work, annoyed with myself because I did let her upset me after all.

It's ten minutes past one when I tiptoe into the office. I hang up my raincoat and hat, smooth down my damp hair with my hands, and check to see if the coast is clear. It is—our doughty supervisor is on the phone with her back to me. So I stealthily zip across the room and slide into my chair. Kitty stops typing for an instant, raising her hands in silent applause at my successful re-entry into Morales-land.

Sam gets on the bus a couple of stops ahead of me. Tonight as I climb aboard, I see his friendly face about half way down the aisle. He stands to let me into the window seat he's saved for me. I settle myself into the comfortable upholstery and snuggle up to him. He kisses me on the cheek and right away asks, "So how was the lunch?"

When I tell him about Cindy's big promotion to director of the Northern California branch, he laughs in an admiring way. Then he asks, "What about that other woman, the one who was the director before?"

"Marigold?" I say. "Oh, Marigold's...*poof*." I waggle my fingers. "Now you see her; now you don't."

As I relate the story of the hapless Marigold, Sam's expression alternates between surprised and amused. He says, "Wow! You've got to hand it to Cindy. Talk about steamrollering your way to the top. So that's why she asked you to lunch? So she could boast about her promotion?"

I murmur, "M-mm," and turn toward the window. It's steamed up and I clear a patch of glass with my hand and look out. Dreary gray streets, dreary gray people scurrying along, bodies huddled over to protect themselves from the wet. It's cozy in this bus. It will be cozy at home too. There's a tasty lasagna there ready to be popped into the oven. *"You make a mean lasagna, Diane,"* she once told me.

Sam says, "What else did she have to say?" His voice is sleepy but insistent as if he knows there's something else. If I tell him, will he think I'm going to leave him? Maybe he'll say, *Hey, that's great! When are you moving?* I turn away from the window and look at him. He's leaning his head back on the seat and looking down at me, half smiling in a lazy way. From this angle, he looks almost handsome. Or at least— I smile—well within the range of what's normal for males.

"Cindy said she'd like Charlie and me to move back with her."

Sam's head jerks forward and he looks at me with his lips half open. Then he says, "Oh, does she! Well, she's out of luck because I ain't never gonna let you go." I rest my head on his shoulder. He puts his mouth down to my ear. "You don't want to leave me, do you, Mousy?"

"Not on your life."

He grins and bends his head to kiss the top of mine. Then he settles back again, closing his eyes. I guess as far as he's concerned the case is closed.

But, as the bus rumbles homeward, I start to feel increasingly sick as the enormity of what transpired today sinks in. In a way, I reflect, it's less stressful when someone dumps you. You have no option but to accept it and get on with your life. Which is what I've been doing since getting that letter from Cindy. But today Cindy changed all that. Now I'm the dumper and she the dumpee.

Shivering, I snuggle closer into Sam, sliding my hand under his raincoat and jacket, up his chest to the place where I can feel his heart beat. I have done what I once said I would never do: put my happiness in the hands of this man. Cindy's parting words keep replaying in my mind. Am I really going to end up with nothing and no one?

"Sam," I whisper, willing him to wake up and talk to me some more.

But he doesn't.

A couple of days after my lunch with Cindy, I arrive home to find a parcel in the mail for me. Or, rather, it is addressed to Charles Alexander Dawson. I look at the somewhat battered package with suspicion. "What on earth is this?"

Sam, peering over my shoulder, comments, "Looks like it's been shipped around the countryside. A bit the worse for wear."

Sure enough, one address has been covered up with a label bearing our Mill Valley address, a "Return to Sender" stamp has been scribbled out. The writing is my sister Hazel's. Peeling off the new label, I see it was originally mailed to our house on Bayley Street.

"Sam, you know what?" I draw in a sharp breath as I remember something. "When we moved from Bayley Street, I never did send my mother or sister my new address. I sent a change of address card when I moved here to Mill Valley but all those months I was living at the Ziebowski place, they didn't know where I was."

Sam, who is busy getting Charlie settled in his high chair, says, "Diane, that's terrible. What were you thinking?"

"Well..." I hope he can understand this. "I wrote to my mother when Charlie was born but she never acknowledged my letter. Not a word. I was so mad and hurt that when I moved I didn't bother to tell her. I haven't made any contact until I sent her the card recently."

He says, "I think you owe someone a call. PDQ. Like tonight."

Before starting on dinner, I open the package. There's a card in it, a "Congratulations on the addition to your family" card—again written by Hazel—and signed "Mom and Hazel." The package consists of baby clothes—blue and white—a knit jacket, cap and booties. New born size. I hold them up to show Sam. "I can't believe Charlie was ever tiny enough to fit into these."

Sam is arguing with Charlie over the necessity of having one's face and hands washed, and doesn't turn around.

Later that evening, I call Hazel. She sounds happy to hear my voice. "Diane, we've been so worried. Our package was returned by the post office, address unknown. It scared the life out of us."

"I know, I'm sorry. You see, I didn't hear anything from you after I wrote about the baby so I assumed you weren't that interested. Also..." The lie springs readily to my lips. "I knew my next address was going to be temporary so I waited until we'd settled in here before telling you."

Hazel sounds apologetic. "I wanted to send a card as soon as we got your letter but Mom wanted to wait until she'd finished knitting the clothes. So, yes, I guess it was a while before we mailed the package. I can see why you thought we weren't interested."

"She knit the clothes *herself*? Since when has she been a knitter?"

Hazel gives a nervous laugh. "It's probably her first effort ever. They looked a bit lumpy to me. I sure hope they still fit him."

"Oh, I'm sure they will," I lie again. "Please thank her and tell her I'll be writing real soon."

"Okay." There's a pause.

Hazel says, "I hope you're all well. You and the baby. And your friend. Cindy, is it?"

"Yes, we're fine. Although, as it happens, Cindy and I have....no longer live together."

"You don't? So you live alone now?"

"No, Charlie and I live with Sam. He's Charlie's father."

"You live with the baby's father?" Hazel's voice has risen to a squeak-like crescendo. "His *real* father?"

"Well, yes."

"For heaven's sakes! You see, we always thought the baby was adopted."

"No, he's my baby."

"So Mom has a real grandson! And you're living with the father?" Again, the squeak-like crescendo. Then she lowers her voice to close to a whisper. "Are you married? No, I guess you're not married."

She sounds so hopeful that I hate to tell her. "No, we're not. So, Hazel, how are things with all of you up there in Shasta country?"

"Nothing new," she sighs. "We live pretty monotonous lives, you know. Here in the country."

While I try to think of a joke regarding swingers like me in the big city, she says, "I'll let you go then, Diane. I'll tell Mom the package arrived safely. Oh, and...I'm so glad things are working out so well for you."

CHAPTER 22

It's the Saturday before Thanksgiving, early in the after-noon. Sam has suggested we go on a little outing to the beach and we're all in the kitchen getting ready. It's not exactly beach weather today—cool and mostly cloudy with an occasional burst of sunshine. But I'm looking forward to a drive along the pretty country roads, curving around and up and down the rolling hills. I sing to myself as I pack a snack to take—juice and oatmeal-raisin cookies still warm from the oven. Sam is struggling to get Charlie's shoes on.

The phone rings and I answer it. It's Phyllis. She says in her hearty way, "Diane, I've decided to give a Thanksgiving party at my house this year. How would you all like to come?"

"That's kind of you, Phyllis. Won't it be a lot of work though?"

"Not for me, it won't. It will be a buffet potluck. I'll supply the bird; everyone else can bring everything else."

"Good for you," I tell her, "It sounds great. Let me check with Sam. I'm not sure what he has in mind."

Phyllis says, "You do that. By the way," she chuckles, "as an added inducement, you might mention to him that an old friend of his is back from South America. She wasn't supposed to be back so soon but she got fed up with the country or her companion or something. I've invited her too."

My stomach falls to my feet. "Phyllis, Sam's right here. Maybe you should talk to him yourself." I hand Sam the phone and take over the job of shoe-ing Charlie. As Sam talks, I listen.

"Hi, Phyllis....That sounds very nice. What would you like us to bring? Diane makes great pies." He smiles at me and I smile back to acknowledge the compliment. The two of them talk a while longer about food and then there's a silence while Sam listens. My ears prick up as he says, "Oh, really!" He turns to look out the window, his back to me, then lowers his voice and says, "No, I haven't heard from her, but then she doesn't have my new address."

Suddenly, I feel disgusted at myself for eavesdropping and leave the room to collect our coats. When I get back to the kitchen, Sam's off the phone. He says, "I accepted her invitation. That is okay with you, isn't it?"

"Sure, it sounds great." What I mean is, it's great as long as that damned Juanita woman doesn't show up. But I can hardly say that.

We reach the ocean about two o'clock. Sam parks in a lot on the cliff top. Taking our blanket and carryall with snacks and beach toys, we wend our way down the narrow path to the beach. In what seems like a sheltered spot on the sand, Sam spreads out the blanket and we all sit down. And *freeze*. Not only is it cold, there's a nasty little wind that blows the sand into our eyes and mouth and hair. Well, I can forget about serving juice and cookies! Charlie is happy enough. He shuffles to the edge of the blanket, and scoops up handfuls of sand, most of which get blown onto us.

Sam sits with his knees drawn up, gazing out to sea. He seems to have something on his mind. No doubt, the something is Juanita. Poor guy. It surely will cramp his style, to use Cindy's words, to have Charlie and me along at such a momentous reunion. Looking at him, I feel a tiny tweak of nostalgia and think of that long ago day when he first came charging up our steps bellowing at the top of his Neanderthal voice.

Charlie moves off the blanket and laboriously clambers over the heavy cold sand. He's fascinated but doesn't really like it and makes distressed grunts as he plows along. Sam goes after him and brings him back. He seats Charlie beside him and uses a plastic pail and shovel to demonstrate what you're supposed to do with sand.

There's a sudden icy blast off the ocean. I pull the collar of my jacket over my ears and cover my hands with my sleeves. How close were Juanita and Sam, I wonder? On what terms did they part when she left the country with her "doctor laddie"? What does her early return really signify? I hesitate to ask him these things although, when you think about it, this Juanita affair is my business as much as his. After all, if he and she start going together again, where will that leave me? To say nothing of my "housing arrangement."

I shiver and hug myself with my arms.

Sam sees me and says, "Whose stupid idea was this anyway?" We both laugh.

"It was a lovely drive through the countryside," I assure him, "so I've enjoyed the outing anyway."

"But now you've had about as much cold as you can take? Me, too."

We both get to our feet and pack up.

On the way home, we come over the crest of a hill and there's a little group of cows huddled near the fence. "Oh, Sam, look." He pulls over to the side of the road and I wind down the window. "Charlie, look at the cows." But Charlie's not in a cow mood today. He looks away from my pointing finger, and idly kicks his legs and rocks back and forth.

Sam turns off the engine. My back is to him but I can feel him close behind me. He strokes the back of my neck with his fingers. "You know, Diane, it kind of bothers me that we...."

But I interrupt because at this moment one of the cows, a pretty chocolate and cream colored animal, pushes her head right over the fence toward me and makes a deep *mm-mm-mm* sound. "Sam, did you hear that? She wants to be friends. What lovely soulful eyes she has!" I lean out of the window and respond to her greeting with a friendly "Moo!" And, over my shoulder, to Sam, "I'm sorry, I interrupted you."

He says, "I was going to say it bothers me we're not married."

What in the world? I twist around to face him. It's hard to read his expression. I make a joke of it. "Is that a complaint or a proposal?"

He says, "Doesn't it bother you?"

"Honestly, I've never even thought about it." Of course, this isn't really true because when we're out together with Charlie, people often take it for granted we're married and I find myself feeling married without consciously thinking about it. But, bottom line, I've always assumed that he hasn't the least intention of marrying me. "So what brought this up?"

Sam draws a breath. "Well, it's occurred to me recently that our current situation is really the worst of two worlds. It's neither one thing nor the other, is it? On the one hand, we're both tied down, to each other and Charlie." He strokes my stomach. "And whoever else comes down the pike. But we have none of the benefits of marriage."

"There are benefits?"

He studies my face, ignoring my smirk. He says, "If we were married, we'd feel more sure of each other, more secure." He expands on this theme in an almost lawyer-like voice. "Children feel more secure if their parents are married. Unconventional family situations leave them open to taunting by their peers. The wife is more comfortable in her interactions with friends and neighbors if she has a socially recognized status. Most important of all, marriage provides critical legal and financial protections for every family member."

In sober silence, I listen. It's not what you'd call a romantic speech, although it has a caring and responsible tone. Also, I question how valid his assertions are. "I wonder," I muse aloud, "if my parents felt more sure of each other because they were married? If so, they were cruelly duped."

Sam says, "Of course, there's no guarantee a relationship will last forever. But when you marry you make some pretty solemn promises to each other. That's a good start, isn't it?"

He's right there, I guess. Even so, it's an effort to get my feelings sorted out. Marriage between a man and a woman has been given a bad rap by most of the women I've associated with in my adult life. Cindy once opined that marriage gives the man the opportunity to do "his power-and-dominance thing" while, for the woman, "it's the end of her life as an independent being."

And yet, the other day, Cindy seemed to imply that Sam's failure to propose meant I was doomed to a life of misery. Cindy must be as mixed up as I feel!

Charlie's humming from the back seat suddenly rises in pitch—a foreshadowing of a change in mood, usually for the worse. Sam and I swing around at the same time to reach for the snack bag on the back seat. We laugh as we bump into each other in our eagerness to find him something to chew. After Charlie settles down with a teething biscuit, Sam and I help ourselves to cookies.

Munching, Sam says, "Remember the first night you spent at my house—I told you how surprised I was at how much I'd fallen for this little guy? In a way, the same thing is true about you. Hey, these things are delicious." He waves his remaining half-cookie at me before popping it into his mouth and wolfing it down. Then, gazing into the distance through the windshield, he reminisces. "Even back in the early Charlie-making days, I did like you. Probably more than I let on. But at that time I never thought of you as someone I'd ever, well, want to spend my life with."

His voice trails off. After a moment, he says, "Then I saw Charlie. I don't mean when he was first born, in the hospital. He just looked like a blob to me that day. I mean the time I first saw him on your living room floor. That's when I really lost my heart!"

I know the time he's referring to. It was the day after he'd bailed me out in the convenience store. Come to think of it, I don't think I ever paid him back that seven bucks. Sam says, "Anyway, after that it seemed the more attached I became to Charlie, the more attached I became to you. As though the two of you were a package." He makes a face as though he finds it odd he should have felt that way.

But his words strike a chord. I say, "Sam, I know how you feel. That's sort of how it was with me too. You so obviously loved Charlie and I started to see Charlie as being a part of you, and vice versa. And then it got so it became hard..." I can't finish the sentence. I was going to say *"to imagine a life with Charlie that excluded you."* I really do think that's how I feel—but it's a disturbing thought.

Suddenly, I become aware of a soggy ball of something in my hand and look down in surprise. It's part of a cookie

I've been unthinkingly kneading in my palm while talking. Embarrassed, I shovel most of the mess into my mouth while escaping crumbs and raisins fall onto my chin and blouse. Sam chuckles as he helps me tidy myself. "What a messy baby."

Then he says, "Diane, you and I get along together so well, don't we? We have the same sense of humor. We make a great team taking care of Charlie. And you're one of the few people I know who seems to love that crazy old house as much as I do."

"I know," I agree. "Moving in with you was amazingly easy. In fact, I can hardly believe what a domestic creature you are." He laughs and I say, "I mean it. I love it that you enjoy grubbing around in the garden with me. You don't mind getting your nails dirty." A fleeting image of Cindy's immaculate nails flashes into my mind. "And it's fun figuring out how we're going to redecorate the place."

"One day we might even have the money to do it."

"Well, it doesn't matter. It's still been fun. But, you know, Sam..." I look at him as he sits with one arm on the seat back to my left and the other stretched across the dashboard to my right, as though he's forming a fence around me. "For all this, I nearly fell over when you mentioned the 'M' word. People keep telling me you're not the marrying kind."

Of course, in truth, "people" don't keep telling me. Only Cindy has ever told me.

Sam snorts. "People are always so quick to make judgments about other people, aren't they? I've always had every intention of getting married some day. Mind you, I wasn't planning on it just yet." He says this with a laconic grin as though he's been the subject of a sly joke.

"But there was the new baby," I prompt him. "Was that it?"

Sam is silent for a moment. "Well, yes, there is that, of course. I definitely do feel committed to taking care of all of you. But...oh, there are lots of things. It's all happened slowly."

Sam stops to ask if I brought anything to drink. I get out a bottle of apple juice for Charlie, which Charlie holds against himself with one hand while he continues to munch his biscuit. Then I pour orange juice into plastic glasses for Sam and myself.

Sam swallows some juice. He says, "You know, angel, I've had lots of girlfriends in my time. Typically, I get the hots for someone, tell myself I'm in love. The fire rages for a while, then fizzles out." *As with Juanita?* I wonder. "But with you, it crept up on me in a sneaky way. Remember that fight we had when I said I wanted to keep up my bachelor lifestyle?"

I nod.

"Well, that night, when I was mulling things over, it dawned on me that I'd be quite happy giving all that up. Just having you."

It occurs to me a distinctly romantic tone is beginning to creep into this conversation. He goes on, "But then what really gave me a wake-up call was Cindy. When she asked you to move back with her. Since then, I haven't stopped wondering what I'd do if you were to go." He adds in a flat, almost matter-of-fact, way, "It would leave such a huge hole in my life, I don't think I could bear it."

Now this is very, very romantic! I whisper, "Oh, Sam."

Sam says, "Sounds like love has walked right in, doesn't it?" He says this in a flippant way—pronouncing it *lurve* instead of *love*. But I understand. I understand he finds this mushy stuff awkward.

I put my arms around his neck and say it again, "Oh, Sam."

Then his summer-sky blue eyes look down into mine and his teeth flash in his wonderful Burt Lancaster grin, and he says softly, "In case you're wondering, I do love you, little Mousy. I love you a lot."

I find my smile freezing in place.

Sam says, "Didn't you hear me?" Then he tosses his head back and *bellows*—his words bouncing off the inside of the car and roaring out the window—"*I love you, I love you, I love you.*"

And that gets everyone's attention. Our cloven-hoofed audience stops chewing the cud or whatever they're doing to look up at us. A couple of them back away nervously. Then a rumbling "*Moo-oo-oo*" erupts from my chocolate and cream friend, and that starts them all off. One *moo* after another echoes around the crowd. A delighted Charlie waves his bottle and tries to "moo" too.

Sam raises his voice above the general racket. "It seems they all approve. So how about it, Diane Dawson, do you love me too?"

And I shout back, "I do, I do."

"And will you marry me?"

"I will, I will."

And we hug and kiss and laugh—and even moo—while Charlie shouts his joyous approval.

Now I really have made my decision, once and for all. I've made my bed and will have to lie in it. I've burned all my bridges.

It feels like a huge burden has been lifted from my shoulders.

CHAPTER 23

That night, after Charlie goes to sleep, Sam and I sit down in the living room to plan our wedding. We agree on two things. It should be small. It should be soon. Sam says, "How about two weeks from today?"

"What! We couldn't even plan an elopement in that time." But I tremble with excitement as I speak.

"Sure we could," he argues. "We can have the ceremony and reception right here at home. We'll have it all catered so you won't have to do a thing."

This seems unlikely but I feel too overwhelmed to argue about it. It occurs to me that feeling overwhelmed is something I may have to get used to, living with Sam.

As for whom to invite… "How about just our families?" Sam suggests.

"Please, anyone *but* our families," I counter. "Too many awkward explanations. I mean, how do we tell your parents about me? And where Charlie came from? Let's just tell them we eloped."

Incidentally, Sam has told me the truth about his relatives. They are respectable but not particularly distinguished. His father is a local bank manager, his mother a stay-at-home mom. But I still cringe to think what they will think of me.

A cheerful Sam says, "Sweetheart, I love you dearly but you must admit you can be pretty weird at times. Downright secretive. My parents know all about us. I've already told them."

"What did you tell them?"

"That I'd fathered a child for a lesbian couple and then later fell in love with the mother. That we're living together in this house."

"Good Lord!" My face feels hot. "But, Sam, I have no intention of inviting my mother and sister."

"Okay, that's your business. Now let's find a pad of paper and make a list."

By midnight, we get it all sorted out. We end up with a surprisingly expansive list that includes a few work colleagues, people from our old neighborhood. Even a couple of neighbors, who probably think we're married already.

One thing Sam leaves completely to me is the issue of whether to invite Cindy, or even to tell her. Telling her might seem like rubbing salt in a wound, but not telling her would be a real slap in the face because she's bound to find out. In the end, I decide to send her an invitation and add a note saying I'd quite understand if she'd rather not come.

After all the excitement, Thanksgiving at Phyllis' is almost a letdown. We arrive shortly after one. Already, the place is humming with disorganization with Phyllis at her cheerful worst. She'd put the turkey in the oven only an hour ago so we'll have to wait hours before we can eat. She'd failed to organize what people were to bring to the potluck so that my pumpkin and apple pies are joined by ten others on a side table, but we have no mashed potatoes or rolls.

No Juanita either. At least, not until just after three o'clock when the doorbell rings and—*ta-da*—there she is. She's accompanied by a thin, dark-haired man with glasses and graying sideburns. Phyllis booms, "Juanita baby, you brought your doctor laddie." She adds, with her customary lack of tact, "I thought you'd had a falling out."

"Oh, no." Juanita smiles coyly at her escort and slides an arm around his waist. Full of indignation on Sam's behalf—I mean, how dare she flaunt her latest lover in front of him?—I turn away without talking to them.

Later on, Sam gets his own back. As soon as we sit down to eat, Phyllis stands and, with a potentially shattering rap on her glass with a spoon, proclaims, "Listen up, everyone. I'm going to make a toast but before I do I'd like my dear friend Sam to make an announcement."

Then Sam rises. "For those who haven't heard," he says, "On Saturday week, Diane and I are getting married."

Cheers erupt from the group. I beam. And catch a glimpse of Juanita's face and beam even more. I stop beaming at Sam's next words, "And you're all invited." But then I start beaming again as I remember that many of them have already been invited and those who haven't surely won't have the nerve to come.

CHAPTER 24

As is often the case, most of the things I'd been fretting about just didn't happen. With such short notice, Sam's family couldn't attend. His parents were leaving on a vacation cruise just before Thanksgiving. His mother talked to me on the phone. She was charming and apologetic as she explained their unavailability. "We'll have a special party for you at Christmastime," she promised, "All the Bradshawes will be there."

As for my family: I phoned Hazel. It's so much easier to lie to her than to my mother. "We're not having a proper wedding," I told her, "It'll be at City Hall with just a couple of witnesses."

Hazel shrieked with excitement at my news. "Mom will be thrilled. She'll say finally the Good Lord has answered her prayers." We both laughed.

Our wedding day is the last Saturday of November. It's a lovely day, sunny and mild. Twenty guests attend. Roland is best man; Kitty is my matron of honor. We have Charlie at the ceremony, which is at noon, but, immediately after, his new sitter takes him back to her house for the rest of the afternoon.

It seems the instant the champagne is poured, everyone in this disparate crowd of work colleagues, friends and neighbors explodes into a noisy, talking, laughing group. They all seem to be enjoying themselves and pretty soon I relax.

The caterers have done a superb job. The table in the dining room, under the chandelier dripping with ribbons and balloons, holds a large assortment of marvelous-looking salads and breads. Then the waiters carry out dishes of delicious-smelling hot food. I walk around the table peeking at the label on each dish: sliced beef tenderloin with shallots, Greek lamb casserole, smoked chicken with shrimp. My mouth waters, but I'm too excited to eat much today.

After a while, I find myself in a group with Phyllis who is voluble after a couple of glasses of champagne. She seems to feel she's "family"—I guess because we were at her house so recently. Now she announces to everyone that she's been predicting this wedding for some time. "Why, Diane fell madly in love with this big hunk the minute she first set eyes on him."

Sam roars with laughter but I bristle and mutter, "That simply isn't true, Phyllis." I would say more but my voice is drowned out by everyone joining in Sam's laughter. Later, when things quiet down, I corner Phyllis alone and try to set the record straight. "I just couldn't *stand* Sam when I first met him," I tell her.

"Well," she concedes, "maybe I exaggerated just a trifle. But really, Diane, I saw the signs a long time ago."

"Signs? What signs, for heavens sake?"

"Remember that party at my house last year? You were pregnant with Charlie and came with Cindy. Sam went over to talk to you at one point. I could see your face as you looked up at him and I said to myself, '*Now what's this? Cindy had better watch out.*' Diane, you looked like a woman in love, if ever I saw one."

There's no point in continuing to argue; she'll say I'm protesting too much. The trouble is, she's almost got me doubting my own memory. From a few feet away, Sam catches my eye and winks. Phyllis must have been feeding him these tall tales too. It strikes me that love stories, like history in general, are always being revised in hindsight to fit with the ultimate outcome.

A waiter passing by with a tray of canapés murmurs in my ear that some more guests are coming up the walk, and I make my way to the front door.

It's Cindy.

She is accompanied by a mousy-looking young woman. I'm really surprised to see Cindy. She didn't send any reply to my invitation. She's carrying a gift-wrapped box, about a foot square. She greets me with a kiss on the cheek and thrusts the gift at me. "Sorry I didn't reply to your invitation. I wasn't sure what my plans would be for today."

Then she introduces me to the mousy one. "This is Julia. I hope you don't mind my bringing her." She adds, "We can only stay a couple of minutes." Julia has a pleasant smile. She also is carrying what appears to be a gift in a paper carrier, but makes no attempt to hand it to me. I welcome her and urge them both to partake of refreshments.

Across the room, Sam's hearty *ha-ha-ha* can be heard above the crowd. The decibel level of Sam's speech in public has not abated during the time I've lived with him. Cindy gives me a knowing smile. I put up a hand to attract his attention and wave him toward us. Sam's face falls when he sees Cindy. He excuses himself to his companions and walks over, looking wary. Cindy holds out her hand and gushes, "Hello, Sam. Heartiest congratulations! I wish you both all the happiness in the world."

Sam shakes her hand and says, "Thank you." I show him the gift Cindy's brought and he thanks her again. The four of us stand in awkward silence for a few seconds. Then someone calls to Sam from across the room and he turns to leave, saying, "Please excuse me. I'll be right back." Like fun he will!

A waiter brings champagne for my two guests and, at Cindy's request, I show them around the house. Cindy's friend Julia is friendly, complimentary about absolutely everything, but Cindy doesn't say much. Her eyes seem to be assessing the peeling wallpaper in the downstairs rooms, the worn carpeting on the stairs, grubby grout in the powder room. I wish we'd managed to get it all redecorated before now.

Even the kitchen, which is practically new, doesn't look that good today with trays of food and dirty dishes stacked everywhere. I apologize for the mess and assure them it isn't always this bad. Julia murmurs, "Oh, you can see it's a marvelous house. Great potential." Cindy says nothing. She seems restless, her eyes roving around.

As we head back toward the living room, Cindy stops at the foot of the staircase and looks up. I tell her, "The upstairs rooms aren't in fit shape to display right now. How about some food? You haven't eaten anything."

"No, thank you. We really should get going." But she and Julia continue to stand by the stairs, exchanging glances.

Abruptly, Julia turns to me and says, "We really were hoping to see Cindy's little boy." She holds up the paper bag she's been carrying around.

"Oh, that's a present for Charlie? How nice. I'm afraid he's not here but I'll be sure to give it to him."

I reach out my hand but Cindy snatches the bag from Julia. She asks, "Where is he?"

"He's at the sitter's house."

The two of them stare at me. Suddenly, Julia's smile has acquired a hard edge. Cindy looks downright hostile. A cold lump forms in my stomach.

Julia says, "Well, would you give us the address?"

It's a simple request, I tell myself. But I have the strongest feeling I don't want Cindy to see Charlie without my being present. And I can hardly leave my own wedding reception. As I hesitate, Julia pleads, "You see, he's the main reason we came today. Cindy so much wanted to see her baby."

"What's going on?" To my relief, Sam has walked up behind me.

"Cindy wants the sitter's address," I explain. "So she can take Charlie a present."

"Oh, does she?" he says. "I don't think so."

Cindy opens her mouth and he says, louder, "No, I'm sorry. Not today."

Cindy's face crumples in a heart-melting look that makes me want to reach out for her. Then she turns and walks out through the front door.

"Oh, Sam." This is a whisper from me.

Possibly Julia takes courage from my softness because she bursts out, "Oh, please. She's got to see him. She's been so looking forward to it."

"I'm sorry, Julia." I glance over my shoulder as I speak, hoping we can't be overheard. "If only she'd phoned ahead, we could maybe have worked something out."

Sam puts a hand on Julia's shoulder and steers her firmly to the door. She turns a stricken face toward me. "It's really not fair, you know. She'll be devastated."

"Too bad," from Sam, as he pushes her through the doorway. By now, I note, Cindy has vanished from sight past the shrubs by the garage.

But now Julia is angry. She shakes off Sam's hand and says, "She's told me the whole story, you know. How could you keep her from seeing her baby? I've never heard of anything so cruel."

Some of our guests are starting to drift toward us. In an angry mutter, Sam says, "I don't know what story she's told you but Charlie is *not* her baby. He's Diane's baby and mine."

Defiant, she glares at me. "Sure, he's legally yours but you manipulated all that. You bamboozled poor Cindy into letting you be the mother when all along she wanted to be. You didn't want her to give up her job because she made more money than you."

Sam has hold of my arm now and tries to pull me back indoors, but I can't let this preposterous statement go by. "What? Julia, that's absolutely not true."

Sam says, "End of discussion. Goodbye, Julia," and firmly closes the door in her face. To me, he mutters, "Goddamned nerve! They're just determined to yank your chain. Don't let them."

Then he turns back into the living room and cheerfully booms, "How about some music? Where's that stuff Roland brought?"

As I go to follow him, my eyes light on Cindy's wedding present which I had set on the hall table. All the other gifts are stacked in a corner in the living room. But now I pick up this box and hide it away in the den. Who knows, there may be a bomb in it!

Somehow, the rest of the afternoon isn't ruined. Not having much of a record collection ourselves, we had asked our friends to bring their own favorites. It turned out to be quite an eclectic collection—from Roland's light rock to Phyllis's Latin American oldies. Before long, the room is rocking with noisy singing and even some dancing. For a while, I stand in a corner, an inward argument with Julia raging in my mind. But eventually the fun is too contagious to resist. At first, I protest when I get dragged into an impromptu conga line—"Isn't this too undignified for a wedding?" But as we kick our way through the French doors onto the patio, I realize I have stopped trembling inside.

By five o'clock, the caterers have cleaned up the kitchen and left, as have most of our guests. Only Kitty and her husband George remain. "Are you sure you don't want us to help you clean up the living room?" she says.

"I'm sure," I reply.

All I want is for us to be alone.

She gives me a kiss. "Diane, it was a truly lovely wedding."

Sam walks the two of them to their car. George is a building contractor and is giving Sam advice about new window frames.

As I stand in the open doorway, waiting for Sam to come back, I take a good deep breath, letting the crisp autumnal air wash over me like a soothing balm. It's been a hectic, sometimes nerve-wracking, two weeks of preparation, and I'm relieved it's all over. But Kitty was right; it really was a lovely wedding. Except for that one incident, of course. The food was delicious. No one got too drunk, or spilled stuff on the furniture, or cast sneaky glances at my belly.

When Sam comes back, I put out my arms and we give each other a big hug. Over my shoulder, he looks through the door at the stack of unopened wedding gifts and wrappings. He says, "Just check out all that loot." I feel exhausted even thinking about it. We go inside. Pretty soon, we'll have to go get Charlie, but right now, I'm going to fix us a cup of my favorite beverage.

Sam says, "What did that stupid woman bring for us?" I lead him to the den and show him the box. Sam says, "Be careful. It could be a bomb." I snicker.

But as I remove the wrappings and open the box and pull out the tissue-wrapped innards, I say, "Sam, I bet I know what it is." And I'm right. It's one of those expensive crystal and gold table clocks. Tiny, beautiful, and completely useless. I explain to Sam, "Some years ago, Cindy and I saw a clock like this in a jeweler's. I drooled over it but said I would never own such a thing because I'd never spend so much money on something so impractical."

There's a card enclosed. *"Just what you always wanted. Love, Cindy."*

Sam says, "She wants you to keep thinking about her." He sounds annoyed. "And as for that disgusting display to-day! How dare she? On our wedding day."

The ache inside me creeps back. "Poor Cindy. I'll always feel guilty about cutting her off from Charlie. In fact, I was going to suggest that when things settle down a bit, we take Charlie to visit Cindy from time to time."

He says firmly, "No way. It's best to make a clean break."

Déjà vu. "Just what Cindy once said about you."

We pick our way through the kitchen—these cater-ers don't do *that* good a job of cleanup—and fix ourselves some tea. Then we go back into the living room to drink it and survey the litter. "Oh, look," I say, "Phyllis forgot to take her records with her."

Sam mimics in a falsetto voice, *"I'd forget my head if it wasn't screwed on."* We both chuckle. Sam looks through the pile. "Tango Time," he reads off one. "We didn't play this one." He puts it on the record-player and jumps to his feet. "Come on, Diane."

He seizes me in his arms and flails me around in what I suppose he thinks is a tango and sings in what I suppose he thinks is a South American accent. *"Ven I feel ju in my arms I get the sheevers."*

I crack up at the gravelly baritone. "Oh, Sam, your voice is—'ow you say eet—'orrible." I add, "Of course, it matches your dancing."

In response, he folds his arms around me tightly and kisses my ear. And then the rest of my face. I struggle in a limp sort of way as he wrestles me onto the couch, but, oh, what a good way to get rid of that internal ache. And there we stay for the next hour or so—cuddling, stroking, and talking.

Around six-thirty, I say, "We really must go get Charlie now."

He strokes my hair. "Feel better now, sweetheart?"

"You mean, about that Cindy and Julia business? Well, yes. Although goodness knows what Cindy's been telling Julia about me."

Sam stretches. "Who cares? Cindy's just doing her usual truth-twisting thing. Julia will find out soon enough what's she like."

I reach up and stroke his face. At this time of day, Sam's "five o'clock shadow" is well and truly advanced. "Sam, I do wish the two of you didn't hate each other so. It's ironic that in the beginning it was Cindy who pushed me into taking you on, did you know that?"

"Yeah," he says. "You've mentioned it before. But you do know why, don't you? She figured you found me so un-attractive that I could never be a competitor with her for your affections."

"I'm sure she isn't that devious. Anyway, I am truly glad she's found someone else. Julia was pretty angry at me today but underneath all that she seems to be a very sweet person."

Sam yawns. "If you say so. Sort of mousy though."

"A fighting mouse." I smile. "Cindy seems to like 'em mousy, anyway. Like me, for instance."

Sam's lower lip curls. "What are you talking about? You're not mousy."

I shout with laughter. "Sam Bradshawe, you've told me some whoppers in your life but this takes the cake. Even you said I was mousy."

"I did not. I said you were like a little mouse and I love little mice. That's not at all the same as being mousy. You're beautiful."

I scoff at his ludicrous logic.

He says, "Come with me a moment. I want to show you something."

He pulls me up off the couch and propels me into the hall. There's a lovely old mirror hanging in the hall. It's one of the few items left here by the old lady that we didn't cart off to the Goodwill. It's big, with an ornate gilt frame, the glass a bit crackled with age. Sam marches me up to the mirror and stations me in front of it. He says, "Now look in that mirror and tell me what you see."

I look into the mirror and my eyes travel upward to Sam's face as he looks over my shoulder. I wonder, as my eyes meet his, how our lives together will turn out. Will he keep all those promises he made today? Will he always make me laugh, feel safe, kiss away the hurts?

Sam says, "Don't look at me. Look at yourself. What do you see?"

Reluctantly, I lower my gaze and look straight at my reflection. And give a little gasp of astonishment. For looking back at me is a radiant young woman. Tousled brown hair that turns to gold where the light catches it.

Sparkling dark eyes. Skin glowing with a warm blush. Mouth turned upwards in a gentle smile that seems to reflect some inner secret.

Sam whispers, "Now, is that a beautiful woman or what?"

Mesmerized, I stare at the mirror. Can this really be me? I whisper back, "How did that happen? What did you do?"

"I didn't do anything. You were born that way."

For a while longer, I keep looking at the beautiful woman in the mirror. I know I wasn't born that way. There is magic afoot here.

And the magician is standing right behind me.

EPILOGUE

Two years go by. It's a Saturday morning in early November. Today, we're having lunch with Kitty and George in their San Francisco home. Our daughter Elizabeth—Ellie for short—is now 17 months old. Charlie will be three in a couple of months.

It's a long time since I've visited the city so, at my request, Sam is taking a divergent route so we can visit places from the past. First stop: the duck pond in Golden Gate Park. We stop and Charlie leans out the window to look at the ducks. "Cindy and I used to bring him here when he was a baby," I say. I don't tell Sam about the ultimatum Cindy delivered to me by the same pond so many years ago.

Charlie leans out the window and quacks in friendly fashion at the ducks. Charlie has a passion for all living creatures that have any potential for becoming household pets. He pleads, "Hey, Dad, can we bring some home? I'll feed them every day."

And Sam's response, "No, Charlie, this park is their home."

Then we drive on to the ocean and along Great Highway. We pass the Beach House where Cindy and I stopped for snacks occasionally, and then head inland again past

Phyllis' house. Sam says, "Better not stop. We'll never get away. Shall we drive by Bayley Street?"

"No," I say, "it's getting late. We'd better head straight for Kitty's." In truth, I've had enough of memories for one day. "You know, I was trying to think when we last saw Kitty and George. Probably just after Ellie was born."

"That long?"

"It's been a while. Too bad really. Kitty and I used to be such good friends when we worked together."

"But now you have a new friend." There's a slight edge to his voice.

He's talking about Helena. She is the neighbor who lent us so much baby stuff for Charlie. When I first quit my job, I was surprised at how much I missed the social interaction at work. Helena is a stay-at-home housewife too and it wasn't long before we discovered mutual pleasure in each other's company. We go to each other's houses for coffee, take turns to drive into town to the stores.

And we talk and talk.

At first, it was mainly about baby issues—teething, potty training, tantrums. And then it was things like marriage. I told her once, "You know, Helena, it feels to me that Sam has changed since we got married. He seems more wrapped up in his job, less domestic than he used to be. Sometimes I wonder if he's lost respect for me since I quit work."

She said, "Oh, it's always that way when you stay home with the kids. The men act like you're freeloading, even though they enjoy having you home."

Recently, our confidences have wandered into new territory. Although she's never hinted that she's had a sexual history similar to mine, she was tremendously interested when I first told her about Cindy and always encourages me to talk about my feelings. This is a huge relief for me because Sam tends to go ballistic if I even breathe Cindy's name.

We pull up outside Kitty's house. Kitty is at the door before we can ring the bell. We greet each with hugs and kisses on the cheeks. In no time, her kids come to drag ours away to the playroom where George has set up a big electric train set. Kitty whispers, "The only time they ever play with it is when we have company." The two men grab beers and retreat in companionable discussion to the back yard. I accompany Kitty to the kitchen.

She chatters while she fixes the lunch. "I hope lasagna is okay. Not exactly an original choice, but it's hard to think of something the kids will eat."

"It smells wonderful."

She smiles over her shoulder at me. "Diane, you look great. Married life must be suiting you."

"It's making me fat, you mean. No, seriously, I'm doing fine."

"How's the house remodeling coming along?"

"Oh, the house." I give a rueful laugh. "Well, I still love the place but we're not making much progress. It's still one giant mess."

"Of course. You can't possibly get much done with the two little ones. But they're what's important right now. Plenty of time for the house later."

"I suppose."

As she busies herself with the dinner, I try to keep the conversation going. It's strange how the less you see of someone, the less there is to say. You'd think it would be the opposite. "Did I tell you my sister came to visit us this summer?"

"No, you didn't. That must have been nice."

"She really enjoyed seeing the kids."

Kitty says, "It's too bad your mother never got to see them."

"Yes," I say.

Her words set me to brooding. My mother died unexpectedly only a couple of months after our wedding, long before Ellie was born. And when she did die, I—who had spent so much of my life blaming her for all that had gone wrong for me—was filled with anguish. It would be nice to say it was anguish born of guilt because I had never tried hard enough to love her or make her life happy. But, in truth, I think it was really anguish that I'd never been able to demonstrate to her first-hand how well things had turned out for me. *See, Mom, you were wrong. I got my man and my children after all, and we're all really happy.*

Kitty slices a loaf of garlic bread, wraps it in foil, and puts it into the oven. She says, "You never heard any more from Cindy, huh? All that business about wanting to see 'her baby'?" Kitty is the only person apart from Sam who knows about that tussle on our wedding day.

"Not a word."

"She probably was just trying to pull your chain, like Sam said. Well, you sure are well rid of her." Kitty turns to smile at me. Her smile fades. "Diane, what is it?"

"Oh, nothing." But my eyes are misting up. I rub them and struggle to speak over the sudden lump in my throat. Finally, I say, "We drove through the park on our way here today and also near the old neighborhood. It sure brought back memories."

She looks at me with a puzzled expression. "Of the bad old days, huh?" I say nothing. Then she says, "Diane, would you find the salad dressing for me. It's in a jar on the bottom shelf of the fridge. Thanks."

I search for the jar of store-bought dressing—I always make my own from scratch—and hand it to her.

Kitty seems to be deep in thought as she tosses the salad. After a minute, she says in a firm voice, "I'm really glad things have turned out so well for you, Diane." She sits down opposite me at the kitchen table and leans forward, her eyes searching mine. She says, "You have the most wonderful life of any woman I know. Sam's a loving, responsible husband and father. And you don't even have to go out to work. What I wouldn't give to trade places!"

"It is a wonderful life, Kitty. Although, you know, after Cindy's promotion she made enough money that I could have stayed home with her too."

"What are you saying?" She looks appalled. "Diane, you would have had a terrible life. Two women raising young kids, one of them a boy. For a start, that's just not good for the kids."

"I'm sure you're right. I just wish that somehow Cindy could be a part of our lives too." I look down at my hands. "I'm going to feel guilty until eternity for separating Cindy from Charlie."

Kitty puts out her hands and slides them over mine. "Diane, don't you think that if Cindy had really wanted to see Charlie, she would have managed to do that somehow over the past couple of years? I mean, what if the situation were reversed, wouldn't you...?"

The oven timer rings. "That's the lasagna," Kitty says.

She jumps to her feet and calls everyone in for lunch.

On the way home, the kids quickly drop off to sleep. Sam glances up in the rear view mirror at Charlie's dark head hanging forward onto his chest. "Charlie sure loved that train set, didn't he? Maybe we should get him one for his birthday."

"Are you sure the train set would be for *Charlie*?"

He smiles and twists the dial on the radio to find the news.

Today has left me feeling unsettled. Coming into the city, driving through the park and the old neighborhood— memories of what Kitty called "the bad old days." How different my vision of my future was then. Me and Cindy— two young women facing the world, happy and secure in our love and our life, on the threshold of becoming a "real" family.

And here I am today: respectable, middle-class Marin County wife and mother. At the end of my life as an independent being? Should I feel fortunate, as everyone keeps telling me, that things have turned out so well for me? That I am rid of Cindy? That playful, clever, beautiful woman on whom the sun had once risen and set for me. The big brass bed still resides in one of our spare rooms, along with the clock Cindy bought us as a wedding present. Out of sight, out of mind. I would like to tell Charlie about Cindy one day, but I know Sam would throw a fit.

Sam listens intently to the radio as he drives. Now he is chuckling at something the announcer has said. His laughter is still as raucous as ever these days—but it is not as frequent. He's developed a furrow between his brows. His conversation at home is peppered with talk like his imminent move up into a vice-presidential slot in his company—or money matters like investing for the kids' college funds.

Kitty is right. He is a loving, responsible husband and father. We are all safe with him at the helm. I love him dearly.

Now, he feels me looking at him and turns to smile at me. "Okay, baby?"

"Yes, just a bit tired."

"Kitty said the two of you had been catching up on office gossip. Do you miss the office?"

"Good Lord, no." We both laugh at my vehemence.

"Although, some day, you really would like to get that degree and get yourself a decent job?"

It's a teasing reminder, but I love it when he's fully focused on me as he is now. I reply, "Yes, I really would, although the prospect sounds too exhausting for words at the moment."

"You know, Diane," he says, in his serious way, "it's important not to waste your potential. Don't go wrapping your whole life around your home and kids. Baking brownies, P-TA, and all that stuff."

"No, absolutely not," I murmur, and turn to look out the window. We're almost across the bridge. It's twilight and the lights of the city are starting to twinkle across the water. We'll soon be home.

And tomorrow is Monday. My spirits rise. Sam will be at work. I'll go visit Helena. We can talk and talk.

About the author

MARGARET DAVIS received a doctorate in Sociology from Stanford University with specialized study in the sociology of the family and the organization. She enjoys writing, reading, walking, travel, and the company of her family. She lives in the San Francisco Bay Area.

Please visit www.margaretdavisbooks.com for more information